ISLINGTON CROCODILES

PAUL MELOY

MONTAG

First Montag Press E-Book and Paperback Original Edition November 2020

Copyright © 2020 by Paul Meloy

As the writer and creator of this story, Paul Meloy asserts the right to be identified as the author of this book.

Montag Press ISBN: 978-1-940233-84-0
Design © 2020 Amit Dey

Montag Press Team:
Editor: Charlie Franco
Cover: Ben Baldwin

A Montag Press Book
www.montagpress.com
Montag Press
777 Morton Street, Unit B
San Francisco CA 94129 USA

Montag Press, the burning book with the hatchet cover, the skewed word mark and the portrayal of the long-suffering fireman mascot are trademarks of Montag Press.

Printed & Digitally Originated in the United States of America
10 9 8 7 6 5 4 3 2 1

This book is a work of fiction. Names, characters, places, and incidents are either products of the author's vivid and sometimes disturbing imagination or are used fictitiously without any regards with possible parallel realities. Any resemblance to actual persons, living or dead, events, or locales is entirely coincidental.

DEDICATION

For Lex

ORIGINAL INTRODUCTION

by
David Mathew
for the 2008 edition:

The tough, generous, interrogatory, course – but above all *resonant* – prose of Paul Meloy has been a delight to me for the better part of a decade. And the tough, generous, interrogatory, course – but above all *resonant* – conversation of Paul Meloy has been a delight to me for the better part of a decade as well.

There, I've said it. I've done what tradition dictates that a writer privileged enough to have been given the opportunity to write an introduction such as this (or a review, or an interview) should do: *I've declared an interest.* And here's my interest. I've known Meloy as a friend and as a colleague for a long time, and it's been my honour to do so.

We met at a British Fantasy Society Convention. Ramsey Campbell introduced us and it was love at first sight. I joke, of course. Paul was sitting – at the time – on his own, and quite frankly was looking miserable. Ramsey had more ambitious thoughts in his head than one of waiting around while I mumbled my way towards a hugely unentertaining anecdote about an editor who is no longer, to the best of my knowledge, working in the field.

It was sort of love at first sight. We certainly got on from minute one, and felt the charge of a meeting of minds; and Paul mentioned his story 'The Last Great Paladin of Idle Conceit', which had been published in *The Third Alternative*. I expressed an interest, I mentioned what I'd been up to, and then (to be honest) we got drunk. That's what conventions are for.

Great evening. It was only later, when I'd had a chance to read said 'Paladin' that I understood – with a sharp intake of breath – what a remarkable talent Meloy had, with his highly *calorific* writing, his original talent. And I've been there ever since. To the point where I'm proud to be his first reader, there to offer opinions on his ideas, early drafts and finished versions of what (slowly) falls from the creative part of his brain. (And by the way, I do mean slowly. There should be no rush on for genius, but it's fair to say Meloy works with the speed – and patience – of a mollusc, going about its chores. Every sentence is honed, picked at, polished, mopped and given a thoroughly good talking-to, before it is allowed into a finished draft. He's a true perfectionist, in this and other senses.) Having read various drafts of other pieces, and having talked through, say, a very early appearance of Rainscissor, I even went as far as to say, in (another) pub, around the turn of the millennium, that I thought Meloy was one of the best short-story writers alive. Drunken talk; but it is not my place here to retract the statement or to rebut the notion, for I do neither.

So, to the book. *To Islington Crocodiles.*

The first thing is, you're in for a treat. The second is, keep your wits about you as you read this extraordinary work. Once lured by the bright lights of a particularly optimistic-sounding passage, we are often immediately dropped down a mineshaft, into the foul-smelling darkness. But that's not all. These short stories are not 'easy reads' (why should *any* short stories be easy-reads?) They do not come into your bedroom to tuck you in and kiss your forehead goodnight; some of them ('Dying in the Arms of Jean Harlow', 'Islington Crocodiles', for example) do not even bother to turn the door handle before entering. As all good resonant horror fiction should do. What's more, it's challenging – as all good horror fiction should be.

But with what do we contend herein? Without wishing to give games away by saying what appears where, I can honestly say that what you're going to find, inter alia, are: some beautifully pungent verbs, certainly(the right word in the right place at the right time) and some astonishing imagery (the ingress of creatures from elsewhere into our world is particularly sharp). We see sadness and confusion. Some bristlingly witty dialogue: Meloy's ear for contemporary vernacular being second-to-none. But this scarcely scratches the surface. What we also can embrace (or be embraced by – now there's a scary thought, given some of what you really wouldn't want to be embraced by, inside these pages) are among the following.

A monstrously distorted-evocation of childhood comic reading (with a fantastic line about a shoal of empty cans: you'll see) a visit from Lenny Bruce, involving an explanation of what stand-up comedy might really be about; and the terrifying Autoscopes (They're coming! They're coming!). We see some great, astutely drawn characters, some of my favourites being Nurse Melt, Doctor Mocking and Ray Cade. The very nature of paternity is addressed, more than once: there are frequent bursts in the texts, and subtexts, about absentee fathers – absent for reasons you'll discover. We see characters attempting, via fair means or foul, to escape the corrosive drudgery of twenty-first century, hooligan-mooned Britain: a Britain raised not on mother's milk but on deep-fry, tobacco, on hard booze and dread.

And, as they say, so much more. One story tells us that pandas roam wild in the suburbs (eating garden furniture); another still, that the most adventurous bank heist of all time might just be a plausible punt.

I'll go no further. Enjoy these calories on your own; get fat on them. It will be worth the weight-loss programme in the following weeks.

Here's to Paul!

But more importantly here's to Paul meloy! Congratulations on this remarkable collection. I'll raise a glass and refuse to touch the blackouts.

CONTENTS

THE MELTING MIDWIFE

An Introduction to
Islington Crocodiles by Paul Meloy
David Mathew

In every gaze, a planet; in every universe, a song…

You hold in your hands a constellation.

Every time you look at the patterns, they will appear different. Any longed-for sense of nostalgia is forbidden. We will not see things in the same way again. Our vision blurs. Sometimes, the stars change position even as your eyes are watering.

Within this constellation that Paul Meloy has coaxed into being and engineered with flawless internal logic – a swirling system, disconcerting and hilarious by turns, often within one paragraph – a famous dead comedian complains to the people who are heckling his routine that they are "laughing at the *wrong stuff*" (author's emphasis).

We might bear this complaint in mind as we explore this unique work. There is much "wrong stuff" to laugh

at – examples where our laughter might seem cruel. Much
to wonder at, too. There are sequences of powerful panic,
where we try to navigate our way into a wider cosmos (but
not necessarily *the* wider cosmos, for it will likely change its
mind, even as soon as tomorrow).

These words are my point of introduction to the deep
sky of Paul Meloy's shorter fiction. In one way, it feels like
reading a brand new book (which, in a sense, it is); in others,
like finding something both perplexing and familiar once
more in the constellation.

Either way, we have all to begin our journeys somewhere.

*   *   *

Re-reading *Islington Crocodiles* after longer than a decade, I
feel compelled to adjust my seat belt in our rocket, and to
breathe with exaggerated gulps. When the first edition of
this book was published in 2008, the author asked me to
write an Introduction, which I did with pleasure. At that
point, Paul Meloy and I had known each other for longer
than a decade. I think it's fair to say that our mutual respect
was a force far stronger than a sneeze; it had seemed like an
instinct.

We had been introduced by Ramsey Campbell, and had
felt, immediately (I believe), the competitive breeze and sunshine of a like-minded individual's proximity. In other words,
we *got* each other – and each other's work – straight away.

Now, with a fountain pen in my hand, the time of
writing is February, 2020; and I have recently submitted a

full-length manuscript of my own, on the subject of nostalgia. Vulgar though it might be, I'll quote from that manuscript now, if I may.

> "Nostalgia is what Sigmund Freud called a screen memory," she says: "a lightly poeticized and sweetened representation of something that did not happen."
>
> ...
>
> She is aware that she is leaning on the delivery of a previous lecture. In fact, she is succumbing to nostalgia, in a sense.

It occurs to me to wonder if I myself, here and now, am piloting the rocket under the influence of nostalgia. However, it takes only a reacquaintance with some of the characters in *Islington Crocodiles* to confirm my earlier impressions. In Paul Meloy's constellation, the astonishing crashes into the everyday, and *vice versa*. Monstrous machinery gives our characters entry points to worlds that they might have believed they could never dream of ... until they did. The healthcare professions might not seem quite as *trustworthy* as you yourself had once imagined. The terrifying Nurse Melt still returns to me from time to time, quite unbidden and unwelcome.

Paul Meloy's fiction reminds us of our earliest forms of fatigue. With something like nostalgia (as strange as it seems), we recall the first time tiredness really *meant* something to us, when we see what it means to some of his characters. A few of them live with a sense of *ennui*; some of them live lives so headache-grey that it's hard not to be frightened for them. The work is muscular and sad, elegiac and poetic. As I hinted at above, it is frequently hilarious as well, coarse and grainy. *Islington Crocodiles* points us to a certain space in our lives, where something has run out (time, a relationship, a reality) and we know that there is no choice but to change. Figuratively speaking, characters climb up ladders of smoke. And these stories throb like a fucked exhaust.

*   *   *

Perhaps we should conclude by asking where any of this leaves us. The strange thing is that such a reading might mess with our tenses.

Where *were* we when we finished?

It is easy to recollect where we were when we started, even if we have to make it up. Even if we have to tell a lie and make ourselves feel (deliciously) guilty.

Inside the mad beauty of the constellation, we might find that it provided only token direction, and sometimes paradoxical sleight-of-hand on a stellar level. Thus, we will have faltered; we will have limped, from time to time. Where we ended up, however, is more of a mouthful. The weather is uncertain. Things have auto-decoded and changed gear. Time itself has grown new bones.

We should take stock – and consider – before, inevitably, striding forward.

THE LAST GREAT PALADIN
OF IDLE CONCEIT

L enny Bruce died the year I was born.

A week ago I woke up in the middle of the night and there he was, in the moon shadowed corner of my bedsit, pissing in my sink.

"Are you pissing in my sink?" I asked him, because I assumed I was dreaming and because that was how his gag went.

He turned to look at me. It was Lenny Bruce for sure: those laconic eyes, half lidded and dark, bulging with eager fallenness; hair short and slick, styled in a long-gone sixties chic; wide, wise-cracking grin at the bottom of his oddly handsome, tumbler shaped face; and that mole to the side of his mouth.

He zipped up. "I just don't think I'm ready to go back into the john just yet, my friend," he said.

He came over and sat on the edge of my bed. I was surprised and a little disorientated by the full weight of him, and I shifted further up against the headboard, totally unprepared for the way the mattress sank beneath him, rolling my hips against his suit-trousered thigh.

Lenny Bruce sat forward and looked me in the eye. "Who're you, Jim?"

"Eddie," I said, quiet and suddenly breathless at the way this dream had blossomed with alarming sensation. "Eddie D'Andrea."

"You gotta help me, Ed."

He got up and strode over to the window and looked out over London through the grimy nets. He rubbed his palm across his lips then ran it down his arm to cup his elbow, which he massaged, thumb pressing into the soft flesh and tendons in the joint.

I took a quick look at Allie, deep in sleep beside me. She lay on her side, facing the wall, her breath huffing softly.

Then I looked back over at Lenny.

When he spoke it was in a hush, so full of longing, debilitating hope it sounded like a man haunted by a lifetime of unanswered prayer.

"You've gotta help me," he said, "I gotta have one more chance."

I told Allie about my dream the following morning as she was getting ready for work.

She shrugged her jacket over a crisp silk blouse and loosely wound a gaudy paisley scarf around her neck.

"Strange, Eddie. Even by your standards," she said, "I never have dreams about anything exciting." She used both hands to pull her splendid ash blonde hair into a ponytail and tethered it with a purple scrunchie.

"It was so *real*," I said for about the fifth time. "But sad, you know, like really moving. Most vivid dream I've ever had. You know, I even got up this morning and checked the sink for urine stains." I laughed, a little embarrassed because it was the truth; it was the first thing I'd done when I'd got up.

"You're pretty bizarre, Eddie." Allie frowned as she stepped into her shoes.

I went over to her and gave her a hug, toppling her back into my arms. One of her shoes hung from her toe in an incredibly sexy way. I kissed her mouth. I felt the silken glide of her stockinged calf against my bare leg.

"Mmm. Bizarre and apparently very horny. I gotta go to work."

I let her go with reluctance. She pried my hands from her backside.

"How do I look?" she asked.

"Like a million lira," I said and got a prod in the ribs. "No, really lovely I meant. Scarf's a bit iffy, but you'll do."

"God! You really know how to treat a lass."

"Treat 'em mean, me. I'll rough you up a bit later if you want, if you're not too busy."

"I'll've had enough pawing when I'm done having lunch with Kimpton, so you can just put that idea out of your mind, matey boy."

I groaned. "That lusty, inappropriate old bastard took the lie out of client and replaced it with little you."

Allie made an exasperated sound and spread her arms. Her small breasts leapt heartily beneath her blouse, all cheeky and delighted with themselves.

"Oh, Eddie, he *loves* me. He eats out of my hand."

"Well I hope that's all he eats out of."

"Eddie!"

I grinned and went for another kiss.

"Right, now I gotta go. Later." Allie opened the door and stepped out into the hallway.

"Watch out for Kimpy."

I'll wear a shark cage. Luv ya!"

And she was gone in a swirl of Coco Chanel and bouncing blonde hair.

I was filling the kettle when I heard a light tap on the door. Forgotten her key, I thought, and went to let Allie in.

"Morning, Ed," said Lenny.

He was leaning up against the wall opposite my bed-sit, half his face in shadow, the other half dimly lit by the watery daylight that slanted in through the small window set in the stairwell. He stepped out of the shadow and I saw the latent urgency in his eyes, still there from last night. I gasped and found my hands covering my mouth in a cartoonish approximation of 'act shocked.'

"No dream, Eddie," he laughed, "You wouldn't dream this suit twice now, would ya? Think about it."

I just stood there looking at him. Dressed in his mid – sixties clothes and shiny shoes, like James Dean, an icon forever preserved in an unequivocal fashion. I did what I might have to anyone else. I stepped back to let him come past me into the flat.

He was shorter than me by at least six inches and I could see the light shining on his oiled hair in silvery bands. He went straight over to the window again.

"London!" He said. "I can see you, you tricky bitch!"

What did I think? What do you think when one of the world's most radical comedians turns up on your doorstep, dead some thirty years, smelling of hair oil and looking like he's just walked out of a jazz club after a particularly trad '50s gig, calling you Ed like he's known you forever.

Personally, I was thinking: *What the fuck?* But we may differ.

I watched him carefully as I dressed. Saw him pace back and forth in front of the window, occasionally leaning on the sill to peer down at the street, then glaring off into the distance, taking in the landmarks and listing them to himself in loud proofs of his observation.

When I was dressed it seemed right to offer him something to eat so I suggested I make him some breakfast.

"Ed, let's eat out." He was at the door and holding my jacket. "You got any dough?"

Lenny Bruce died the year I was born. In 1966, in a bathroom, from a Heroin overdose.

He became known, inaccurately, as the "sick comedian," inaccurate because, like a finely ground mirror, he reflected back nothing but the hypocrisy he perceived beneath the surface of his culture. In his day he delivered it up undiluted and difficult for some to bear.

When Lenny said cancer, people walked out. When he said cocksucker he got arrested and tried for obscenity. They all missed the point: he didn't talk about tits and ass to incite prurient thought; he was talking about tits and ass because nobody else would, and some shit needed airing.

We sat in a café in Denmark Street and ordered coffee and toast. Nobody was paying us much attention, so I assumed that my companion went unrecognised. I was still overwhelmed by the feeling that someone was sure to walk in at any moment and point and say: My god, that's Lenny Bruce! He's dead!

It was possible, but probably unlikely. Lenny had never been particularly well known over here and what black and white television archive there was of him was rare and late on, when he was rambling.

People definitely saw him though, especially the waitress who had stood and held his gaze while she took our order, her pretty brown eyes looking straight into his as she scribbled on her pad. He had given her an easy smile and gazed after her as she went off with the order.

"Nice tuchus," he informed me once she had gone.

"Yeah," I said absently. "Lenny, could you please tell me what I'm doing here, having breakfast with a dead comic, because the shock's going to wear off soon and then you'll have lost me."

Lenny looked me in the eye. "No doubt you are playing host to a wide range of emotions, Ed. Let me put you on the level. I'm back because I should never have gone to begin with. And I'm back because bad things have begun to happen and they're going to get a lot worse." He took a bite from his slice of toast and chewed slowly, his eyes never leaving mine.

"You're going to explain all that, right?"

"Look, let's crack it wide open. You're a comedian yourself, Ed, you gotta understand this."

"Have you heard my stuff? I've done supports and warm ups for TV shows. That's about as good as it's going to get. I'm under no illusions, I'm not that good. My agent nearly hired one of my hecklers."

"No, no but you've heard *my* stuff. You know my work. You know what I do best and that's all I need."

This was true. I was a second rate warm-up man. I was never going to play the big rooms, as Lenny might have said, but I did know my history. I knew all about the greats, and I considered Lenny to be one of the greatest.

"When I was doing my stuff," he continued, "I was taking chances. I was on the fuckin' edge, man. All the time there were people walking out on me, there were clear lines of demarcation, so it was: *fuck them*. They thought they were decent, they thought I was sick." He picked up his teaspoon and hit the top of the salt seller. "*To* is a preposition." He hit the side of the sugar bowl: "*Come* is a verb."

His expression was now openly challenging.

"To come," he tapped the salt pot and sugar bowl again, building up a rhythm. He added his coffee mug to the repertoire.

"Didja come? Didja come good? Didja come? Didja come good?"

He laughed and the people sitting around us began to stare a little.

"Lenny, man – "

"Don't come in me! Don't come in me! Don't come in me min me min me min me!" he sing-songed.

The waitress came over. "Everything all right?" she asked wearily.

Lenny smacked the spoon down on his empty plate. "I can't come!"

"What the fuck was all that about?" I said once I had mollified the waitress with a further order for coffee.

"Were you shocked?" Lenny asked.

I shook my head. "I don't think she was too amused."

He sat back on his bench and hooked an arm over the backrest. "You know I never got to play in England."

"Yeah, you were deported before you even got off the plane."

"That's it. My reputation preceded me. I was fuckin' hounded to death. Heat wouldn't leave me alone. The world got rid of Lenny Bruce and now he's back and you're going to help me play here and put things right."

"Oh right. I'll just give my agent a call and see if he can book you in for a slot at the Comedy Club. Lenny Bruce live and fucking undead!"

"No, no, Ed, you're not digging me. If I don't play here, if I don't fulfil my destiny, things are going to get crazy. Let me give it all to you."

He sat up and surprised me by taking hold of my hands. They were cool and oddly delicate.

"When I was around, there were taboos to break. I had my pick of them. But I didn't do it because it was easy. It wasn't. Then it was the hardest place to be.

"Now look, thirty years later, anything goes. How could things have changed so fast? You can get up on stage now and shit your pants and you'll get big laughs. I used to get cops at my gigs just to ensure I didn't say anything unconstitutional. Now..." He looked into my eyes, searching with that jagged urgency dancing just behind his; I was slightly alarmed to see them filling with tears. "Now there's nothing left to make people feel uncomfortable." He released me and smacked his palms flat on the table top. "The new fuckin' rock and roll! Look at the audiences, Ed, look at 'em trying to crack up at stuff that just ain't funny. How'd it get like this? I died for my stuff. I gave my fuckin' life for it!"

Horribly, he had begun to cry. Huge tears ran down his cheeks.

He was right in many ways. Some years ago I had read his biography, a surprisingly fair and compassionate study of Lenny by Albert Goldman, probably the biggest pop biographer of his time and a man not renowned for prettying things up. But it was impossible, especially if you were in the business—however small-time you were—not to get a sense of Lenny's struggle to represent something, to get something across that would truly shock us at a level fundamental enough to open our minds and face stuff we were afraid of. To Lenny, that's what his art was.

Lenny had pulled himself together. "Sorry, Ed but I can't take this. In thirty years it's got so nothing matters anymore. Don't you see? They thought I was sick but I wasn't. I was keeping it fresh in their minds. Without that, things start to fly apart. Haven't you begun to notice?"

"Lenny, it isn't all bad. There are some real great comics out there. Great observers. Bill Hicks. Henry Rollins. Real power."

Lenny looked at me with an expression of deep concern.

"Hicks is dead, man, case you haven't noticed. And Rollins was this close to getting it he's never going to come to terms with it." He leaned forward, "There's something out there, Ed, and it wants us to shut up. That's why I'm back. If I don't do what I was stopped doing thirty years ago everything's gonna blow wide apart."

"You think you were stopped from playing here by something other than convention, Lenny? You've gone way past me."

"Look. If you lose the edge, you're numb. That's what's happening. If I'd played here—Lenny Bruce at the fuckin' Palladium—I could've kept things together. When that got out of whack, it had won. It got rid of me. You're gonna think I'm an asshole, but I was one of the last great paladins of idle conceit. And don't go grinning at me like that, I didn't come up with that one. There were others before me and there have been some since, but none of them as powerful or focused. They're being taken out, man, and what's taking their place is comedy promulgating feeble, popularised *inelegant* crap. It won the moment I ended up in repose on the floor of my crapper."

"What won? For fuck's sake."

Lenny ignored me.

"It filled up the next thirty years with a lot of unimportant shouting and a lot of cussing and what people thought was groundbreaking obscenity. You know what the truly obscene is, Ed? It's shouting *fuck* and getting a laugh. It's standing there on stage with your dick out despising the audience by giving them stupid nitwit crap, despising them by expecting to be laughed at simply because they don't know what's funny anymore, and despising them by knowing it. And now here we are with nothing left to brace ourselves against, nothing left to draw gasps from us and show us what we are, to stop it all coming apart. Look."

I turned as the door crashed open.

A young woman wearing jeans and a tight sweater burst in and let out the most wretched scream. Wretched, because within it and upon her face, all the articulations of every worst nightmare were apparent.

Her arm shot out and the bundle of woollen blankets she was carrying flew apart, sending their contents spilling to the floor. The people at the table nearest the door rose as one, their mouths open to make the usual pointless noises of indignation a scene like this always seemed to provoke.

"Oh god," I said as what between the chair legs reached out tiny hands.

There were squashed chips and peas on the floor around its head. Beyond the mother, who was standing shuddering with horror, both rows of teeth showing in a frightful, disgusted sneer, a woman had paused in passing and was peering in, her fists full of shopping bags.

One of the waitresses had gone to comfort the mother while another—our bright-eyed lass in fact—bent down between the tables and chairs and scooped up the mewling bundle. She cooed and fussed, looking into the mite's face and smoothed its fine blond hair with her hand.

Together, they walked the trembling woman to the back of the café and sat her down behind the counter. When the child was offered back to her, she cringed and held her hands up as if to ward it off. Further ministrations from the girls eventually persuaded her to resume contact with the child, but she held it with terrible care, exploring its face with her panicked eyes, her breathing rapid and shallow.

"Come on Ed, let's split." Lenny was up and out the door, looking back at me, still sitting with a mug of coffee frozen halfway to my lips, wondering what the hell was going on.

We made our way back to my flat, the streets smelling of that curious and repellent blend of diesel and sick particular to the west end at most times of the day.

"You ever heard of Norville Laughton, Eddie?" Lenny asked me as we walked.

"Huh? Rings a bell," I said, still so deeply disturbed by what I'd seen in the café that I had been walking in reflective silence for the past five minutes.

"I've got quite a bit more to tell you, Ed, so listen up. Norville Laughton was a small time player in the silent movies. Played a Keystone Cop a coupla times, extraed in some of Keaton's later films, even made it into one or two of the Laurel and Hardy talkies. His greatest moment was in the gorilla suit. Remember that one?" He threw back his head and pealed a great whoop of delight. I was beginning to smile to myself, a little at the memory of that great hairy brute lumping around in a tutu, but more so because to was Lenny Bruce himself, out on the streets of London at last, howling with great humour in the late morning sunshine, who was telling me about it.

"Well, he rubbed up against all the greats. Harold Lloyd, Chaplin, the Marx Brothers, all of 'em. And he got close. Laughton was a big guy, big personality, big sense of humour. You know the type: great guy you know, just never going to make the big time."

"Not unlike me, then." I said, smiling.

"Right! So he got close to the greats, got to be a friend with the legends. Confidant of Harpo. Best buddies. Anyway, so it goes, Harpo was sitting backstage one night with Laughton and they were really tearing into the booze and Harpo says, 'Do you want to know the real reason I don't speak in the movies?' And so Laughton, curious, says 'Uhuh' and Harpo leans in to him real close and says, 'Because what I've got to say ain't funny'.

"So Laughton asks Harpo what he means, and Harpo tells him that he knows things, things so terrible that no one could possibly be ready to hear them. He says that in time only the funniest, only the most powerful, *visceral* voices are going to be able to keep everything from flying apart.'

"'That's what you keep saying. Flying apart. What's going to fly apart?"

Lenny had stopped outside a souvenir shop. He span the post card rack. Smut revolved in a flicker of tits and ass. "Reality, Ed. The very memory that confines our structure." He looked at me with his eyebrows raised, an incredibly open expression on his face. "Harpo told Laughton a story about when he was a kid. He woke up one night in total darkness. He said how this was odd, since there was always a little light coming in through the curtains, but he couldn't see shit. Like he'd gone blind. And when he reached up to touch his face, the little fingers that were growing out of his eyeballs seized his hands and squeezed and wouldn't let go. Imagine the terror, Ed. Harpo said that they held on so tight he still had the bruises between his fingers the next morning. He screamed and screamed and brought the fuckin' roof in till his folks came in and put on the light. He said he was just sitting there in a puddle of piss, staring at his hands like they'd turned into claws. 'Never was a good sleeper after that, Norv,' he'd said, and, as Laughton put it, 'laughed, but with desperate tears in his eyes.'"

Lenny walked on. Unbelievable, I wanted to say, but I couldn't get the picture out of my head of that baby lying there on the scuffed lino-tiled floor, tiny pale arms reaching out, and just for a moment—such a brief, flickering instant, and then it was gone—I had been sure I had seen another, much smaller face staring out at me within its bubblegum pink, toothless mouth, wheezing with awful effort to be delivered.

I put two mugs of tea on the table and sat facing Lenny; the stereo was playing Pat Metheney.

"I'm a progressive jazz cat myself, " Lenny said. "but this ain't bad."

I broke open a pack of Marlboro and lit up.

"So you're telling me that what happened to Harpo Marx is going to happen again?"

"Kinda. Except that what happened to Harpo has probably happened countless times before, to countless numbers of people."

"Yeah, but hands in the eyes? Stuff like that I'd've noticed."

"Not necessarily. How many asylums full of people who're there because they've seen something they can't understand? How many people driven to madness not because their minds are failing, but because the very fabric of what they're a part of has lost its way for awhile. How much has gone unnoticed by dull eyes?" Would you want to admit to seeing things crawling out of the walls, Ed? I know you've seen it. I *let* you see it. Brief, right, but the anticipation of seeing it again won't leave it now. Just like with Harpo. Just like Laughton, who started to notice things almost constantly towards the end. Just briefly, like things swelling and waving at him from the corner of his eye where someone's face should be. Features not aligned properly, missing blemishes, new scars, then all back to normal again in the fraction of a second. And he reckoned it wouldn't be long before the changes happened at a catastrophic level. A permanent breakdown in the constituent design of reality."

I'd smoked my cigarette down to the filter. I tapped off an inch of ash and stubbed it out. I lit another. Lenny got up from the table and paced the room.

I said, "What's this got to do with you, Lenny?"

"Laughton became obsessed. Obsessed with the sadness he saw in all these fuckin' clowns. Obsessed with seeing what was behind our need to make reality seem ridiculous by laughing at it. Life wants to be taken seriously with all its random tragedy and subtle ironies, all it's cataclysms and fineries. He thought that maybe we were weakening it by drawing strength from laughter and that it was trying to fight back and create something else from us, something less likely to ridicule it. And he was right!

"And now nobody knows what's funny anymore. When I was doing my stuff, it was pretty fucking clear to me that I had a line to cross and I crossed it often as I could. If we ain't got somebody to show us our hypocrisies, Ed, it's us that become ridiculous, and that ain't right."

"Anyhow, Laughton wrote it all down before he died back in '53." Lenny reached into his jacket pocket and pulled out a folded sheet of paper. "He came up with the idea that when things got rough, people would appear who could alert us to the state of our complacency, writers and comedians, wits and playwrights, taking the kind of risks that would make them for a time incandescent, standing between us and the thundering indignant power that made us, and attempting to move us on up the ladder toward higher thought before we could be irrevocably changed into something dumb and compliant. Paladins of idle conceit, he called them. What a guy!"

Lenny handed me the piece of paper. I unfolded it and read: *We are almost something else. We stand on the brink, a canted rhythm of atoms. Modify the orbit and—monstrous!—we are a counter product. The relentless irritation of variables and the unending urgency of chaos; there is an alchemy inherent in my parts, the colossal and eternal process holding everything together has a drive to decay-I am in uproar!*

"Drove him bugfuck, poor bastard. Look you gotta get me a gig somewhere. If I can do my stuff, maybe there'll be a fuckin' *renaissance*. Ha ha."

"I'll make that call," I said and dialled my agent.

I was supposed to be warm up for some lousy sit-com audience later that evening. Some three in a bedsit thing flogging a flimsy premise and getting big laughs for every cleverly applied knob gag and an apoplexy of rebellious mirth for a really gratuitous wank-inclusion. How far we've come.

That was it for me, really. A TV studio full of students dressed in witless-chic is about as low as you can get, but I knew the form and I knew what to give them to get through fairly unscathed.

I told my agent that I was sick with something and couldn't make the gig, but I had someone willing to stand in.

"Is he any good?"

"He's better than me, Mike."

"Is that a recommendation? What's his name?"

"I looked across at Lenny for inspiration.

"His name… his name is Frank Dell, dean of satire."

Lenny was loving it.

"Get him to the studio by seven thirty." Mike said, and hung up.

The idea was to get Lenny there late, so late in fact that Mike wouldn't even have time to get a good look at him let alone ask to see his equity card. I'd left Mike high and dry, I knew. He'd only hired me for this gig because he couldn't get anyone else, so I knew he'd be a little lax over the formalities. Warm-ups for these kind of shows were thankless, often arduous nightmares; the audience has got in free and they don't owe you a thing. You're out there stepping over cables and lighting rigs, getting obscured by shifting scenery, having all your punchlines blown by the director when they want to get on with the shoot. You're comedy's equivalent of elevator music basically, or one of those irritating jingles put over the phone line when you're on hold.

"No problem, chum," Lenny said when I explained it all to him. He was pacing the flat, wrapped up in going through his routines like it was still 1963. It was wonderful to hear him, his beautiful, broad, sonorous voice rattling those famous schticks out just for me, and after a while I just sat there on the sofa and listened to him, tears in my eyes, letting the master work.

We were at the studio by eight. Mike was outside, chewing on his cigarette, his coat collar turned up and a jaded look of disenchantment on his face as we arrived.

"Mike," I said, this is Frank Dell." They shook hands.

Mike didn't even bother to acknowledge me and I had a feeling there wouldn't be much more of this kind of work coming my way after tonight.

"You've done this kind of thing before, Frank?" he asked.

Lenny beamed and clapped him on the shoulder. "Sure, Mike. Been a while, but I think you'll dig my stuff. Got it all down."

Mike led the way along the corridors backstage. "You've got about three minutes, Frank. Place is full, so just get out there and enjoy yourself."

He let Lenny slip past and I saw him, just for a moment, framed in the doorway leading out to the studio floor, rows of people up on scaffold seating to his right, and I knew what he was thinking. He knew that he was going to go out there and *murder* these people.

Mike turned to me and said, "Where did you find this guy? Stars in Their fucking Eyes?"

"He's just a little old fashioned," I answered.

"I thought you were supposed to be sick, anyway."

"Migraine."

"Well you've given me enough frigging headaches, Eddie. OK, Frank?"

Lenny stepped out into the lights. London lights. Not exactly the Palladium, but then he'd hooked up with D'Andrea not Izzard.

Notwithstanding, the last great paladin of idle conceit was back on his game.

I suppose my greatest mistake was letting Lenny entrance me so easily. Seduce me into believing he was some kind of talisman against what would happen later. I should have guessed, really, that things were different now. Too different.

If you listen to recordings of Lenny at the height of his power, along with the sophistication of his delivery, his timing and his phenomenal ability to improvise, you'll also get a sense of his vulnerability.

One of Lenny's most famous routines was about the Palladium. If you were anybody you played there, if you played there you'd made it. The story goes that a rising young comic leans on his agent to get him a spot there, insisting he's played his last Vegas lounge. He's ready for the really classy rooms now. In spite of his agent's misgivings, he lands him a spot on the bill. The rest of the story describes in gorgeous detail his ensuing and inevitable humiliation.

You have to bear in mind how long ago it was that he did his stuff, the climate of his time. Things *have* changed.

Lenny bombed.

I think it was undoubtedly the most painful thing I have ever had to watch. It started almost the moment he stepped out and the audience got their first real good look at him. He played to utter silence for the first five minutes, and then, predictably, the hecklers found their voice. That wasn't such a great problem because Lenny could deal with them, it was just that he couldn't get his routines to work. He began to sweat. The filming began and he wouldn't shut up for it. He just carried on, pacing the floor, whipping the microphone lead behind him, his face white and strained, while the audience clapped and hooted. When the director went across to him and

yanked the arm of his jacket, Lenny shoved him off, calling him a 'fuckin' nitwit' and ploughed on with his act.

The crowd erupted with delight. A rogue warm-up
was better than any of them could have imagined, and
they showed their appreciation by howling and cat-call-
ing. When finally, inundated by airborne seat cushions, his
face a mixture of panic and furious affront, the director
pulled the plug in desperation and called security, Lenny
was screaming. Screaming that they were laughing at the
wrong stuff. I watched all this with a terrible feeling in my
heart of inevitability and guilt. Inevitable, because things
have changed so much in so short a time, and guilt because
I should have told him it would never work and didn't
because I'd had Lenny Bruce back and all to myself and
I'd been enjoying myself too much.

I left Mike standing there, his big face blotchy with
fury I knew was directed solely at me, and walked back out
onto the street.

I could still hear the crowd in uproar as I put my arm
out for a taxi. I thought it would probably be for the best if
I forgot about comedy for a while. I didn't feel like laughing
much now anyway.

I never saw Lenny Bruce again after that night, but I began
to grow aware that some of the strange and random changes
he had warned me about were becoming more frequent.
Allie, I knew sadly, had also become more aware of the new
changes within me.

Our usual banter was grimly forced now, and I felt that soon perhaps she would become sick of seeing my dreary mug first thing in the morning, but there seemed little I could do about it. My mind was elsewhere now. And I just didn't find things particularly funny anymore.

How do I know these things? Well, I've begun to see it everywhere now.

The other night I came back from the pub with Allie; she stormed off ahead because I had spent all evening feeling sorry for myself and had got drunk and maudlin, and there had been a man kneeling in the gutter, his back to us. Allie had stomped straight past him and gone up the steps to our flat, but I had seen him more clearly. I had seen him trying to pull the soft, segmented things from out of his mouth and shove them down the drain.

And now, the most awful thing.

I was awakened last night by a scream from outside the window. As I staggered across the room, I kept misjudging the distance of things and barked my shin on a chair and slammed my chest up against the window sill.

I fumbled with the net curtains and pressed my forehead against the glass. And saw, as if looking through the wrong end of a telescope, two men and a woman fighting in the road. The woman was dragging at the clothes of one of the men, trying to pull him away, her mouth a toothless 0 of froth, while the second man held onto the lapels of the other's jacket and gored at his chest with the sharp plate of stubby horns his lower jaw had become.

I stepped away from the window, knowing I was either mad or that things were degenerating at a terrible rate, perhaps to the state of permanency forewarned by Lenny.

I did not expect to have this insight so quickly confirmed by my reflection in the dark mirror of the windowpane: incredibly, huge as a horse's, filled with a dumb and humourless understanding, my solitary, lidless eye gazed implacably back at me.

There was a light tap at the door.

I glanced back at my reflection, just once, and saw my face looking in at me as if coming up from a tank of dirty black liquid. Now two eyes again.

Normality in an instant, and enough to make me wonder if anything had really happened at all. Below, the street was empty.

Not sure what I was really doing, I stumbled across and opened the door.

A short, stocky man stood in the total darkness of the hall. I could see nothing of him but his bulk, but when he spoke, I knew the voice at once. Plumy with a hint of weary cynicism, a voice unheard since he had overdosed in a squalid rented room in Australia so long ago.

"Eddie," said Hancock, "I just need another half hour. Can you help me?"

I gently shut the door.

I wanted to laugh.

RAIDERS

It was early, nearing five in the morning, and Barwise was casting about in the back of a taxi. His restless posture alternated between lying on his side with an arm pressed beneath his hip and his boots jammed under the driver seat, or holding onto the door-mounted arm rest and forcing the side of his face up against the cool misty window in the hope that sweating, ashen flesh and condensation-fogged glass would form a seal robust enough to keep him from keeling over again.

"Yeah, thanks, anywhere here," he said, fumbling for the door handle as the taxi idled around the bend past the Co-Op. He paid the tenner and climbed out onto the cold, damp High Street. His dandelion clock silver wig caught on the top of the door frame and dragged back over his head like a hood.

He watched the taxi pull away and stood there, swaying on the pavement. He readjusted his head-piece, smirking like a hopeless bastard. He wobbled on his hired silver platforms.

By all accounts he'd had a good night. New club in town called Glitter Dammerung, late seventies, end-of-an-era glam nightclub. A barroom blitz of retro groove. Tonight was Afrogeddon. Hence the outfit. Hence the fuckin' *outfit*.

Barwise had loved the jaded magnitude of the Seventies. He recalled his childhood vividly: a sudden disgorgement of cultural tastelessness spewed unchecked from the black and white parenthesis of the sixties; a time he mused when his parents had become strangers in a world they had taken for granted, a world emerging humbly from the war. Something else had taken over, something chaotic and buggering and coarse. Everything slipped momentarily into a sudden spacey future furnished with lousy technology. The minimalist's nightmare; a science fiction envisioned millennium but with Ronco hardware.

He teetered on the curb, going through pockets for keys to his flat, and as he did so he was suddenly aware of something huge blundering across the street to his right and disappearing into the entrance to the station on the corner. He whipped his head around, which proved unwise. His ankles buckled and he went over. He lay there, distantly aware that his wig had come off and was blowing up the road in a stiff breeze, like glamorous tumbleweed. He sat up and felt the sudden, bitter flood of saliva puddle under his tongue, which at this juncture of the proceedings can only signify one thing.

Having divorced his evening's consumption of extortionately priced bottled lagers in a messy and drawn out affair, Barwise tenderly made his way to his feet. A little clearer-headed, he wiped his mouth and frowned, remembering the charging shape he had glimpsed in his periphery a moment earlier. The station was closed this time of night and should have been gated, but he was sure he'd seen it go in under the darkened sign. There was no way something that big could be huddling out of sight, even if it was standing there pressing its bulk against the gate. Why was he thinking about the thing trying to get out of sight anyway? There *had* been something furtive about the way it had shot across the road like that and disappeared, a bit like it had been lurking on the corner waiting for him to look away before making a dash.

He decided against investigating. In his state. Could have been anything. He retrieved his wig from where it had lodged in a doorway and crossed the road on rickety legs. He jabbed at the lock with his key, trying to accuse the door into opening, and stumbled into the hallway.

"Fuckin' what?" he inquired of the darkness as he walked into a cluster of obstacles barring his way into the flat. He lost his balance and threw an arm out to steady himself but the fist clutching the slippery nylon wig slid against the gloss painted wall and, if anything, precipitated his collapse. He shot forward and nutted himself insensible on the substantial plaster architrave surrounding his bedroom door.

He lay there unmoving, splayed and thickly bleeding amidst the tumbled pile of Trish's bags.

"I'm going to live with Martin," Trish said, realigning her bags by the door.

"Mar-?"

Trish held up a hand, bossy little palm outward, fingers stiffly together like a policewoman on traffic duty. She always looked away, eyes closed and chin uptilted when she did this to him, long disdainful of his excuses, and it was a gesture that never failed to stop him in his tracks.

"I don't want to hear it," she said.

"You don't want to hear me say 'Martin'?"

Trish rounded on him, "I don't want to hear your voice at all, okay? I've had enough and I'm leaving." She gazed at him sitting there on the sofa, knees together, clutching a frizzy ball of silver material in his lap like some laughably pampered cat. His face trembled with remorse and the unhinging pressure of a cast-eyed hangover. "I'm going to live with Martin," she sighed.

"Martin?" Barwise said in a small, tearful voice.

Trish didn't slam the door. She closed it with a tightly controlled snick that resounded nonetheless with decibels of finality. Barwise stood at the window looking out onto the road and watched the taxi driver loading Trish's things into the boot of his Cavalier. They shared something; a joke perhaps, because Trish smiled, then laughed, and then looked back at the flat. Her eyes shone with that cold righteous vindication she could summon effortlessly to confound any attempt he made to justify himself to her.

I won't miss that fucking look, thought Barwise rancorously. Loaded up, Trish climbed into the front seat and they sped off. Sped off to Martin. Martin, that preposterous little Amway rep whom Barwise had come home one afternoon to find setting out his stall in their living room. Trish enrapt and giggling over his patter, his demonstrations of eco-friendly cleaning products ("Yum," he phonemes absurdly, dipping his finger into a pot of drain pep and sucking the cream greedily into his mouth), his gleam-eyed affiances of wealth and his curt dismissal of Barwise's derisory opener, "It most certainly is *not* pyramid selling!"

"Bollocks. I'd like you to leave now." Barwise had said, stepping unmindfully through Martin's picnicked out wares. He threw himself onto the sofa and switched on the telly to watch the snooker up loud.

"Gather your goods, my man." Barwise dismissed, and Martin, having mutely complied with the wishes of the master of the house, exited. "I would be happy to continue the demonstration another time, Tricia." Martin said at the door. As, it appeared, he had.

"Little cornholer," he said, "prissy little tit was the same at school, astronomy club-type, nibbling on a Penguin at break time all on his own with a copy of Angling Times and brown shoes and one of those Adidas satchels with the adjustable strap and front pocket for your folders that they don't—surely mustn't—make anymore. We did him over once, tipped all his pens out. You know what we found at the bottom of his bag? A ten pence and two pence cellotaped to the plastic. His mum had put them there for emergencies. Fucking emergencies, like if he got done over and had his bus fare nicked. Ten p for the bus and the two p for the phone. Fucking marvellous!" He chuffed, "so we nicked it. Christ," he said, suddenly serious in his reverie, "two p for the phone. Those were the days, Trish. You could get the shit kicked out of you, phone your mum in tears and still have change for a cream egg."

"You *cretin*!" Trish had yelled at him, "How dare you treat Martin like that?"

Barwise, who had gone off on a tangent in his head, suddenly snapped back to reality. "Trish, love, I thought you'd be glad to get shot of the mutt."

She stood by the door, slowly shaking her head and glaring at him with unconcealed disgust. "I like Martin, he's kind and not a bit like you. He respects people and he has ambition."

"He's a door to door salesman selling detergent flavoured yogurt."

Trish flounced across the room and picked up a magazine. "There's an article in here about you." She flapped the magazine at him. "Julie Burchill's right; you're a Manboy. All Playstation and Loaded and crying over football matches. Useless. Martin's the real man." She threw the magazine onto his lap then turned and huffed out of the room.

Barwise raised his eyebrows at the TV. "Martin's a cunt," he muttered and returned his attention to watching Jimmy piss another frame up the wall.

Initially, Barwise had enjoyed a period of brief elation following Trish's departure, that strange fugue men often find themselves in immediately after the breakup of a longstanding relationship. He was free. He could do as he pleased. He could stay up late, play his music loud, go down the pub all the time, eat shit, watch snooker, not bathe, fuck other women.

He charged around the flat with a bin bag clearing out the rest of Trish's stuff: books, magazines, ornaments, videos (aerobics workouts that he'd bought her and she'd never used, Friends, This Life, a whole set of Branagh's Shakesploitation movies) and photos. A pitifully small remnant of her presence in his life for the last six years.

He was free. He could do as he liked. He could sleep poorly and wake up alone, spend too much on drink, get undernourished, watch videos alone, be spoken to at work about his poor self-care, have existential panic attacks in the small hours and question the entire direction of his life, terrified of a lonely future, realise that he'd forgotten how to approach women and come home from the pub alone each night for a shamefully hollow wank.

He held a copy of a sweet film he had watched and enjoyed with Trish, something they had both had in common, and began to fill up. He put the bin bag gently down by the front door, went over to the sofa and had a cry.

"I'm in bits, Micky. I feel like I've had a *raison d'ectomy*." Barwise informed his friend.

"Eh?" Micky mouthed through the froth at the top of his pint.

"She was my reason for living, Micky, my be-all and end-all. My baby." A grimace spasmed his eyes shut and sorrow-masked his mouth into a grim bow of torment. "And now she's gone. Shacked up with that little dopper from school." He rummaged savagely in a packet of dry roasted.

"Martin Glomerulus," mused Micky, "old Emergency Bus Fare. Still I s'pose he's come on a bit since then. Drives that Subaru, innit?"

Barwise tipped the peanut dust into the palm of his hand and got it into his mouth with elaborate loose-lipped puckerings, like a horse taking a sugar lump.

"I haven't eaten for two days," he said. "I can't go round the shops on my own. It makes me feel like a loser. I could eat the arsehole out of a dead rhinoceros, should the opportunity present itself, but I just can't be fucked to cook. I think I'm getting depressed."

Micky, who didn't come down the pub to talk about emotions, shifted uneasily on his stool.

"I keep bursting into tears," Barwise lamented, wells of dampness gathering at the bridge of his nose.

"There's Dave!" Micky ejaculated hoarsely. He scooped up his pint and left Barwise sitting alone, blinking in moist regret. A while later he began staring shark-eyed at a table full of seventeen year old girls over by the triv machine until they became uneasy with his attentions.

Feeling a free-floating kind of depersonalisation, an hour later he went home and got the porn out.

Maudlin, Barwise sat picking at his microwavable New York Takeout with a grubby fork, last night's microwavable Thai Noodle remnants clogging the tines like forensic toe-jam.

The phone rang. Barwise shuddered and let it ring. The last time he'd answered the phone it had been Trish, concretely businesslike, arranging a window to pick up the rest of her stuff. Appropriate really, seeing as he'd defenestrated the bin bag in a pissed rage a couple of nights ago, leaving the contents strewn across the back yard.

The phone continued to ring. He sighed and went to answer it.

"It's Micky. Fancy a couple of polite ones?"

Barwise thought for a moment. He had work to do, a half-finished cartoon strip that, despite his most fierce avoidance, was resolutely refusing to draw itself. He just didn't feel inspired. Whenever he sat down at the board he felt a swamping tide of panic well up into his chest like dark water. His pen shook and his vision blurred. He needed to urgently visit the bathroom.

"I'll see you down there," Barwise heard himself say. At least down the pub he could be more his old self and it certainly helped him go off to sleep.

Much later, his upper body a febrile jack-in-the-box on the oafish springs of his legs, Barwise allowed himself to be ejected from the pub following a nasty incident with a crippled local.

He'd been sitting at the bar with Micky. They'd got looking at the charity boxes and discovered they both had some opinions to explore around the issues highlighted by the plights of others less fortunate than themselves.

"Look at that," says Micky; pointing to the SCOPE box, "do you remember those little crippled statues outside the supermarkets, kids in callipers. Spastics."

Barwise nods, distantly remembering how the little doll-faced girl with the money-box and gammy leg had curiously aroused him as a small boy. She'd had dried bubble gum pushed into one of her eyes and one morning he'd spent some time chipping it out with his fingernails. Like a good deed. He'd gone home and spent a fair part of the rest of the day with the bright, jolly smell of Hubba Bubba on his fingers and a troublesome sensation in his pants.

Micky continues, "Now what I want to know is, they change the name to something more politically correct, like SCOPE, then they go and blag a big sticker on the box saying 'formerly the spastics' society'. I mean whassa point in that? I mean."

Barwise grows bored with Micky's thrust and says, "Don't you know what it stands for? It's one of those anachronyms."

"A what?" goes Micky.

"A nacronism."

Micky nods.

"It stands for," and this is when Barwise's luck falters, because some of the chaps from the local hostel for young people with disabilities have come in for a night out with their carers. It is, after all, quiz night.

"It stands for," he says again. His eyes squint with mirth.

Micky is still nodding, pint half raised, now not so sure that what is coming will be as educational as he might previously have thought. His eyes dart uneasily over Barwise's trembling shoulders.

"It stands for *spastics can't often propel 'emselves*! Ahh-ha HARR!"

Outside, in the steady drizzle, Barwise's misery was complete. He craned his head back and looked to the dismal cloud cover for some sort of sign. Fine rain rinsed his unshaven face and webbed his tormented eyes. He blinked to clear them and placed his head in his hands like someone gently laying a cold dying animal into a merciful grave.

A short while later, he composed himself and looked up and across the road at the curry house. Sitting at a table in the window, bathed with mellow light in the brothelish, crimson interior sat Trish and Martin, tug-of-warring impishly over a peshwari naan.

"Oh," whispered Barwise, "Not *our* table." Bitterly he recalled nearly proposing to Trish at that table, suffused with romance and Kingfisher lager.

Unable to tolerate any further pain, Barwise spun and bolted up the high street. He skidded to a stop on the corner, his back to the station, panting, feeling sick. He remembered that night coming back from the club. Falling over bags. The pain, the loneliness, the wig.

And something else he recalled. The big thundering shape that legged it into the station. He'd forgotten about that. He wheeled around and was surprised to find that the entrance was ungated and that a small light still shone from the newspaper kiosk. The last train came through at about eight forty-five and it was getting on for eleven. Curiosity and a need for distraction led Barwise to venture under the awning and take a peek along the concourse. Twelve yards of black-and-white tiles and another set of steps leading up onto the windy darkness of the platform. Set into the right hand wall, like a secret door in a role-playing game, was a little booth which sold papers, magazines, fags, etcetera. From within Barwise could distinctly make out rustling and a tuneless yet nonetheless elated species of humming.

He pursed his lips. Perhaps he could grab a quick packet of Royals and a Mars bar for supper. He had a dig around for some change and as the jangle of coins echoed along the concourse, the rustling and humming stopped abruptly.

Barwise froze, suddenly and unaccountably fearful. He slowly removed his hand from his jeans with pick-pocket caution and let out a careful breath. He'd stumbled onto a robbery. Someone was doing over the kiosk and he was about to march up and ask for a fucking light snack.

Then a voice came from the concealed recess.

"Can I help you, sir?"

Barwise belched a throatful of beer as the tension broke. He took a couple of steps further into the station and peered into the kiosk.

Barely tall enough to see over the counter, wearing a dark green sun visor and what actually looked like a butchers apron, stood a little bald man with eyes and grin that hinted at a substantial degree of mental disorder. He reached down, disappearing momentarily, then popped back up with an effortful groan and swung a pile of newspapers onto the counter by their frayed, knotted string. He winked at Barwise and produced a rusty, ivory-handled straight razor which he used to hack at the string and free the papers.

He stood back and stared at Barwise with grimy eyes.

Suddenly a gust of wind sheeted down from the platform and Barwise turned in time to get a faceful of the stink that carried on it. It was an awful smell, like dead wet dogs and savage wild dung. Like having the bottom of a caged animal held up to your face. He wheeled away from it, choking, and felt the beer rise again. Something heavy

thumped along the platform up there, resolute and somehow impatient.

"Got something for you," said the little fellow and he
ducked down again and brought up another parcel. He used
the razor to cut the string and turned the parcel of papers a
hundred and eighty degrees to face Barwise.

Barwise frowned and watched the man fan them out. His
eyes widened and he said, "No way," and stepped right up to the
counter and leaned over, unmindful that the man had grasped
the razor again or that something the size of a garden shed had
begun to take the steps down from the platform behind him.

Barwise looked up, but the man was busy paring his
fingernails and was humming tonelessly again. There was
a tremendous oily clatter from behind him. Barwise turned
in time to see the diamond hatched gates slam home across
the bottom of the platform steps, compressing and springing back like a concertina with the force of their closure. In
the darkness beyond he made out the shape of something
massive plodding back up the steps.

He looked blearily back at the little fellow, feeling con-
fused and suddenly drunk again. His hands gripped the
edge of the counter and he narrowed his eyes.

"You can't make a monkey out of Gus," the proprietor said, grinning even more widely. "Oh, no." Then he
laughed, which Barwise found rather horrid.

But Barwise couldn't stay uneasy for long, because his
attention had been drawn back again to what lay splayed out
on the counter as if for him alone.

"I don't fucking believe this," said Barwise and he rummaged about in the pile. He looked up at the proprietor again. "Are these, are these actually *new*?"

The man nodded and grinned more widely. There was a gleam in his eye Barwise struggled to read, intimating not only secrecy but an almost gangland complicity.

"They mean a lot to you, yes?"

Barwise took a step back and ran a hand through his hair. He didn't know what he felt. "Well, yeah, I guess. I mean, yeah!" He shook his head to dislodge a heavy feeling over his eyes. He wanted to sit down.

He reached out a hand suddenly afflicted with a coarse tremor and snatched up the top copy of a comic called Monster Fun. He used both hands to steady it in front of his face. On the cover a gleeful and mildly unhinged Frankie Stein gawped out at him. Barwise lifted the comic to his face and sniffed it. It smelt of cheap ink and mass produced grainy paper. He looked back at the counter and grabbed for a fistful of the remaining comics: Buster, Shiver and Shake, Jackpot, Whoopee, Whizzer and Chips, Krazy. EVERY MONDAY they blared. Today's date. Price 8p.

Barwise took a breath in order to say something but let it out through a tight grin. A grin not unlike the gleeful and mildly unhinged grin Frankie Stein was modelling this day in fact, a good twenty years after the comics he had appeared in, comics Barwise had adored as a kid and which had inspired him to create his own strips, had disappeared off the shelves and into hazy oblivion at the cliff edge of his childhood. A small part of him had missed them terribly ever since.

Barwise grabbed the entire pile and scavenged for his small change. "I'll take the lot," he said, spilling his money onto the counter. In his state of arousal Barwise failed to notice that a small boy had descended the platform steps and was standing amongst the litter and softly stirring leaves gathered at the foot of the drawn gate. Had he turned, Barwise would have glimpsed only a short, fat silhouette, its round hairless head inclined at an angle connoting curiosity. Pale fingers slid through the grating and gripped the cold iron, and one might have noticed in the slight shift of posture a more subtle anticipatory attitude, as if the boy was eager for release.

Still staring at his comics, Barwise jolted suddenly as a harsh unfolding rattle sounded and he looked up to see that the kiosk shutter was now pulled down. He frowned but was in no mind to question the emphatic closure to their business because he had an armful of his childhood and wanted to get home in order to facilitate its recapture.

Barwise peered through a crack in the curtains.

On the step, Micky fished in a carrier bag and broke a can of Heineken off its four pack. He thumbed the ring pull and sloshed back a long swallow, wiped his mouth with his wrist and stood staring at the front door with a perplexed expression.

Barwise stepped back from the window and peered around the gloomy lounge. He prodded at a pile of empty

foil containers with the toe of his left foot and watched
with bafflement as they resettled themselves with a hollow
silvery rattle, dribbling bits of chicken tikka and aloo gobi
onto his sock. He pressed his hands against either side of
his face and massaged his temples with his fingertips, feeling the bristles on his cheeks scrape his palms.

He went back to the window and took another peek,
thinking, *Fuck off, Micky.*

As requested, Micky had indeed taken his leave, having tired of pressing Barwise's buzzer for the last ten minutes. Barwise returned to the spicy semi-dark of his living
room, stepped over a shoal of lager cans and made for the
bedroom, rubbing his hands together. His right foot came
down in a foil dish but he didn't seem to notice and continued through the hall with it stuck there, wearing it like
a futuristic slipper. He slouched into the bedroom and to
his dismay came upon the small head of Micky peering in
over the window sill, his brow furrowed beneath the narrow
chevron of his widow's peak.

Their eyes met and, reflexively, Micky grinned and lifted
a hand in relieved greeting, but the wave aborted halfway
and all expression emptied from Micky's face as he saw the
state Barwise was in.

Barwise skipped nimbly across the room and scooped
up the comics scattered over his bed. He clutched them
to his chest and stood, breathing in short agitated breaths.
Micky stood there watching him with a blank look in his
eyes, mortified that he had just caught Barwise having a bit

of a wank and thinking how was he going to busk his way out of this one.

Barwise decided to be proactive and came around the bed. He gently placed the pile of now dog-eared comics on the counterpane and reached over to unlatch the window. He lifted the sash.

"Micky," he said. "Can I be of assistance?"

Micky looked at Barwise and saw little he would normally describe as healthy: the greasy hair sticking up at the crown of Barwise's head, the sallow complexion, the progressing beard, the bloodshot darting eyes and the licks of primary coloured food stains at the corners of his mouth. With a half-hearted gesture towards the bag at his feet, Micky said, "You could assist me with these if you like."

Barwise sighed and stepped back from the window. "Come on, then," he said and walked off, leaving Micky standing occluded with indecision, actually wondering whether Barwise had meant for him to climb in through the window. He shook his head, gathered his bag of lagers and headed round the front.

Micky knew Barwise hadn't been too clever lately but when he saw the conditions in which he was living, his stunted empathy cranked up a notch and he said, "Fuck sake, look at this shit hole. Are you all right? I haven't seen you all week."

Barwise sat down on the sofa and disturbed Micky further by smiling brightly. "I'm good, Micky. Very good indeed." He sat back with a sigh and crossed his legs. He noticed the container stuck to his foot, appeared momentarily at a loss, and then idly flicked it across the room. "Why do you ask?"

Micky's attention was on the kitchenette. He said something inexact, something which entirely failed to sum up the enormity of the squalor he saw there.

"Been busy," Barwise said, still smiling into the far distance.

"Busy losing the plot?" Micky said with a weak laugh.

"*Au contraire,* Michael. In fact I have a plan. A plan to regain my lost love."

Micky was becoming sensationally uneasy. "Trish?" he said.

Barwise exploded off the sofa. "That fucking bitch! I'll get her back, Micky, I'll get Trish back!" Barwise stood in the middle of the room, panting with venom. Then his shoulders slumped and he turned to Micky with a terrible haunted look. "I've got friends." he said in a small, tired voice.

Micky had exhausted his coping mechanisms. He backed up to the door and pulled at the handle. Barwise tilted his head to one side. "I'll get her, Micky," he said again.

"Keep the beers!" Micky said with a bright and terrified shrillness and bundled out into the street.

Barwise blinked. He shook his head in four short tight jerks. He smiled and went back into the bedroom to be with his comics.

Monday again day after tomorrow. He looked at the pile of small change in an old ash tray by his bed and grinned and skipped gleefully from foot to foot.

That night, as Barwise slept, his friends came into the back yard and gathered under his window. Their black outlines and cheap colouration paled down in the moonlight so that they looked like sinister double exposures. They moved across the concrete, past the washing line, through the shrubs, to take their places outside Barwise's rear window as if summoned.

Aroused by their murmuring, Barwise sat up in bed and squinted towards the moonlit window. He slid his bare legs from under his blanket and crept across the room. He smiled through the glass. There were more than ever tonight, and they had brought things with them to help. He waved.

One of them gestured and Barwise said, "Oh, right," or thought he had, and opened the window. He was vaguely uneasy, as if he had done this before recently and the result had been unsatisfactory. Nevertheless, he leaned his head out and said, "Hi!" He was so happy to see all his old friends here. There was Martha, Faceache, the guys from Scream Inn. Odd ball sprang about morphing into all manner of hilarious shapes and creatures. Ray with his specs, Brainy with his Monster Maker. And his favourite, Pete with his bottomless pockets. Marvellous. At the back, like a door-man minding the back gate, Frankie lifted a huge green sewn-on hand and waved. Barwise was delighted and was about to clap his hands when one of them stepped forward to speak.

It was Sweet Tooth. His one huge, white prominent tooth stuck out over his top lip. He had his toffee apple, which, for some reason, reassured Barwise enormously. Sweet Tooth opened his mouth. A big white bubble slid out and hung above his head. There were words in it.

Barwise read them with a solemn expression. He nodded with great seriousness. Other bubbles popped up above the heads of the crowd. Barwise took the time to read them all, which made him feel very tired. He felt his eyes start to close, so he lifted a hand, bade his friends goodnight and slid the window shut, hoping he wasn't being too rude. A bit like that chap in the station kiosk really, he thought, closing up business for the night. Not impolite, merely efficient. That reminded Barwise again that it was nearly Monday. Monday was comics day, always had been, always would be. Dad used to bring them home with the newspapers and they'd sit together at breakfast. Dad with the Mirror and the Star, little Barwise with his own stack of colourful tabloids. Each one full of monsters, and kids with the kind of additions to their toy boxes any responsible father would confiscate immediately. Particularly Brainy's aforementioned Monster Maker which, as the name implies, made things substantially bigger. Barwise's smile faltered. It wasn't long after Dad left that the comics stopped coming out, he recalled.

He climbed back into bed and lay on his side. He stared at the small pile of coins on the bedside table. He felt a nostalgic longing overwhelm him.

As he drifted off to sleep, he murmured, "I'll get you back." But behind his eyelids it wasn't Trish he saw. It was his father.

There was a little pot of cream and a matchbox on his window ledge in the morning. It had rained in the night; Barwise could smell the creosote on the damp fence. He looked out across the yard. The gate was shut, the gap between the bottom of the gate and the concrete clogged with fallen leaves. Some of Trish's belongings were still strewn in the flower bed.

Barwise picked up the items on his window ledge. He unscrewed the lid of the cream jar and sniffed. Memories went off in his head like fireworks; this was the smell of Trish at night. The cream smelt just like her moisturiser. Amazing, because it was far from being ordinary moisturiser. He pushed open the matchbox with a thumb and nearly fell over when out popped a little pink sponge. It was highly porous and about the size of his thumbnail. It smelt faintly metallic.

Delighted, he took these through to the lounge and sank down onto the sofa. He would spend the day planning. And tonight he would get Trish back. Delicately he placed the matchbox containing the Iron Eater on his bare right knee and Martha's pot of Monster Make-up on his left knee. He sat back with a contented sigh and contemplated his plan.

Barwise stood looking up at the fire escape at the back of Martin's building. He checked his watch. They wouldn't be back from her mother's for a good hour, plenty of time to lay his traps. Another thing he didn't miss were those trips round to see the old girl every Sunday afternoon. Not that she was a cow or anything, it was just the stifling gas fire-cooked smell of cheap tabloids, beetroot salads and the dismal war-torn honk of farts that oppressed him. It made him want to clamber out of the scullery window biting back screams. Those visits would stop when he got Trish back. He chortled throatily and patted his pockets. Lovely. He glanced up and down the alley, stepped over a haul of bin bags and began to climb.

He reached the fourth floor, his footsteps like dull chimes on the wet ironwork of the fire escape. He ducked beneath the small kitchen window and sidled up to the back door. His foot slipped on the metal and kicked one of Martin's pot plants into space. Barwise swore and peered over the railing. He watched the plant plummet into the alley, spiralling leaves, and detonate with a splintering thud at the bottom of the fire escape. As he looked down, Barwise could make out the furtive withdrawal of indistinct shapes into the shadows of bins and gateways all along the alley. He smiled and raised a hand but they remained hidden.

Barwise turned back to the door. He took the match-box out of his pocket and slid it open. He tipped the Iron Eater onto his palm. It felt slightly oily when he picked it up between his thumb and forefinger. He placed it against the mortise lock.

There was a brief glugging sound, like water going down a plug hole, and the lock was gone. All that was left was a ragged hole in the wood. Barwise was astounded. He plucked the Iron Eater out of the hole (it was now the size of a snooker ball), and held it up to his face. "You were hungry, weren't you fella," he said. He stepped forward and pushed against the door. To his delight it swung open. He stepped over the threshold and began tearing little bits off the engorged Iron Eater until he had a handful of little pink pieces each about the size of a pea. He lobbed the tiny Iron Eaters out onto the fire escape, scattering them.

Barwise went into the kitchen and pulled a small Mag-lite out of his back pocket. He trembled with excitement as he shone the narrow beam around the room. He went through to the living room. When he saw Martin's shelf full of Laurel and Hardy figurines he felt a sudden and vicious urge to smash everything up, massive as a heart attack. He stood breathing hard, a tremendous, thick pounding at his temples.

Barwise steadied himself. Stick to the plan. He dug in his pocket for the Monster Make-Up and pulled the little jar out. Living with Trish had taught him one thing: she was a woman to whom routine meant everything. He looked around, located the bedroom and went through.

He had braced himself for the rush of unpleasant feelings he had anticipated on seeing their intimate little boudoir. He let out a harsh, involuntary bleat of laughter when he shone the torch on two single beds. Marvellous. No shagging, Martin. I need time. He spoilt me, Martin. Barwise rejoiced.

He went over to the bedside cabinet. There it was: Trish's night cream. Every night before lights out, she plastered herself with that shit. Barwise unscrewed the pot and scooped the cream out with his fingertips. He looked around, shrugged, lifted the rug up with his foot and wiped the goop off on the carpet.

Barwise took the lid off the Monster Make-up and decanted the contents into Trish's now empty cream jar. Barwise wasn't surprised to see that it was the same consistency and colour. It had the same smell. He put the lid back on and replaced it on the cabinet. Very carefully, he secured Martha's pot; he didn't want any of that stuff on him. He put it back in his pocket and stood up. He took one last look around, smoothed the bedding and returned to the living room.

He looked at his watch. If the past was anything to go by—and with Trish it was as reliable as a seeing-eye dog—they would be home within ten or fifteen minutes. He went to the front door and let himself out into the hallway.

There was a little boy with short spiky black hair standing there. He was wearing a black blazer, stripy tee-shirt, shorts and shiny shoes. He had a little pot belly and wavy lines were emanating from the side of his head with words between them. *SHOCK HORROR*, they said, and *IMMI-NENT FEELINGS OF DREAD.*

Barwise looked at Faceache and was about to say something, when he heard footsteps in the stairwell below. He heard Martin say something.

"Fuck!" Barwise said and ducked back into the flat. He looked frantically around, spotted the broom cupboard adjacent to the front door and pulled it open. He shoved the vacuum cleaner aside and got in, clattering the ironing board with his knees. "*Shit!*" He pulled the door shut and squatted in the dark, panting.

Seconds later the front door opened and Barwise heard Trish and Martin come in. He held his breath.

"That was a very pleasant afternoon," Barwise heard Martin say.

From the living room: "I think she liked you, Martin. Especially when you found her pads."

"I haven't had beetroot for goodness knows how long," Martin said, and in the darkness, Barwise choked.

Trish said, "I think I'll turn in early." Regular as fucking clockwork.

Martin said something else and then Barwise heard the bathroom light ping on. He stood in the cupboard, knees bent and beginning to threaten cramp. He straightened up and felt his head connect with the low ceiling. He hoped Martin was keen to hit the hay too, maybe try for a bit of topside. *Don't even think about it, tosspot*, thought Barwise, *it just ain't worth the pain.*

Eventually, Trish emerged from the bathroom. She said, "See you in a minute, then." Martin made a hideous kind of appreciative grunt and then the TV went off.

Barwise jigged from foot to foot as quietly as he could. When he heard the bathroom light again, he decided to get the hell out of there. He bent over the Hoover, trying to avoid clanking the ironing board again, and opened the door a crack. He put his eye to the gap and saw that the living room was all quiet. From the bathroom he could hear Martin's electric toothbrush humming. Satisfied, Barwise stepped out into the lounge, heart thumping and reached out a hand for the front door handle.

Trish screamed. Barwise froze, his hand halfway to the handle. There was a crash then another scream, this time louder and lungfully sustained. Barwise turned and saw Martin step out of the bathroom with a dumb look of uncertainty on his face. He made for the bedroom, saw Barwise cringing in the doorway, stopped, looked back at the bedroom and was only galvanised into action when Trish screamed a third time.

He reached the door just as she emerged.

Her head was the size of a horse's. Pupilless eyes blazed from a wart-studded forehead. Teeth like sugar cubes gnashed behind meaty, rippling gums and ropes of filthy saliva flew in thick, grey clots. She lowered her head and bellowed.

Martin staggered away from her, eyes wild and horri-fied. He seemed to see Barwise for the first time, and came towards him, arms raised. "What have you done to her?" he said in a shrill, accusing voice, but didn't reach Barwise, because Trish reached Martin first and sank her claws into the flesh beneath his chubby arms. She wrenched her wrists and Martin's face crumpled in shock as she lifted him off his feet by his armpit hair. There was a brief tearing sound and Martin shrieked. He sank to the floor, red-faced, arms crossed with his hands pressed beneath his armpits. He twisted his body away and looked up at Trish. Huge boils had broken out across her cheeks and chin. She no longer had a left eye but a long splintered horn curved from the socket, dirty-looking and slathered with fluid.

Barwise gaped as Trish bent forward and hauled Martin to his feet. He beat at her arms, but she was too powerful. She dragged him through the lounge and into the kitchen. Martin went down on his knees, weeping now, and saying "Don't, don't." over and over. His knees squeaked on the linoleum.

Barwise followed, trying not to miss anything, and saw Trish reach out and throw open the back door. It flew open and hit the worktop so hard the frame split. Barwise stood at the entrance to the kitchen and watched as Trish lifted the gibbering Martin to his feet, snorted hot yellow steam into his running eyes, tensed, and tossed him out into the night.

Barwise shrieked. Trish turned her monstrous face away from the darkness outside and made a foul-tempered rattle at the back of her throat. Barwise took a step back, shaking his head. Trish tilted her head and returned her attention to the door overlooking the alley.

From below, Barwise could now hear a familiar murmuring sound. He wanted to see so badly that he actually came across the kitchen and stood directly behind Trish. His eyes widened with surprise and wonderment, for there was no longer a fire escape. He looked over Trish's slumped shoulders. There were a few denuded stanchions still bolted to the wall, but little else. In the alley, pink spongy medicine balls sat gleaming amongst the rubbish. There was a great crowd gathered in the alley, gradually taking on substance. A hundred familiar faces looked up at him, imploring him to make them live again, make them real. Beside him, Trish shuddered and let out a soft cry. She glanced up and Barwise saw blue eyes.

He looked down again and saw bubbles popping up above the heads of the crowd. They drifted up towards him. Trish was crying, one manicured hand holding onto the door frame for support. Barwise rubbed his chin with his fingers. He frowned and stepped back into the kitchen.

"You can't make a monkey out of me!" He crowed, laughing like a loon, and shoved Trish out, too.

The police found him the next day. He had somehow broken into the concourse of the disused station and was pounding on the rusty, screwed down shutter which concealed the old newspaper kiosk. He was shouting. When the policemen put locks on his arms he howled, a terribly empty, let-down sound that reverberated the length of the concourse and could be heard quite a way down the weed-ridden tracks in either direction. They took him away and charged him with the double murder of his ex-partner and her new lover. A certain Micky Mitre had informed the law in his statement that he thought Barwise might be planning a drunken revenge. "He kept saying he was going to get her back," Micky could be heard saying down the pub. "He got her back, all right. Chucked 'em both off the fucking fire escape. I mean! Yeah, I'll have a pint, mate. Cheers."

Barwise sat on his bunk with his head in his hands.

They had been found at the foot of the fire escape, dead from the fall. His prints were all over the flat, his bootsoles matched the muddy tread marks on the back door from where he had kicked it in. It wasn't meant to be like this. What had he been doing this last week? Nothing seemed to add up. He looked around his cell, broken-hearted. "Trish," he said in a bewildered voice. No way out of this, they had told him. He curled up on his bunk and stared at the graffiti on the wall a foot away from his nose. No way out. He shuddered.

There was a noise in the corner of his cell. He sat up quickly, eyes adjusting to the gloom.

A small boy stood in the corner by the door. He grinned a mouthful of tombstone teeth and put a finger to his lips. He had close-cropped hair and fat, pale cheeks. He put a hand in his trouser pocket and Barwise watched with amazement, as the smiling boy pulled a parrot in a cage from it. The boy frowned in a comical, exaggerated way, and put both hands in his pockets. Out came a step ladder and a set of golf clubs. Barwise clapped. A tear trickled down the side of his nose.

After a few minutes, the boy was almost totally obscured by junk. The cell was getting full and Barwise was becoming uneasy. What if someone came to check on him? At last the boy pulled something from his pocket, showed all his teeth in a mad crescent of satisfaction, and chucked the object on the cell's only table. Barwise looked at it. He was aware of a dimming in his periphery and he looked up to see that he was alone again in his empty cell. All the junk was gone. Well, all but this one thing. For a while, Barwise remained sitting on his bunk, dimly aware of how hard his heart was beating.

He got up and went over to the table.

Barwise stood looking at the rusty straight razor for a long time. There were tiny strands of coarse string caught where the blade was hinged to the ivory handle.

Smiling, Barwise picked it up.

DON'T TOUCH THE BLACKOUTS

I looked up from the counter and Bismuth was there, standing tall in his knee-length coat, head slightly tilted back and staring down at me with those eyes like tiny tiger-heads rammed in his face. His mouth was hidden completely behind a neglected topiary of beard. His hair was like an armful of bats blown back off his skull and frozen, matted into tangled, greasy wings.

I blinked and wiped my hands on the front of my apron. My shop had emptied. Outside, the arcade stretched ahead like a walk-in kaleidoscope to the street at the far end where there was a rectangle of natural light. Across this aperture snow and traffic and people blew back and forth, constantly refracting through my pebble-glass shop window.

Bismuth opened his mouth but he had already begun to cry.

"I don't want you to die," he said.

At first, Bismuth had only come to me in dreams. Last year he appeared in my shop where I discovered him crawling on his hands and knees at the back of my stock room, weeping over the things for which he was searching. We didn't speak. I just left him and went home, locking the shop behind me. I didn't look back as I walked down the arcade, past the other small units, and turned left on the street to cut across the bombsites.

Sometime after that I was at the Triangle bar drinking coffee and eating a pastry as I did every morning before opening up my shop. The Triangle bar is at the neck of the arcade and is a great place. Peter and Johnny own the Triangle bar and if you want to get served you have to speak French. My French was poor but has been slowly improving. I can pick out whole sentences from the French stations on the wireless now and get a gist of the news from the papers they lay out on the counter.

It was snowing again. A couple of young lads came in under the awning and stood shaking snow out of their hair. The gas under the stainless steel urns was roaring. I could smell pecans and rich, salty butter.

Then, Johnny tapped me on the arm. "Qui est-ce que?" he said, and pointed out into the snow.

Standing on the pavement outside was Bismuth. Snow was blowing around him like rose petals.

I stood up and walked to the door. Bismuth turned away and began to walk down the arcade. I went out onto the street and followed him. The other units were beginning to open up and we walked past flower stalls and cabinetmakers and booksellers until we came to the door of my shop right at the end. Pigeons were fluttering amongst the struts and flues that ran beneath the corrugated roofing high above us.

Bismuth was staring into the shop. His eyes shone with a distracted form of hope. I took out my key and unlocked the door. He stood aside for me to enter then followed me in. I went behind the counter and waited for him to speak.

"I need my Instruments," he said. His voice was slow and deep, thoughtful, like I knew it would be.

I smiled then, because not long after I had found him weeping and searching through my shop that time, I had discovered beneath my cash register some curious, arcane looking objects.

I nodded and pulled open the drawer beneath the till and lifted them out. I placed them on the counter and watched as Bismuth reached trembling hands towards them.

"I don't want you to die."

There was nothing I could say to him but I smiled as kindly as I could and reached out a hand. He responded, in turn reaching out and taking my hand in both of his. I knew what he had come for; they had appeared only this morning, in the drawer beneath my till. His Instruments. They were always here when he needed them.

"What is it this time?" I asked him.

"I don't know," he said, "I don't know. I just hear them calling."

"Do you have to go?"

Bismuth made a soft sound in his throat, like a sob, a lost, imploring affirmation. "Of course," he said.

I drew my hand back and pulled open the drawer. I gave him his Instruments—his Compass and Levers.

The Levers were like two old-fashioned brakes from an antiquated automobile, slender rods of tubular steel with a sprung brass handle and grip. The Compass was just a small disc the size of a coin that opened like a pocket watch. Its face was the colour of parchment and it had no cardinal points, just a slender silver needle that swung and spun abruptly as if sensing out its lodestar rather than responding to its pull.

Bismuth put the Compass in his pocket and took up a Lever in each hand. I stood aside to allow him access to the back of my shop. There was only a narrow aisle between the counter and the back wall of the arcade. There was a small door at the end of the wall, almost concealed by the shelves of goods piled up next to it. I kept it locked because it opened directly onto the bombsites and there was nothing out there beyond grey dereliction.

My apron was hanging on a hook on the back of the door. I took a small brass key from the front pocket and slotted it into the lock, turned it and pushed the door open. Outside, the snow had intensified and now resembled something of greater substance than particles, more like a blinding condition agitating deep and cold within my head. Bismuth stepped past me and walked out into it. Before he disappeared into the blizzard, as he became a vague,

shredded outline, I saw him lift his right arm and bring the
Ingress Lever down, slamming it into the ground. He would
compress the handle now, I knew, clenching the sprung,
shoehorn shaped switch against the grip and the Gantry
would appear for him. An access to somebody's grief would
for a moment be shored up and he would be able to step
through and locate them. And try to free them from their
cycle of despair.

I shut the door. I walked back onto the shop floor and
drew a blind down over the window. I left the *closed* sign
facing out and relocked up. I went back behind the counter
and sat down on the low stool I kept there for standing on
to reach the top shelf. I put my head in my hands. I tried to
imagine the tenderness of his heart, the might of pain that
drove him. I don't think I came close. I could not begin to
perceive the hurt I had been unable to prevent causing him
that kept him trapped in his own loop of bargaining and
denial. That which kept bringing him back here.

Bismuth did not subscribe to linear time and by strength
of will existed at all points simultaneously. It was killing him.

He holds the Compass open on his palm as he walks
towards the buildings. The needle swings, sensing out its
objective. Occasionally it appears to jump a little and he
has to cup his hand slightly to counter the sensation that it
might skate away on its own. He looks up and notices that
he is heading down a tarmac road running through a modern looking estate of houses and small flats. The buildings
all look alike with their dark coloured wooden porches and

communal entranceways. Each building has a metal box the colour of pewter next to its front door, with either one or four buttons on it depending on whether it is a single house or flats. He looks up and the rooftops seem to rush away from him, thrown into relief against the racing ochre sky. The verges and squares of grass between the buildings are the colour of pondweed. He feels there is no life beneath the earth, nothing crawling, and nothing there to satisfy the roots; there is moisture but it is like dew on a corpse.

All he can hear are his boot heels gritting on the tarmac. He looks down at the Compass and sees that the needle has settled. It is pointing just a little above North West. He stops and looks in the direction of the needle and sees the flats. He crosses the road and walks up to the door. There are four vertical panes of grimy frosted glass set into the wood, like slots. He can see nothing through them. He reaches out and presses one of the small square buttons on the intercom. There is a hiss and crackle of static like a hollow electronic exhalation and he feels an appalling sensation overwhelm him, standing there on the concrete step beneath that dreadful sky. He fears for a short spectacular moment that somehow he has opened up a connection to a dead room in there, to a terrible mortified enclosure within the building that will suck him forever into this nightmare.

He takes his finger off the button and the connection cuts off with a sudden harsh implosion of silence. He tries the door and finds it open.

He steps into the hallway. To his right, stairs go up to the first floor and a narrow landing. There are two small flats up there, their doors facing each other. Ahead of him are two more doors. The flat to his right has an entrance beneath the stairwell. He glances at his Compass and sees that the needle is pointing towards that door.

He approaches the door. This is the flat enclosing those dark, implacable eddies, he thinks. He does not know what form the loss will take but he knows that he is needed, that somehow he can apply his gift inside. He takes hold of the handle, twists it and goes in.

He is immediately aware of a voice, raised in anger. As he crosses the hall he passes a small kitchen. It is basic, with a small Formica-covered worktop to the left of the sink and spaces clogged with greasy dust where appliances have been removed. The linoleum flooring is rucked and discoloured. Ahead of him are two doors. The carpet is brown and faded, the walls and ceiling are blotched and webbed with fine cracks. A single light fitment hangs above him on a cord amber with nicotine-stained dust. The bulb looks blown. He looks again at his Compass and it is pointing to the left hand door.

The voice is still raised but it has an imploring tone, an almost bewildered, importuning quality to it, as if the speaker is begging for someone stubborn to respond with love.

Bismuth enters and sees a young man standing in the centre of the room. The walls have faded but there are brighter rectangles where posters have been removed. There is an empty bed frame and an old brown sofa. There is a large French window in one wall with a net curtain hanging across it. The curtain is torn in several places. Through the streaky glass, he can see the bombsites have appeared. They have displaced the estate of the young man's dream with the bleak desolation Bismuth has brought with him.

The young man is talking in that pleading tone but now it has an edge of anger to it again. He is weeping. There is a sense of loneliness in that room so profound, Bismuth has to close his eyes tightly against it for fear of being overwhelmed.

And as his eyes close him off from the sight of that room, he gets the full impact of the man's loss.

They have shared the flat for seven years, the two boys. They are best friends and although there have been times when they've probably wanted to kill each other (his friend being an idle slob sometimes and he being an overemotional neurotic tidy-upper) pretty much every day has been a great day, full of the kind of laughing that makes your stomach ache and can actually make you fall over with its surreal stupidity. They've both had girlfriends throughout their time together, off and on, but in truth they are both pretty content just to sit on the sofa all night, drink beer and play video games, indulging themselves in their own private jokes to the exclusion of the girls (to their despair) and have pretty much resigned themselves to bachelorhood and insidious liver-failure. Seven years go so quickly.

Then one evening, he is waiting for his friend to get back from work so that they can go to the pub for a drink and be back for a late night with a few tins. He was in the bath when the phone rang, so he missed the call and was briefly perplexed when he played the message back and heard nothing much except some voices in the background of what sounded like an office of some sort. Cold caller, he thinks, trying to flog something. He makes himself a cup of tea and waits.

The intercom buzzes. He lifts the handpiece and says hello. He hears static and the sound of traffic but no more. Frowning, he goes out into the communal hall to open the street door.

There is a policeman standing on the step.

His friend has been killed.

Bismuth opens his eyes.

The young man has been coming here in dreams for many years, stuck as he is in the anger of his grief. He walks these empty rooms, knowing that somewhere in the small flat his friend is back, waiting for him. In the dream his friend has just been away for a long time. The young man is both furious and hurt that he went like that without saying goodbye, but feels such strange, desperate relief now he is back, now things can be the same again, that his heart is aching with the confusion of feelings.

And he does find his friend but he is not as he remembers him. He hopes for some kind of remorse, some explanation, but his friend just stands there and looks terribly, miserably lost. There is no recognition. This boy has died and should not be here, should not have to suffer this recurring, broken-hearted reclamation.

The young man always begins to shout when he can elicit no response. He just wants to know where his friend has been. Is that too unreasonable?

And he knows that he will eventually awaken from this room into another and know this dream for the false hope that it always is, and he will remain lost in the greyness that unravelled his marriage and kept him drunk at the end of most days.

Bismuth moves further into the room until he is standing next to the young man. There are only the two of them in the room, but Bismuth feels a third presence. It is not the young man's friend, however, it is something alien and wrong and now Bismuth knows that time is running out. The bombsites have encroached so far that there is a pile of grey masonry pressing against the base of the French window outside. It is becoming dark out there, dark like the electronic connection that whines between dead places. Bismuth senses a sudden change in the pressure within the room, a bizarre sensation as if something is applying itself with great force against the wall of the building. There is a sudden splintering sound and a crack appears, radiating from the bottom of the French window to the top.

The young man starts and looks up. He sees Bismuth but does not react unexpectedly; he reacts to quantum changes in the way one normally would in dreams. Bismuth has seen this unsettling behaviour many times before.

He speaks to the young man. "You can let go," he says.

Sometimes, for whatever reason, whatever guilt, shame or trauma occasions it, they cannot let go.

There was a woman, bent double, pulling at her hair, screaming. The Gantry had opened and, never knowing his destination, Bismuth had emerged to find her contorted before him. They were outside and the bombsites were all around. He had a sense of desperate belatedness. He scrambled over boulders, kicked up clouds of cement dust. To his left, half a tenement collapsed with a sound like capitulation. He stumbled on a loop of rusting cable and went down. Still the woman screamed and tore at her hair. He reached out for her, but she was moving away from him as if on ice, sliding towards the object that stood like an archetype on a dais of concrete in the middle distance.

Bismuth got to his feet and went towards it and saw what it was. It was a refrigerator, rusty and paint-chipped, but it blazed against this charred and objectionable background.

The woman drew up alongside it. She turned then and for a moment her eyes met Bismuth's. He watched her reach out and grasp the handle.

Bismuth could not get to her. He cried out for her not to do it, not to open the refrigerator door in God's name, but as the words left him another building went down and drowned him out.

He watched her turn from him then and use the handle and he sensed the presence for the first time. And saw it, coming at them from between the demolished shells of buildings, the monstrous, curious shadow of the devil-in-dreams that came at the moment of deepest sorrow and fed itself fat on the misery it found there.

The woman pulled at the door and it opened and she screamed a mother's scream at the sight of her child blue and dead in there. As she had done every night since they found her boy after weeks of searching, cold and dead at the city dump, in the rusting refrigerator where he had hidden and then died.

As she screamed, tearing again at her hair, scratching at her eyes, she was engulfed by the darkness and Bismuth had time to raise the Egress Lever and bring it down, summoning the Gantry to escape this awful place. He knew what would happen when she awoke from this. This time she would take the tablets she had been staring at every morning for the past three months.

Sometimes they could not let go.

The man says nothing at first. He just stands there looking at Bismuth for a moment. Then, as Bismuth had hoped, he walks into his arms and begins to weep. Sobs, like iceberg flanks calving great mountainsides into the ocean, break away from him and Bismuth holds him.

Something booms against the wall outside and the nominal grey light from the window is blacked out. Again, that sensation of pressure change, more an implosive potential, and something opens in Bismuth's mind like a piece of space. He bites down on his lower lip hard enough to draw blood. His sinuses clatter and cold needles slide into his ears.

Keeping one arm around the young man, Bismuth half turns and begins to drag him with him out of the room and towards the hall. The man complies, sobbing still but with less intensity, and together they get to the street door. Bismuth steps out into the darkness and draws the Egress Lever from his belt. He turns his head and there the devil-in-dreams stands at the side of the house. It darts its awful face at them, its grin the mock-amused look of something that has seen all your secret shame, and tries to bite the man away.

Bismuth pulls the young man across the road and feels the eager blackness wheel away from the side of the house and hit the road close enough to send gravel spattering up the backs of their legs.

Bismuth does not look back. He has never seen this thing so close before and does not wish to see it again. He lifts the Egress Lever and punches it down into the verge. There is a sound like a bladder of sour air being punctured and the Lever is in the earth. Bismuth compresses the handle and the Gantry opens. He can see a white aperture of snow and he hauls them through. The thing at their backs howls with rage, but the Gantry swirls shut before it can rear up again.

I let them in.

The young man stood there, staring around my shop and blinking snow out of his lashes. I smiled at him.

Bismuth walked around to the front of the shop and unlocked the door. The young man nodded and followed.

For a moment they stood in the weak light that filled the arcade and then Bismuth stood aside to let the young man walk out of my shop. Bismuth didn't watch him go, he just closed the door quietly behind him.

Bismuth came over to where I was standing and looked at me over the counter. His eyes were shining. I knew what was coming.

"Son," I said, but he cannot hear what I have to ask him, cannot tolerate me asking him to let me go, to liberate me from this dream of bargaining and denial he has created for us, with its dream implements and fantastic gifts of healing in which he believes.

Outside, I saw the arcade darkening as the blackouts rolled down.

From miles distant I heard the low, almost indolent sound of renewed detonations.

Something was coming.

"Dad," Bismuth said. He had started to cry. "Why did you die?"

THE LAST PLACE
ON EARTH FOR SNOW

There's a photo of you somewhere in one of the old albums. I'll have to get them down one day and we can go through them together, before my eyesight gets any worse. You're very little in it, probably no more than two or three. You've got a big thick coat on with the hood up and you're standing in front of what you've made from a big pile of snow. Do you remember? No. You were so young I'm not really surprised. I must get the albums down. Perhaps you can go up and get them one afternoon. We'll sit together by the fire and have a good look at them. I remember thinking at the time how important it was to take that picture. I had an old fashioned camera, one you opened at the back to put in a roll of film. Probably worth a fortune now. Well, probably not, but it would certainly be pretty funny today, wouldn't it? I remember that day so well and with such happiness. We had great fun out there that morning, all wrapped up, breath frosting out in clouds, throwing snowballs. Snowballs! Can you imagine? Your mum was quite a hot shot, I remember. There really isn't a sensation in the world quite like getting a snowball in the neck and feeling that icy water dribble down between your shoulder blades. Your granddad made you a sledge that winter, too. I remember him towing you around the back garden on it. He was a clever man, your granddad. There didn't seem to be a thing he couldn't fix. He brought me an old typewriter home one day, my first one. It was a big, heavy metal frame with a greasy clamshell of stalks at its centre, each stalk embossed with tiny letters. There were big push buttons and a big rubber roller on top to wind the paper into. Anyway, one day I broke the carriage the roller ran on. A lot of the little teeth were chewed up and the entire roller had come off. There was no way I could fit it back together. It was just very old and well-used. I have to say, things lasted for a long time when I was a boy but even so, even so. I was heartbroken. My beloved typewriter, I know, but I was only young and, well, you know how much you wanted to be an architect, well, that's how much I wanted to be a writer. So your granddad took a look at it and shook his head and said something like, "I'm not promising anything." He disappeared down his garage and I probably got on with something else. Later, he called me down from my bedroom. I thought he was calling me for dinner, but when I went into the dining room, there was my typewriter on the table. I knew at once by the way dad was grinning that he'd fixed it, but I couldn't believe it. I took hold of the little lever and ratcheted it back and the roller flew along the carriage like new. It made that wonderful, unmistakable sound like a huge, heavy zipper snarling open; nothing makes a sound like that these days. Yes, he was a clever man. He'd never make promises but he didn't need to. Anyway, look how the time's gone. Next time you come, we'll get the photos down. Definitely get the old albums out. We'll find that photo of you in the snow. It might jog your memory. It would be good for you to remember that day. You can tell little Lucas when he's older that you actually played in real snow. Isn't it hard to believe that it'll never snow again? Even down in Antarctica where the Americans are building their new cities, there's just a few months of snowfall a year up in the mountains. The last mountains on Earth where you can still ski on real snow! I bet those resorts are pricey, eh? I know you submitted some of your drawings for the new city buildings on Antarctica, that's why I mentioned the photo. That was the last year it ever snowed. You don't remember, no. If you get the contract, take Lucas. Take little Lucas to the last place on Earth for snow and take a photograph. You can email it to me!

RUNNING AWAY
TO JOIN THE TOWN

t was a wild and moving drama that slouched into town, lit by darkness, old beasts and fiends and conjurers adrift on a river of rising mist. The black canopies of the hoop-crimped fabric wagons rocked in the muddy tracks, snapping like washing on a long, sullied line. And rain fell upon them, darkening further the heavy cloths and coverings stretched over the great creaking cages, drumming on the tarps, lifting a dust from the hay that hung in scarecrow hands from between the bars, until all was saturated, steaming, dark and elemental.

A driver sat at the head of the procession, reins tight between his fists like a garrotte, riding the ruts with a seagoing ease. A great, oblong coach lamp swung from a hook above his head. It lit the front of the wagon and the greasy backs of the horses with a tawny, guttering light. His shaven head shone like an ostrich egg and the rain ran in his hollow temples and down the long lines in his cheeks and dripped from the bristled bulb of his chin. The driver's hearse-black eyes surveyed the road ahead. It forked, becoming a long, narrow high street and a road that wound away to the next town along. The fork made a triangular green that was bordered on the adjacent with a stand of elms, their branches against the night like the bones of clouds. He turned and looked back along the length of the procession. At intervals the smoky yellow light of lamps banded the winding convoy, where the other drivers sat nodding, smoking their pipes or taking nips from their pewter flasks. He gave a low whistle, which was the sign to pull in, and directed his team up onto the green.

So, without invitation—for surely none would ever be freely extended, not to this, this low-slung and slumbering pandemonium—did Rainscissor and Morgoder's Autoscopic Cavalcade arrive on this poor town's fair green and prepare to deal in disquiet.

Marcel's greedy eyes surveyed the astonishing thing that had grown up on the green over night. Entranced, he pulled away from his mother's restraining hand and drifted with glazed eyes across the street. He stood gazing at the ring of caravans and cages that sat on the green. Amongst them, burly men strode carrying stanchions and parts of machines, mallets, trunks, heaps of fabric, bales of hay. He watched as a man pulled aside a heavy swag of material to reveal the mysterious interior of a cage. He bent and pulled a hank of raw, dripping meat from a tin bucket, which he slung between the bars. Something vast and black arose there in the hidden dark. There was a moment of scratching, snuffling excitement and a sudden blast of wet slobber. The man with the food pail turned his back in time to avoid being sprayed with a coating of filthy straw, dirt and drool.

Marcel was afforded a momentary glimpse of something massive as it blundered against the bars and seized upon the meat. The entire cage rocked on its axles as a caked, nostrilled cone slammed between the bars, dragging mottled lips away from an ochre octave of teeth. He heard a wet guzzling sound and felt something within him *give* like a primeval, digestive appreciation of that beast's savage devouring. Marcel's stomach rumbled.

As he stood watching, a group of children came running down the steps of a painted wooden caravan. They shrieked and skidded in the already churned-up mud, pulled faces at each other and tumbled across the green to where a group of men were assembling a bulky metal machine. They crowded up against the legs of one of the men who turned, laughing, and shouted, "Get away, you buggers or I'll put you in Dicer's cage for the rest of the day! See if you like that!" The children shrieked and scuttled away.

They flew untamed back and forth across the green. Others joined them until there was a group of nine making mischief. One of them saw Marcel and stopped tormenting one of the smaller boys in order to stand and return his gaze. Marcel gulped and took a step back, back into the shadow of his waiting mother. The boy smiled, then. It was a wild, gleeful gash of teeth, full of waywardness and destruction, but Marcel thought, as he was dragged gently away by his resigned and selfless mother, stumbling and peering back over his shoulder, that it was the most breathtaking smile he had ever seen.

So, to the bakery and a bag of cakes and pasties to help Marcel through to lunch. His mother watched the boy standing at the counter, shrouded in the somehow promising fragrance of newly baked bread, and believed her sadness to be lifting a little. She smiled at the attentive, pouting expression on her son's face and allowed herself to hope that perhaps today might be a better day for them both. It was hard bringing up a son without a father and Marcel was such a strange boy, with his tantrums and hungers and sullen defiance, that she often wondered whether she was doing him more harm than good. She did spoil him. No wonder he was getting so plump.

Marcel reached up and snagged the bag of pastries being offered across the counter. He pulled open the top and peered in. After a few moments, he looked up at his mother and his expression seemed to accuse her of some great neglect. "Is that *all* I get?" he said. There was a dusting of icing sugar on his chin and in his eyebrows. Despite his disenchantment with the contents of his bag, he nevertheless clutched it tightly against his chest, causing a further sprinkling of sugar to puff out of the top of the bag and whiten the lapels of his blazer.

Crestfallen, his mother sighed. She handed a note and some coins across the counter, feeling embarrassed beneath the look of unwanted sympathy being offered by the baker's assistant. "I can't afford any more, Marcel. You're a greedy little boy sometimes."

Marcel huffed and stomped out of the shop. His mother smiled thanks to the baker's assistant and followed him out onto the street. She resolved to take a firmer approach with her son before she ruined him completely. He would have to make do with biscuits and whatever she could find time to bake herself from now on. No more treats.

Marcel had drifted off towards the carnival, magnetized by the hooligan industry of it. A tall pole had been raised in the middle of the green. Stalls were being constructed and big, complicated clockwork machine parts were slotting together to become the rides. Marcel could hear the alien sounds of exotic animals and above it all the high, shrieking delight of children unchained by constraints and conventions (although Marcel would not have thought in these terms, the word he would have used to describe them was *free*.)

As he watched, a figure detached itself from a group of people working on one of the stalls and ran across the green. It grabbed something out of a crate and then ran towards Marcel. Marcel felt the first flutter of uneasiness in his stomach and looked round for his mother. She had begun walking the other way, towards home.

The figure was a boy. It was the boy who had smiled at Marcel as he had watched the children play on the green.

He charged up the street with something flapping from his hand. Marcel stood as though rooted. The boy skidded to a stop. Marcel took a step back.

The boy was tall and good-looking, probably about twelve or thirteen. He was wearing a red shirt and black trousers that were torn off just below the knee. He smiled, blue eyes flashing with that open, unrefined charm. "Here," he said, and held out a hand.

Marcel looked down. The boy was offering him a piece of coloured paper. Torn between trepidation and fascination, Marcel looked back again at the retreating figure of his mother, then reached out and snatched the paper from the boy's hand. He held it up and looked at it. His eyes grew wide with wonder.

It was a fly-poster for the carnival. It was printed on coarse-grained paper in red and black ink. In the foreground stood a small figure, a clown with a face so cheerless it might be the very embodiment of the word *unloved*. He held a large hoop and framed within its circle was the bulk of some huge black creature that glared through it with fierce crimson eyes. Marcel thought it must be a wolf or perhaps a bear. There was something about the way the shoulders rolled and the gut belled out that leant it a dishevelled savagery to some extent beneath the slender menace of the lions and tigers Marcel was hoping he might see. Overarching the image were the words RAINSCISSOR AND MORGODER'S AUTO-SCOPIC CAVALCADE present a congress of spectacular entertainment and a colossal combination of all that is breath-taking and implausible.

"Only show's tomorrow night," the boy said. "Eight o'clock."

Marcel nodded, still gazing at the poster.

Then he looked up, might have asked how much the tickets would be; but the boy was gone.

The next day, Marcel was sitting at the big table in the kitchen. He looked down at the plate of small, overcooked biscuits in front of him. He picked one up and held it between his thumb and forefinger. He tapped it against the side of the plate and stared up at his mother with dark and dangerous eyes as the biscuit made a stony *chink!* against the china.

His mother took a deep breath and reminded herself not to be drawn into shamefaced excuses and undignified retractions; both were responses she often found herself resorting to beneath this particular perilous gaze.

Marcel dropped the biscuit, sat back and crossed his arms. His mother reached over and took the plate away. "If you don't want these, Marcel, then you'll not get any more," she said.

"Is that a promise?" Marcel replied.

"Marcel!" she cried and, to Marcel's horror, burst into tears. The plate tipped and the biscuits – lovingly but ineptly baked – spilled onto the tiles where they shattered like fragments of unglazed pottery.

Marcel stood up. His mother had turned away and was sobbing. Marcel opened his mouth, perhaps to say the one thing that might mend his mother's heart, but he could only think of the weeks, the months following his father's disappearance when she would do this: dissolve in front of him and pitch his own grief-stricken world into an even darker and more desolate place. He would reach out to her then, but, being so small, and finding no comfort, would heap up blame and internalise the guilt, and the gulf between them became inexpressibly vast and unbridgeable.

Marcel withdrew to his bedroom. He took the poster from beneath his pillow and held it up before him. Tonight, he thought, transported. He sat down on his bed and rocked with delight.

"You're not going," his mother said. Her eyes were red from crying; she looked exhausted and tousled by sorrow. Marcel's eager expression became a mask, draining away like excited waters flattening to a deep, cold calm.

His mother stood in the doorway of his bedroom. Marcel had been reaching for his jacket as his mother had uttered the unexpected refusal.

He sat back on the bed. "*What?*"

"You're not going to the carnival, Marcel. I'm not paying for tickets because you don't deserve to go."Marcel felt panic rising. He clasped his hands before him in a gesture of supplication. "Oh, mama, *please*," he said. "It's only for one night and I've never seen the animals – "

His mother held up a hand. "I've had enough of you, Marcel. You can stay up here and think about how horrible you are." And she stepped back into the hallway and slammed the door. Marcel clutched at his temples as the key turned in the lock. He ran to the door. "Mama!" he shouted, but she did not respond.

Marcel opened his bedroom window and looked out. He could hear the sounds of the carnival carried on the wind; the foggy lowing of the pump organs and the inveigling cries of the Barkers, the vivid, metallic melodies of the calliope and the general clamour of the gathering crowd, all rose up into the twilit sky and filled Marcel with such an insupportable longing he felt he might lose his mind.

The drop to the yard wasn't too far. Marcel reckoned he could squeeze backwards out of the narrow window and dangle from his fingertips, leaving a distance of about six feet between him and the flower bed beneath the parlour window.

He pulled himself up onto the sill and shuffled round so that he was kneeling with his bottom sticking out of the window. He slid his legs out and manoeuvred himself on his belly until he was hanging, as he had imagined, about six feet from the ground. He closed his eyes and let go of the sill.

Marcel landed in the flowerbed. He toppled backwards and sprawled on the cold concrete of the yard but picked himself up, unharmed by the fall.

He ran to the gate and flung himself at the carnival.

When Marcel arrived at the green he marvelled to see so many people. It was as though the entire town had turned out. He wandered up onto the grass and began to make his way through the crowd. Everywhere he looked he saw stalls selling treats and offering entertainment, rides and slides and secretive curtained entrances to tents and kiosks. The sight was wonderful, as were the smells and the sounds, all competing for his attention; Marcel drifted, seduced.

And in the middle of the green, surrounded by caravans and cages, loomed the circus tent itself. Hitched to its pole by a taut network of ropes, it draped its pastel canvases like skirts to form a squat pavilion into which the crowd was artfully funnelled.

Marcel joined the queue and edged towards the gash of canvas open to admit the people. When Marcel arrived at the entrance he was surprised to see the boy who had given him the poster the previous day. He was dressed in a bright red tasselled jacket with four huge brass buttons on the front, black trousers and a pair of shining black boots. He was collecting the tickets and putting them into a slotted wooden box placed on a trunk beside him.

Marcel approached the boy. "How much are the tickets?" he asked.

The boy smiled. He gave Marcel a price. Marcel searched through his pockets but could not come up with anywhere near the required amount.

He looked up at the boy with a fretful expression and held out the coins.

The boy laughed. "That's not enough," he said.

"It's all I've got," Marcel said. His lower lip began to quiver and the gently mocking face of the tall blond boy blurred as Marcel's eyes filled with tears.

"Look," the boy said, "I can't give you a ticket for that handful of coins but if you go round the back of the tent I'll lift a flap for you and let you sneak in when I'm done. It's me who asked you here after all. Can't have you missing the show."

Marcel wiped his eyes. "Oh, thank you," he said.

"About ten minutes," the boy said.

Marcel nodded and withdrew around the side of the tent. He slipped between a caravan and a pile of wooden boxes and found himself in a small square of muddy grass at the rear of the tent, walled on three sides by large, barred cages up on high, wheeled wagons. Two were empty, but the third held something; it drew Marcel's attention and he approached the cage.

Marcel stood on tiptoe and peered through the bars into the cage. He could distinguish the shape of something huge and bulbous, rising and falling in time with a thick rattling sound. It could have been a great stack of mats, dragged sodden from beneath abattoir benches and left flyblown and animate with decay, or perhaps the abdomen of some vast and distorted freak spider, ripe to bursting with foul matter, and bristling with agitated hairs. The smell was unbelievable, like something dragged weeks dead from the bottom of a lake combined with the raw and tarnished odour of blood and something more organic still.

Marcel lowered himself down. Against a stack of barrels leant a long metal rod with a hook at the end, a sort of grappling iron. Marcel seized it up and returned to the cage. He took a stance bracing his weight on his back leg and swung the rod so that it clattered between the bars and landed with a heavy thud on the floor of the cage. He leaned forwards and slid the rod in until he felt it sink into the bulk at the back of the cage.

There was the sound of mucus rattling in the chambers of a cavernous sinus as the creature at the back of the cage woke up and lifted a huge, heavy head. It swung towards Marcel, made a thick, furious grunt – undomesticated and bitterly savage – and fixed great bloodshot eyes on him.

Aghast, Marcel stumbled backwards and tripped over a tent rope. He sprawled in the mud between a stack of packing crates. He yelped.

"What *are* you *doing*?"

Marcel yelped again and sat up in the mud and stared around. A figure came into view. It was a small clown, his face made up with grease paint to represent unreserved despondency. He was carrying a large wooden hoop.

"S-sorry," Marcel stammered, trying to rise, but the little clown stepped between the packing crates and pushed the rim of the hoop into Marcel's chest. Marcel was shoved against the odd, clammy canvas of the circus tent.

"You shouldn't aggravate Old Dicer," the clown said.

"Who?" asked Marcel from his seat in the mud.

"Dicer Herod, the performing bear." The clown jerked a thumb towards the great black creature in the cage behind them. It was standing at the front of the cage, breathing thickly through its mouth. "Well, not that he strictly *performs* any more. Not since he got into the audience last time. Terrible disarray. No, we just keep him along as a mascot, kind of. I look after him. Name's Bumpo the Clown. You are?"

"Marcel," he said. "You're the clown on the poster, aren't you?"

"Oh yes. Marcel, tormentor and prodder of our performing bear, what are you doing here?"

"My mother wouldn't let me come to the circus so the boy taking tickets said he'd let me sneak in. I was just waiting for him."

Bumpo's eyes misted and his shoulders sank. "A mother," he said. "I never had no mother."

"You're lucky!" Marcel said. "You can do whatever you want. You just have fun all the time. You can have my mother!"

Bumpo narrowed his eyes. Behind Marcel, there was the sound of a fanfare. Dicer Herod paced his cell, suddenly restless, a rope of drool swinging from his chin.

"You don't know how lucky you are," Bumpo said. "You've been loved. You've been – oh! – you've been *held*!"

"You can have all that! I want to go to the circus *every* day," Marcel cried, pushing the hoop aside and springing to his feet. Where was that boy? Marcel turned and started to scrabble at the hem of the tent where it met the mud. He could gain no purchase. He pulled, but to his wonder and rising horror he realized that the fabric had wormed itself into the earth and could not be freed. He pushed past the clown and ran around the crates. The fabric was rippling as it sank itself into the ground like a giant pastry cutter. Marcel swung around. There was another fanfare, but this one harsh, *serrated,* like a dying breath amplified through vast rusty pipes. He heard a voice: *"Let the carnival begin!"* But to Marcel, it had sounded like "Let the *carnage* begin!"

Marcel felt something cold on the flesh at the back of his neck. He was jerked forward and fell to his knees. The little clown was standing over him with the hoop encircling Marcel's neck. The clown was smiling.

"What's happening?" asked Marcel. He jumped as something hit the side of the tent. The sudden roar of great steam-driven machines filled his head and the entire big top began to vibrate and shudder.

"You should ask Mr. Morgoder," said little Bumpo, and pulled Marcel over onto his belly.

And then a silhouette blocked the light: a great, broad, cowled and caped thing smelling of the unearthed long-dead, which reached down for Marcel with fingers fused and fisted, more like trotters than hands it might be said, and Marcel heard it speak some atrocious words before the screams began in the shut-in tent and he fainted dead away.

Bumpo the clown stood beneath the narrow, open window. He had left his hoop at the circus and wiped his face clean on a towel before slipping away. He might not be missed at all if he had done his work well enough. He saw his reflection in the dark glass of the parlour window; how strange that he resembled that boy so closely. He smiled at the plump little face regarding him rather smugly from the depths of the glass. He went up to the wall and grasped a trellis. He felt such love for his mother then; he would lie in her arms and be her good little boy forever.

He began to climb.

The jolt of the wagon awakened Marcel. He opened his eyes. His mouth was dry and full of straw. He wiped his lips and looked with bleary eyes at the white grease paint that came off on his fingers. He was lying on his side on a wooden floor. The world shook again and Marcel heard a sound from within the cage; it was a sound that caused his mind to freeze: an ill-tempered, mucid grunt. Trembling, Marcel reached his hand around behind him and felt thick, oily fur. Something cold and damp nuzzled the back of his hand then blew phlegm across his knuckles as it began to growl.

BLACK STATIC

Doors bang and diesel-black rooks maraud the dereliction. On the station platform, Doctor Mocking
alights amongst a rattling litter of umber leaves. It is
November and Doctor Mocking is cold. Overhead the sky
is white. It begins to snow. The train pulls away on a roller
of steam and Doctor Mocking walks through the double
doors into the ticket office. There is no roof, just more
sifting white of sky. The one wall that remains has a dark
booth behind it but no occupant. Outside, there is a slip
road that slopes past a silent foundry. There are factories
but the machines are idle. Doctor Mocking shifts the heavy
leather bag he is carrying from his left hand to his right. He
rotates his shoulder in its socket and narrows his eyes as it
cracks. He looks down and sees something lying on the path
by his feet. A fine dusting of snow covers it. It is a small
brass detonator cap, sheared neatly in half by the explosion.
Doctor Mocking bends down and picks it up. He brushes
the snow off with a gloved hand. He examines it and puts it

in his pocket. Above, the white late afternoon sky is giving
way to an ocean of cloud coming in from the west. The setting sun lights its leading edge and Doctor Mocking thinks,
*It blew down on a stormfront's lip, humid jaws gashing atmospheres to
strands.* There is a blizzard coming. It covers the entire sky
like a blackout.

Doctor Mocking pulls his collar up around his throat
and looks about. There is a chain link fence following the
contour of the slip road to his right. It is intricately sewn
with a dead and desiccated climbing plant. He reaches out
and takes a handful of leaves. They splinter in his hand
with a sound like grating teeth. He allows the remains to
drift through his fingers like rust. Through the links in the
fence he can see the railway tracks. Snow is settling on them,
between them. It settles on the windowsills of sheds full
of levers. Junction boxes hum. Doctor Mocking pushes on.
He can see where the slip road ends, cresting gently a hundred yards further uphill. It joins a silent, untraveled road.
He reaches the road and turns right. This takes him over a
bridge that crosses the tracks. He glances down and sees
that the snow is falling so thickly now that soon the tracks
will be entirely covered. No matter; there will be no more
trains through here.

Over the bridge the road curves into town. Doctor Mocking can see the bombsites and the edges of buildings that
have thrown themselves to ruin in the blasts. The grey walls
have unseamed and now lean apart, crenellated as broken

cogwheels, draping roof and floorbeams and great yellow skirts of plaster. They look like the cabinets of terrible, burst clocks.

Doctor Mocking pauses. He is listening for the sound of water flowing quickly over pebbles, a lovely soaking sound. There is such a silence within the snowfall that he can actually hear the sound of snowflakes landing on the brushed wool of his coat, a minuscule ticking, the sound of absorption. Doctor Mocking feels absorbed; it is as if this terrain is welling up around him and holding him fast. He tilts his head and tries to catch the sound of the stream and thinks, yes, there it is. Like a glittering twirl of swarf in his mind's eye, he hears it. And can just make out its inexplicable blind spot, too, that miraculous beat of stillness between two bridges where it does not flow and stands as flat as pond water. This is where he must cross.

Doctor Mocking treads through the snow, across the bombsite. He doesn't stumble but is wary of what lies beneath his feet. He keeps his eyes fixed on what he can see of the distance (which amounts to little more than a vague impression of something high and dark obscured by the blizzard) and his mind focused on the sound of the water. Eventually he comes to a park bordered by railings. He continues along a path for some time until he finds a gate and enters a large and untended orchard. Doctor Mocking follows a track that winds through the trees and all the time the sound of the stream grows louder. There is some shelter here beneath the trees and he is delighted to find yellow crocuses in abundance, amongst the roots where the snow is light, their little fractured goblets open like the beaks of bright baby birds. At the bottom of the orchard is the stream. It flows into the orchard on its slender, hectic business, disappears under a dark stone bridge and stops. Further, beyond a second bridge, it flows again, not picking up speed or trickling past an obstruction, but continuing remarkably from where it left off as if ripping out of stasis. Doctor Mocking stands between the two bridges and looks down at the still, unmoving water. His face is set in an expression of thoughtful caution, not in any way afraid or apprehensive despite the strangeness of the terrain. Doctor Mocking is a Firmament Surgeon and they are mostly strangers to fear, what few of them remain.

On the far bank of the stream at the end of the orchard is an eerie row of derelict shops. There is no reason for them to be there; they are follies. There is no glass in the windows and, within, snow whispers and drifts against counters and shelves that have never held stock. One, a chill and desolate laundrette, contains nothing but a stack of old washing machines piled up which stare out through their darkened drums like the face of a vast and dreadful steel spider found nesting there. Beyond them, perpendicular to the stream and running off into the distance is a dark road bordered on both sides by high and crumbling tenements. The road is flooded and somehow sunken; the tops of streetlamps rise from the dark water like periscopes. Things float at the edge of the water, gathering in a scum against the walls of the buildings. A narrow wooden boardwalk has been constructed, rigged to the sills of the great sash windows of the tenements. It stretches the length of the road, above the floodwater, battening occasionally to the frames of fire escapes, and disappears into darkness. Doctor Mocking can see a crude wooden sign on the far bank of the stream. It says WELCOME TO THE WATERLOGS, OLD TOWN DISTRICT OF QUAY-ENDULA.

Once he crosses the stream he is committed. He feels the weight of the detonator cap in his coat pocket; it is neither comfort nor threat. It is fact. He knew it the moment he saw it on the ground outside the station. Each time it is different, each time it appears for him and each time he has the choice whether to pick it up. It gives no indication of its use or for whom it is to be used. Some of his kind choose their Instruments before they go in, some carry them permanently and they remain fixed and never transmute. Doctor Mocking always finds his and never once has he suffered anxiety that he would not. And as he crosses the stream and the cold water rises above his bootstraps, he looks down past the indolently rippling surface to the streambed and stops dead.

Lesley Morning is brought to Quay-Endula in a hot air balloon. She sits in the basket contemplating her journey while above her head the great, ornate brass gas burner roars and splutters. Lesley peers up through the crosshatch of struts that hold the burner to the basket and watches the air waver and ripple the inside of the massive purple balloon.

She has been drifting for some time now across a mapless expanse of snow. She is so high up that the balloon casts a shadow like a tiny keyhole, which slides endlessly across the landscape as if hoping to encounter its mechanism somewhere beneath the ground. Lesley thinks it looks forlorn and it saddens her to look at it. She knows she's being silly but these things are symbols. She knows what a symbol is because this place is always showing them to her. She knows what *forlorn* feels like too and knows she is projecting her own feelings onto things but can't help it. That's what happens here.

There is nothing in the basket but Lesley. She sighs and looks up again. This time there are stars in a twilit sky and the balloon has changed from a huge purple pod into a billowing fabric tiger's head. She can see inside it and likes the way the convex orange stripes flutter and glow like flames on the wall of the balloon. It is like being beneath a vast lambent mask. The gas from the burner glows green and is speckled with yellow sparks. It purrs constantly in the tiger's throat.

Lesley likes this balloon; it changes with her mood.

Lesley sleeps, curled up in the bottom of the basket. Above, the balloon glides across the night, its hollow throat a pulsing hoop of orange snarls.

Lesley dreams within a dream.

This is her gift: these focal rifts within her subconscious; like tiny gemstones glimpsed at the bottom of a wide, fast-flowing river, they lie still and complex, endlessly repeating their structure while the dark fractal waters thunder overhead. They are beautiful, these faults, and like all things rare and priceless, they have their hunters.

Lesley jumps to her feet and peers over the lip of the basket. She has heard something.

In the distance she can see a tiny speck bobbing and slaloming through the air. It is coming towards her at quite a rate. Lesley gasps and thinks, oh no.

It's Nurse Melt, coming to get her on her dreadful old iron microlite.

How it ever gets off the ground, nobody knows. It looks like a huge, florid wrought-iron gate, buckled by terrible impacts, and sent airborne by a small, oily motor and kept there on wings of fabric stitched over complicated frames. But old Nurse Melt can ride it. Her huge bulk slung over the crossbar, the engine yapping beneath her ragged skirts, she grips those cowhorn handlebars, pulls back on the throttle and, hooting and pulling at her long red hair, she rockets skyward.

Nurse Melt can really handle that old cloudbike.

Lesley feels real fear as she watches the old woman gain on the balloon. She can hear the testy little engine grumbling. She steps into the centre of the basket and looks around.

Her flesh is creeping and now her breath feels caught in her throat, buoyed up there by her quickening heartbeat. She wrings her hands and thinks she might burst into tears. She wants to wake up but knows she can't, not now, not on this visit, because it is the most important trip of her life and someone else depends on her. She must remain here and fight what comes at her, however horrible it is. And she must get to Quay-Endula. Then she feels the lump in the front pocket of her corduroy jeans and gasps. She reaches down and pulls out an object that at once fills her with luminescent hope and causes her to utter a laugh of such genuine bright surprise that Nurse Melt, who is drawing close with alarming speed, actually almost within grasping distance of the edge of the basket, looks up and cocks her head at the sound. She can see just the top of the back of Lesley's little blonde head and that laugh makes her face twist with fury. Nurse Melt takes her hand off the throttle and reaches out for the basket.

Doctor Mocking bends his knees and blinks. He removes his glove and reaches down into the water.

Lesley turns and sees Nurse Melt's great, mad, broad face hanging over the edge of the basket. Her hand is clawed, nails digging into the weave. She grunts with effort, somehow controlling the microlite with her left hand. It drops and sways beneath her but she clamps her thighs around it and pulls down on the lip of the basket so that it tilts and Lesley begins to slip. Lesley shakes her head. She can hear the burner above sputtering as the gas starts to give out. They will sink to the middle of nowhere and Nurse Melt shall have her. A tear spills down Lesley's cheek; Nurse Melt's grin grows wider and the gas jet falters.

There are strawberries growing at the bottom of the stream. They seem quite happy there, small and flawless, a clump of crimson amongst the pebbles, no bigger than fin-gertips. Doctor Mocking twists one from its stem and puts it in his mouth. It is icy cold and sweet and he closes his eyes with pleasure. There are six or seven more strawber-ries and he gathers them all. And as he picks the last one he feels a slight sensation of gentle movement around his feet and sees that the stream is flowing now between the two bridges. He puts the strawberries in his pocket and crosses to the far bank. He walks past the shops and turns into the drowned and sloping road. He feels momentarily uneasy; there is something about slopes he dislikes. They draw you down.

The basket is sloping towards Nurse Melt. Lesley makes a supreme effort to jump backwards and manages to grab hold of one of the sand bags that hangs from a hook on the wall of the basket. The microlite's engine makes a muted *thump-thump* sound as it idles in neutral beneath the ashen slabs of Nurse Melt's haunches. She takes her other hand off the bike and uses it to add leverage to the edge of the basket. Lesley feels the bottom tip alarmingly and she clings to the sandbag with all her might.

"Wake, you little bitch!" Wake *up*!" Nurse Melt hisses.

Lesley shuts her eyes and remembers her dream within this dream. The cool flowing water and the rubies in among the stones. The basket lurches again and the wings of the microlite rock like a seesaw. Nurse Melt's hair flies about her head and her lips smack and her wicked eyes roll. She starts to heave herself off the saddle and into the basket. A bare knee comes up like a lumpy, uncooked loaf.

Lesley opens her eyes. Nurse Melt teeters on the edge of the basket and glares at Lesley from beneath the burner's copper struts with a gloating and moronic glee.

Lesley can only think to do one thing.

"For Anna," she whispers, and uses all her strength to unhook the sandbag from the wall of the basket.

Nurse Melt's expression changes.

Doctor Mocking stands for a moment at the foot of the splintered, sand-coloured wooden steps that lead up to the planks of the tethered walkway. He looks up and sees a line of wires strung taut against the lightening sky. Time has no logic here; it is already dawn. He mounts the steps and starts out along the walkway. There is a rope guide rail at waist height but he ignores it and walks straight and true, passing windows on his right, ducking and stepping through the frames of the fire escapes. His steps sound like yelps in the throats of wooden dogs. The water below lies flat and deep and dark. Occasionally something knocks against the underside of the walkway like the tiller of a boat bumping the side of a quay. Then something catches his eye. He turns and peers through one of the large sash windows into the unadorned room beyond. The room is so huge he cannot see the far wall. There are machines in there with pulleys and flywheels connecting them and great gray belts plunging through slots in the floor. Curving, flaking pipes buttress the ceiling from which hang fitments and rows of complicated, segmented ducts. He can smell the heavy oil and bare metal through the glass. He is about to try the sash when he feels movement beneath his feet. He turns.

Ah, he thinks, here you come.

Nurse Melt just has time to scream as Lesley crashes into her and the point of the hook connected to the sandbag slides into her mouth and through her cheek. As Lesley heaves it over the side, the weight of the sandbag jerks Nurse Melt's head sideways and she is flung off the microlite and into space. Lesley stands on tiptoe and watches as she drops like a stone into the white chasm of air. The microlite stalls and swoops into a spiralling nosedive after her. Lesley closes her eyes and sinks to her knees. Her foot connects with something and she looks down. Bronze John glares up at her with his fearsome eyes, his black lips peeled back in a grin revealing tiny, sharp white teeth. He is grubby and has a plastic front leg caught between the weaves in the bottom of the basket. His tail curls back like a tiny orange crook. He is a four-inch long, die-cast plastic tiger with faded black stripes and he has been Lesley's constant companion for over two years. Lesley took him off the dashboard of her father's car the day after he died. She talks to him and Bronze John listens, his small orange muzzle wrinkled in a knowing grin.

Doctor Mocking watches as Fluffplupps comes sagging up the walkway. His head is nodding and his saturated cloth fists are dragging two perished dogs behind him. They leave a trail of soot and carnage. There is the sullen activity of flies. He holds the dogs by their muzzles but still they utter a continuous servile whimper. Their eyes are gone; leather buttons have been pushed into the empty sockets. Their hindquarters have been stamped flat and savagely burned. The fur peters out just below their forelegs and becomes a sodden, matted, carbonised sack. Fluffplupps lifts his flat face and sees the Firmament Surgeon step out from the shadows beneath the sash window and halts. His bone-coloured eyes glitter and he utters a furious hiss. He lets go of the muzzles of the perished dogs and they drop to the planks. They writhe and mewl there, leaking and foul. Fluffplupps lifts his arms and Doctor Mocking can see the sharp, rusty cables that articulate him piercing the stinking cloth of his body. Fluffplupps lurches forwards and Doctor Mocking turns quickly to the window and lifts the sash. He hoists himself into the room, then closes the window just as Fluffplupps slips and staggers up to the sill. They stare at each other through the smeary glass. Fluffplupps puts a hand against the window but does not have the strength to open it. Fluffplupps is feeble; he is here to distract and alarm, not to hurt. Something else would do the hurting, something much worse than Fluffplupps. Doctor Mocking turns away from the window and crosses the room. He can hear the sound of Fluffplupps' exposed wires scraping and jarring against the glass.

And here in the balloon, a wonderful thing is happening. As the balloon loses height and drifts towards the ground, Lesley asks Bronze John for help. She holds him in the cup of her palms and whispers and chats and kisses his head and *believes*.

There is a tremendous elemental sound, as of a vast pack of beasts bursting simultaneously from wild and baking undergrowth. Pressure and turbulence rock the basket. Lesley squints and lets out a small cry. Her teeth ache and she bites her tongue.

She opens one eye, and everything is tiger.

Doctor Mocking negotiates the machinery. There are turbines and generators and great constructions of slats and dials that he cannot identify. There are ranks of gas cylinders labelled with letters and atomic numbers from the periodic table. He knows that many of the cylinders contain elements that could not possibly be held in a gaseous state under normal circumstances; he sees Nitrogen, Radon, Helium, but also Antimony, Bismuth, Silver. Somehow these tall, slender tanks stir strange memories and he gazes up at their dusty shoulders and compass-sized gauges with a longing he has not felt for a long, long time. He shifts his bag from one hand to the other and flexes his fingers.

He walks on, across a floor of dusty blue marble, between the engines, until he reaches a door at the far wall. Without hesitation, he opens it. There are two sets of stairs. Those that descend progress into darkness. There is something down there, and Doctor Mocking thinks, *Bismuth, wandering lost through a basement of brass looms,* with a sudden and inter-locking clarity. He puts his hand in his pocket and feels the detonator cap. He smiles. *I'll help you,* he thinks.

But not yet. He takes the ascending stairs. And as they curve and become steep and cold, and as the concrete begins to darken and stink, he knows that he is getting close. Eventually, the stairs open out into an alcove containing the entrance to a corridor and an ungated elevator shaft. From hundreds of feet below he can hear mechanisms clacking and whining as the elevator continuously rams the wrenched and twisted walls of the shaft. There is a balcony boxed in with reinforced glass. He goes over and looks out. There is a new darkness approaching. Great black juggernaut slabs of it, high as the cloudbase. *Humid jaws gashing atmospheres to strands.* It's the devil-in-dreams, come to feed.

The devil-in-dreams brings your sins with him. Some-times they are white and vast and tower above him, feature-less and blind, and shudder dumbly in his wake; others are like fluted blown glass things that scamper and come at you. When your dreams are of failure or longing he is never far away. He is that presence you feel abroad somewhere in the dream town with the wide dusty streets lined with gaslit, slumbering bars. He despises these less-than-angels, these

Firmament Surgeons who sanctify the spaces they travel, so that all around on conscious planes people can come awake, and wipe their eyes in the fragile hope he wants destroyed. He wants no resolution, no healing of deep wounds. He wants your loss because it sustains him and stocks his vacuity; its mass is the gravity that binds his whole.

Doctor Mocking puts down his bag and turns as the elevator batters its way past the obstruction and begins to ascend. The devil-in-dreams is at his back, a colossal membranous mass bearing down on the building. *How it has grown*, thinks Doctor Mocking, and with a dawning submission to the fact: *There aren't enough of us to contain it any more.*

Bronze John turns his huge head to look down at her. Lesley digs her hand into the fur at the top of his haunch. It is soft as feathers. She looks up into John's eye. The sun reflects in it and for a moment, Lesley Morning can see nothing merciful in that eye. She wonders for a moment how she could have spent so long gazing into it and seeing sweetness; not in a tiger's face with its furnace of rebel flags, its tremendous awareness of its earthbound might. A tiger thinks: W*hat could I have been?* Bronze John looks up at the tall, bright sun and sees a forsaken place, a veldt of world-high fronds and knows he is the only animal fit for that sun. He might mourn a little for his languid lifelong roam across those roaring plains, the relentless hydrogen jungles of the sun.

Bronze John expands his chest and drops his barrow-load of jaw.

Doctor Mocking walks to the lip of the shaft and looks down. Rising toward him is a large, cubic machine made of metal bars and dark wooden struts. It is climbing the shaft using a complex collection of fitments that strike out and haul it upwards at terrific speed. He can see its workings, the belts and pulleys and wheels that drive it, revolving and threshing. At its heart is the driver, pinned and shackled to its levers, shrieking amidst the ferment: the *vitreophim*, the devil-in-dreams' own murderous acolyte. Doctor Mocking has heard talk of such things, strange rumours picked up over time, of constructions made to house these forged attendants; Uproar Contraptions they are called and here comes one now, a clattering frame of shearing edges, with its driver's maddened face turned up and glaring with eyes like calid holes of steam.

Lesley shivers and smiles a fierce, tight little grin. Her eyes narrow and her shoulders hunch. She can feel it now, starting inside there, not far from where her hand is grasping lava-bright fur, an inner striking of flints; a whoosh within the great cat's trunk and upwards it comes, ablaze.

Fuming. Triumphant.

Bronze John roars.

Doctor Mocking feels the building rock. He stumbles backwards, away from the clambering horror rattling up the shaft, turns and starts to run down the corridor that stretches away from the alcove. As he runs, the Uproar Contraption reaches the opening and flings out an array of filaments. Their tips come down like pickaxes, impacting the concrete floor in an explosion of gray shards. It ratchets and grinds against the dull stainless steel edges of the elevator door as it heaves itself through. The vitreophim squeals and its eyes glow in the darkness of the alcove. The devil-in-dreams is massing against the side of the building and the vitreophim shudders and chatters when it sees him, the blown glass limbs crazing with exertion; something fractures and a chunk of it slides off to be ground to dust in the teeth of the machine.

Doctor Mocking's heart is racing. For the first time he is beginning to feel afraid. This is taking too long. *Where are you?* he thinks. Behind him, the Uproar Contraption has begun to pull itself into the corridor. He can hear it building speed, scraping along the walls and pulverizing the unlit rectangular light casings built into the ceiling as it squeezes beneath. They explode with a sound like windscreens punching out in a head-on collision.

Bronze John roars and the sound is like a mile of shale cliff face crashing into the sea. The balloon is filled with it, and as it begins to rise Lesley looks over the edge of the basket. She leans against her marvellous tiger and feels his soft bonfire flank against her cheek. She can see the outskirts of Quay-Endula in the distance. Something dark is walking there. She looks up at Bronze John who is standing with his head and shoulders between a rack of copper struts. He rests his massive paws on the lip of the basket and narrows his almond eyes. John sees the darkness, too, and his instinct is immediate and all-consuming; he wants to fight it, to kill it, to tear it apart. He tenses. Lesley reaches up and strokes his back and can feel the low, almost subsonic rumble of his molten purr, like some slow, heavy core revolving in the dark heat of his belly.

They continue to drift in this fashion and soon they are above the great waste of the bombsites. Snow fills the craters and adorns the battlement edges of blasted buildings. Lesley sees the orchard and the stream that winds through it. There is a vast tower block dwarfing the rows of tenements that line a sunken road. And beyond that, the glutted mass of the devil-in-dreams presses its eyes to the walls, and applies its pressure. The block shudders and the back of the building begins to drop away. Masonry thunders.

Doctor Mocking feels the building quake and he staggers to a stop. He turns, leans against the wall and watches with a feeling of absolute, existential hopelessness as the Uproar Contraption comes into view. The vitreophim burns in its middle, a purple incandescence to match its rage, and the light it disgorges throws a sliding frame of flickering shadows ahead of it. Suddenly, Doctor Mocking is jerked backwards as the corridor twists violently. There is a piercing shriek and the Uproar Contraption is caught, jammed between the sharply compressed walls. Cracks appear and a section of concrete smashes to the floor about a foot away from Doctor Mocking. He feels the tremor as vast sections of the building crumble away and he is suddenly left standing, like a high diver, as the end of the corridor and most of the floors above peel out and drop away. He is exposed to the deep distance, and has no time to throw himself back-wards because the girders are moaning and warping and a fissure has jagged between his feet and the floor is gone. So, Doctor Mocking falls.

This place, this Quay-Endula, where Lesley comes so many nights, mostly alone, mostly seeking something almost always within grasping distance but never quite…this place from which she wakes with an emotional flatness, a kind of bleak nostalgia, with its complex lanes and twilit shop fronts, its canals and tired, crumbling beauty, is her safe place, her hid-ing place both for herself and, as she will discover, for those she loves. Lesley doesn't know what her gift is yet but is learn-ing, and this meeting place, this Quay-Endula, is where she comes to find herself.

But now something else has found it, too. Bronze John snarls low in his throat. His black lips ripple and show red gums and huge, ferocious teeth. Impressed by those ter-rible, exciting jaws, Leslie is caught by surprise as bronze John suddenly tenses and, like lightning, lashes a paw over the side of the basket. She cries out and takes a step back.

He closes his eyes as he falls. No slow dream-tumble, this; he drops towards the ground like a piece of iron. He wonders what will happen now that he is gone, who will stop the devil-in-dreams before it becomes so mighty that it fills the sleeping heads of all humanity and finally darkens hope for good. There will be no more healing, no more peace. Doctor Mocking feels a crushing wave of regret overwhelm him. Suddenly, an enormous weight thumps against his back and a branding heat cuts into his shoulder blade. He gasps and opens his eyes as he is swung through the air like a toy on a fairground grab. When he comes face to face with the scimitar grin on a tiger's blazing face he feels a sense of recognition as intense as *déjà vu*, and dangles there from a paw, trying to think. Then he sees the little girl, and she sees him, and now he no longer has to think. His sinuses fill with a rush of hot, desperate emotion. He lifts his arms as he is carried over the edge of the basket and is put down by the child. He falls to his knees.

"Oh, hello, love," he says.

"Hello, dad," says Lesley and bursts into tears.

Together, they steer the balloon towards the ground at the bottom of the orchard. It lands quite gracefully, the balloon sinking slowly between the trees like something wistfully fainting. Bronze John is a toy again. Doctor Mocking holds him and smiles. He hands him back to Lesley. "I'm glad you saved him," he says. Lesley looks up at her father. She has such love for him she feels she might break apart. "Are you here to help Anna?" she asks. Doctor Mocking puts a hand on her head and feels the warm softness of her hair. He closes his eyes tightly. "In a way," he says.

He puts his hand in his pocket and pulls out one of the strawberries. He gives it to Lesley and watches as she puts it in her mouth and eats it. Lesley is in an extremely happy place right now. Her dad is back. She has red juice on her lips. Doctor Mocking runs the ball of his thumb softly across her mouth, presses the thumb to his lips, kisses it.

They sit for a while in the bottom of the basket, Lesley cuddled up against her father. They say very little. When Doctor Mocking feels Lesley's head nod against his ribs, he looks down and sees she has gone to sleep. He carefully gets up, rearranging his little girl in a more comfortable position. She lies curled up, a faint smile on her lips. He takes a moment to pick up Bronze John and look at him. He smiles, remembering how it had made Lesley laugh when he had stuck him on the dashboard of his old car, a mascot to keep him company on his long drives. He puts the tiger down by Lesley's head. He bends down and kisses her then he straightens up, clears his throat, wipes his eyes and steps out of the basket. "Sweet dreams, love." He says and heads back towards the suspended wooden walkway. There is a room down there, and an old friend, wandering lost in a labyrinth of brass looms. Doctor Mocking puts his hand in his pocket and takes out the detonator cap. His Instrument; his key. He squares his shoulders and mounts the steps.

Lesley sleeps. She dreams within a dream.

Something is coming down the wooden steps, quietly so as not to wake her. It creeps past the sign WELCOME TO THE WATERLOGS, OLD TOWN DISTRICT OF QUAY-ENDULA and crosses the grass. It reaches the balloon and places its cloth hands on the roll of weave at the top of the basket. Bent and rusty wires, sharp as needles, tick against the wickerwork. With a grunt, Fluffplupps hoists himself up and into the basket. He looks down at the sleeping girl and his bone eyes gleam.

And a moment later is thrown against the wall of the basket by a wave of pressure that literally knocks the stuffing out of him. Bent double, he looks up and can find no will to utter a sound; he can only weep a filthy tear as Bronze John bears down to finish it.

Lesley kneels at the end of her bed in a tangle of sheets. She looks down at Uncle Michael, who lies unmoving on the floor beside her sister's bed. His face is contorted and blue and he is quite clearly dead. Next to him, torn to shreds, are the remains of the horrible little cloth doll, Fluffplupps. Something has chewed it to ribbons. Uncle Michael would use it to pacify Anna on the nights he came in. Anna hated it; she said it felt full of thorns and wires, and it smelt of unwiped bums, but she would hug it anyway, and close her eyes and make sure Uncle Michael never, ever touched her little sister the way he used to touch her.

Anna's bed is empty. Lesley turns bronze John over and over in her hands. She climbs off her bed and goes over to Anna's side of the room. Uncle Michael has knocked Anna's side table over and the digital alarm clock is flashing a crimson 00:00 from beneath the bed. The room strobes queasily and Lesley bends over and unplugs the clock. She stands for a moment by the side of Anna's bed, then reaches out and places Bronze John on her pillow. He reclines there, grinning. Lesley is content; wherever she has sent Anna, she knows she will be safe now.

Then Leslie turns and kneels by Uncle Michael's head. It is twisted towards her and his lifeless eyes stare up at her from a patch of shadow beneath the bed. Leslie is so sure of what she needs to do next that she does not even remotely question how strange it is.

Using both her small hands, she prizes Uncle Michael's mouth open. To Lesley's relief, his mouth is quite dry and opens without too much effort. His tongue is slumped in the pouch of one cheek. She hunches her shoulders and puts her nose to his mouth and sniffs. The unmistakable, cloying smell drifts up out of his mouth and Lesley, with a deadly serious expression, puts her fingers in and pokes about. She pulls a face but nonetheless continues rooting until her fingers touch the thing lodged in his windpipe. It feels fleshlike, a pulpy lobe grown across his throat. Leslie removes her hand and peers at her fingertips. They are stained a darker pink, like watery blood, and she holds them delicately to her nose.

Yes. Strawberry.

DYING IN THE ARMS OF JEAN HARLOW

I found a couple of pandas consuming my garden furniture this morning. Ever since they found a way to genetically modify the bastards to *mange tout* with an infusion of goat protoplasm or suchlike, and some bleeding heart Animal Rights activists liberated a facility and set a breeding pair free, you can't move for them. No natural predators, see, the East Anglian panda.

I ran at them, waving my arms and shouting, keeping eye contact and ducking my head in the way set out in the leaflets. One of them looked up, languidly masticating a chair arm, and began to lumber away down the garden. The other one just sat there in its charming iconic pose and arced a stream of urine onto my shoes, unresponsive to my government-endorsed panda management.

"Fuck the Public Information," I said. I took a Browning automatic out of my coat pocket and shot the monochrome bastard in the face.

Gun smoking, I looked about. I could see a herd of them bolting away across the fields, alarmed by the echoing gunshot. Some of their cubs tumbled after them, all paws and fluff. I drew a bead on the smallest and let off a couple of rounds. I think I took an ear off.

I stood with my hands on my hips, shaking my head. I was curious to see how effective that *pandavulax* virus might be. The government had authorised its release into the countryside last month using a couple of infected captives as vectors. The other day I'd found one in the lane on the way to the pub, lying on its back on the verge. It was breathing weakly and had froth round its chops. Its eyes were like dabs of toothpaste.

I holstered the Browning and examined the damage to the patio furniture. I cursed myself for not dragging them into the conservatory last night, but I'd been too drunk to bother by the time we turned in. Always the way, isn't it? The one time you forget, you get the pandas.

I went into the garage and had a rummage for the disposal bags. The government had made the local councils issue them to all households. I found a couple (it was policy to double-bag) and began the job of clearing up.

The panda was a big boy and I had only managed to drag the bag under half of it, leaving the upper body and head still lolling on the grass when I heard a voice say, "Hey, mister. What you doing?"

I paused, breathing heavily, and wiped sweat from my brow. My hair was soaked and I had huge sweat rings under my arms like plague spots. I cursed under my breath. It was that little Lolita from next door.

"The panda's had an accident," I said with a regretful look on my face. "It fell down…"

"You shot it in the face," she said. "I saw you from my bedroom window. You blew its brains out. I'm telling the police."

I couldn't believe it.

"You're mistaken." I said, but the evidence was there at my feet. I stepped in front of the panda, hoping to conceal it.

She craned her neck, appeared momentarily perplexed and stood there chewing softly on her lower lip. Her eyes unfocused a little and she used the ball of her bare right foot to rub distractedly the fondant instep of her left. It was a cute gesture, I can tell you, but it didn't mean I was going to try and fuck her again, okay?

I just wasn't getting this panda disappeared.

Technically it was illegal to grease them on private property. It was government policy to call in the exterminators but the insurance was up in the ionosphere, even with a full no-claims. Still, there were the reward points.

I left the panda where it was and wandered back indoors. I poured myself a glass of beer and leaned against the bar dreaming about the girl next door and a handful of kumquats.

I was still thinking about that when the door opened and Frank walked in. He was barechested and was drying his hair with a bath towel. Frank was my brother-in-law.

I drained my glass. "Want one of these, Frank?"

He looked up at the clock. "Not early enough for me," he said. "Did I hear gunshots? Fuck." He walked into the conservatory. The muscles on his back looked like a tray of loaves.

I got myself another beer and went out to join him by the pool. He was looking down at the panda.

"He shot it," the girl said. She was wearing a bikini. She came over and stood beside Frank. "Hi," she said. "Can I have a swim?"

Frank looked down at her. He grinned wildly and put a hairy arm around her shoulders. "Hey, baby," he said. "Want me to pick you up by the ankles and *lick* you like an *ice* cream? How 'bout that?"

She smiled. "I dunno."

I took a sip of beer. Indoors, the phone was ringing.

There's a town on the coast called Invidisham-next-the-Sea. Rory Reeks doesn't like it there very much. It has a cramped, cheerless atmosphere, full of pound shops and joke shops that don't really sell jokes in the sneezing powder and whoopee cushion kind of way he remembers as a boy, but are emporiums of smut instead. He finds this kind of humour demoralising and unsettling; to Rory, it's like he co-exists with a coarse sub-species intrinsically oblivious to taste. These people must lack proper stimulation, he thinks. That, and their cheap packets of Richmond cigarettes and deleterious gene pool.

Invidisham-next-the-Sea has a long concrete promenade with no jolly lights or powder blue railings. It has
no pier and no gardens to speak of, merely a large sloping
expanse of grass that's really a bit too steep and which on
wet days—and there are plenty of those—can endanger the
elderly population by accelerating them beyond their optimal velocity as they attempt to pick their way down from
the tea shops at the top to the edge of the promenade at
the bottom.

Rory saw an old girl go over once, whinnying like a race-
horse, and she didn't stop until she hit the beach. He was
fairly sure she was quite badly injured.

There's a row of disconsolate looking beach huts down
there on the front. They're poorly maintained and draughty
and are used predominantly for defecating in and sex acts.
Rory assumes this, actually, but it's on the cards.

The other concession to beachfront cheer is the crazy golf
course. It has nine oblong concrete concourses carpeted with
mangy fabric the colour of kelp. Each hole has a hazard to
negotiate, like a castle with a narrow drawbridge, for instance,
which you attempt to scuttle your golf ball over. Some of the
hazards, particularly the fibreglass crocodile, he finds rather
sinister. One of them, a squat, ruddy-faced policeman lying on
his side out of whose fat bottom the ball is supposed to pass,
is just offensive.

There's an amusement arcade at the back of the car
park. It's not really an arcade, more of a warehouse full of
video games. Rory believes a lot of crime is formulated in

that arcade to be perpetrated later around town. Where's the amusement in that?

Last season, there was a desultory old busker called Drinky who set up outside the arcade. He really was the least attractive and able entertainer Rory had ever seen. He was dressed like a tramp and had a wide, yellowing beard covering his mouth and throat. He wore a filthy tan fabric hat with little black pompoms arranged vertically from its tip to its brim. One of the pompoms had come off at some point and all that remained was a little sprig of black cotton between the pompoms above and below. It reminded Rory of a hairy mole. He had a big red clown's nose on, but it wasn't mirthful, just a little misshapen and grubby.

He had an old acoustic guitar slung over his shoulders and his performance amounted to little more than strumming its slack, tuneless strings and shuffling from foot to foot.

Rory once watched a group of men come out of the arcade and surround him. Drinky just stood there, continuing to strum, when all at once, one of the men stepped forward and kicked him with incredible force where his low slung crutch hung beneath the curve of his guitar. Old Drinky went down really hard and the men just laughed and pointed, then went back into the arcade.

Rory works at the supermarket on the big estate outside town. Well, it's more a grocery outlet that sells cheap brands you've never heard of to people on supported incomes. There's a sign at the till that says NO QUIBBLE

GUARANTEE. Rory can't make up his mind whether *quibble* is a word that is either underused or too ridiculous to be used at all. He supposes quibbling is really the kind of thing you'd only find people doing at the checkouts in one of these shops, perhaps pointing out the dent in the side of a can of economy lychees, purchased to add zest and mystique to a trolley full of poor quality staples.

At weekends it's basically Rory, Milton, his Workability-provided assistant, and Derek the Golden Greeter (HERE TO HELP! his large-print badge declares, although all Rory has ever witnessed Derek muster is a kind of wilful hindrance in his approach to customer care—an example of this was the time he announced his availability as bag-packer to a struggling mother by scooping her baby out of the trolley and rolling it clumsily from its swaddling blanket onto the conveyer belt whereupon it was whipped away and got its fontanel dented on a four-pack of reduced-to-clear All Day Breakfasts). There are the checkout girls but no one has much to do with them because they badly arouse Milton and traumatised him quite profoundly once by showing him the edge of one of their mons. Rory thinks they must have to demonstrate an obligatory love bite and history of terminations to meet the criteria to work on the tills in this shop.

Rory was outside, watching Milton careering round the car park on the end of a rattling conga of trolleys. He'd seen him take a couple of wing mirrors off already so he was none too impressed with Milton's morning's work. He was, in fact, trying to remember the Makaton for *fired*, but then his heart sank as he saw Dean Brazil drive into the lot in his delivery truck. He went back into the store and through to the delivery yard, or *glory hole,* as Dean liked to call it, showing off to Milton with goatish winks.

There was a sudden, bright clattering sound and a yell and Rory knew with a heavy despondency that Milton had seen Dean arrive and had propelled his trolleys right up onto the forecourt and into Derek in his eagerness to get out to the yard and greet him first. The doors flew open behind him and Milton waddled past at speed. Rory heard, *"You bandy little cun-"* and looked back to see Derek feebly trying to push himself out from beneath a pile-up of trolleys. He looked like he'd been ambushed by a group of skeletal daleks.

Rory followed Milton into the yard. He had already seized the small palette forklift and was shoving it with the same rampant and regardless glee with which he handled the trolleys. His shirttail flapped and Rory winced to see the dark vertical seam running down it, evidence that he was still tucking it too far down between his buttocks and *inside* his pants. Had he been outside like that?

Dean had parked up and was already engaged in a monologue with one of the checkout girls who had slid out for a cigarette: "Yeah, I used to do a lot of banger racing up at Arlington. That's a tight old track up there. Tried a Rover once. 3.5S. Old wedge shape. Give it a massive handful.

They tend to push out a bit…" He saw Milton and grinned. "Get us a cup of tea, Julie."

Julie pouted around her Raffle. "What did your last slave die of?"

"Repeated kicks to the head, Jules. White, two sugars, there's a good girl." He turned away and began to undo the buckles along the underside of his truck which released the taut fabric flank. "I bet she goes down faster than a pint of lager on a hot day. Had some of *that* have you, Milt?"

Rory wished Dean wouldn't talk to Milton like that; it sends him demented and then you can't get any work out of him for hours. He just disappears into the toilet for the rest of his shift.

Milton threw back his head and flared his nostrils, giving Rory a view of the chartreuse flakes barnacled to his sinuses.

"All right, Rory? Come on Milt, let's get this lot unloaded." Dean went over to a stack of crates and perched on a leading edge. He took out a pouch of tobacco and began to roll a cigarette. Milton pumped the handle of the trolley until the forks were level with the first palette on the back of Dean's truck, then he slid them through the wooden slats, gave it one more crank and tried to pull the load backwards out of the vehicle.

Dean was going, "Took my missus to Felate last night. It's marriage guidance for couples where the wife won't give blowjobs anymore. Look at your face, Rory. You're the kind of bloke who'd catch the head of his prick in his zip and say,

'Actually, I meant to do that'. Stroll on. Come on, Milton! Pull it like you're pulling a black man off your mother!"

To say Milton was overdoing it was something of an understatement. In his desire to please Dean he was jacking palettes off the back of the truck with the urgency of a looter at the face of a riot-damaged shop front.

Julie came back out carrying a grimy mug with the generic name of some optimistic-sounding antidepressant written on the side of it. She put it on the crate next to Dean and flounced off.

Dean watched her depart. He lapped along the edge of his rizla. "That Julie," he said, "I've seen more meat on an otter's cock."

I noticed Frank hadn't finished getting shot of the dead panda. He'd shoved it in the pool. It floated face down, its stubby arms and legs splayed out at its corners, stabilising it. A filmy pink medium drifted about its left ear like toad-spawn and tomato pips. The girl from next door had gone. I wasn't surprised.

I told him about the phone call. "Fuck," he said.

We hit the road in Frank's old Chevy Kodiak flatbed. He'd had it shipped over from the States for twelve grand. It was low to the ground with a wide, jeep-like cab. He'd always wanted one and, now that he had it, he used it for little other than cruising around the fens picking up girls from the traveller camps and driving at pandas. If I tell you it kept him happy, you'd have to believe me. Saints and psychopaths. The only truly happy people. No tension, see.

We were aiming to head across country as far as the coast then take the sea road north until we got to Invidisham-next-the-Sea.

On approach, as you wind along endless dusty fen roads, Invidisham-next-the-Sea backs evasively away into the Wash, giving you glimpses of a flat industrial roof here and a staggered row of terraces there; it shrugs into the rough grey waves as though trying to slope off without drawing attention to itself. But you eventually catch up with Invidisham-next-the-Sea, and then it squares up to you like a middle-aged drunk apprehended hanging around outside the girls' toilets, full of ready bravado and the habitual, companionable routine you've grown sick of hearing time and time again.

After the ambulance had taken Milton away, everyone went across to the Macebearer's for a debrief.

Dean had an arm round Julie. He was shaking his head. He had the misty look in his eyes of someone nostalgically recalling some moronic achievement. "Milton," he said, "can't believe it. Kept the secret of his dodgy ticker from his colleagues." He shook his head again and glanced down at his pint. His dirty grey T-shirt had pulled up out of his trousers, allowing a hairy crescent of belly to pout over his belt. His prolapsed navel was defined against the taut fabric like a ramekin full of gristle. He picked up a menu from the bar. "You hungry, Jules? "

Rory looked around the pub. A couple of girls sat in the corner heckling their restless toddlers through an unrelenting haze of fag smoke. They were as thin as council house carpet and wore matching plasters on their heels where their Achilles tendons had rubbed raw on the backs of their cheap stilettos. Rory imagined them shopping at Motherneglect, buying Silk Cut and Ritalin over the counter and noshing your hood for a kind word. Genetic litter, Rory thinks.

The Macebearer's atmosphere was dominated by the dry, cheerless smell of the carvery; under baking lights beneath a glass cloche lay a slew of computer-grey turkey slices and a few brittle rinds of pork gleaming like infected wounds. There was a well of scummed-over, meconium-coloured gravy.

Dean drew Rory's attention to the menu. "Wild rice and gourmet lemon grass and one thing and another. By the time they serve it up it just tastes like a fuckin' pocknoodle. I'll have the chilli. Know what I'm getting, Jules?" Delayed shock and alcohol were disinhibiting Dean more than ever. He started going on about porn to Derek who, in turn, was staring up at Dean with a look of unanchored dismay.

"This big black bloke's giving her one from behind and I swear it looks like he's trying to nudge a *dachshund* up her gary-"

The estate had grown up around the outskirts of the town, effectively ringing it in against the coastline, around thirty years ago; it was the vision of a local architect, whose philo-sophical rarefaction allowed only for bleak concrete clads piled into oblongs, cubes and hexagons, creating flat rain-laked rooftops, switchback overpasses and a network of alleyways that occasionally debouched onto a patchy rect-angle of space which might be called a recreation area or merely an accident of ground hemmed between four indif-ferent, identical walls; it would depend on whether there was a metal climbing frame or a lone swing dangling from some hollow iron pipe. The architect had passed some time in East Berlin, it appeared, and had been inspired by the panorama of ochre hexagonal structures he had seen from his hotel window, spread out beneath him like a vast, industrial beehive. The estate resembled some great inverse, primordial Gormenghast, a looming, sullen structure, all poverty and neglect, with what real money there was scat-tered around the arc of its outer perimeter. No Hall of Bright Carvings here. Just the crocodile-eye reflection of drear skies off the windows and gritty little pools beneath the climbing frames. And the only Titus, hepatitis.

If you follow any number of the concourses that lead into the heart of the estate, you will eventually come across a broad, paved plaza. High walls containing flats overlook it, each balconied floor accessed by stairwells ascending from the square's four corners. At ground level are the shops and, making up half of a whole side and separated from the *VAL-YOU!* Bargain Market by the arched entrance to the square, is the Macebearer.

Rory was in the toilet. Dean was creating a radius of discomfort which had grown to encompass everyone at, and behind, the bar as his voice had become more penetrating and its content more off-colour.

Both Rory and Dean had flats that overlooked the plaza. Rory felt trapped and stultified having to live in an insubstantial, narrow enclosure as papery as a wasp's nest and dreamed of days ahead when a florid fiction of romance and opportunity would blow into his life and whip him away through some rift in the Undeniable Progression of Life continuum; Dean just wanted to do his place up (in his mind's eye, Dean saw rooms full of black self-assembly shelf units, red mock-leather sofas and a flat-screen TV the size of an upended pool table. Lots of brushed silver aluminium appliances in the kitchenette.). Now, Rory was thinking about knocking off so he could go up to his flat and spend the evening adding links to his Jean Harlow website. He was pretty pleased with it as far as it goes. She was so captivating. Did you know that Rin-Tin-Tin died in her arms? Rory thinks that's so romantic. Nothing like that ever happens here. No glamour in his life. Only his on-off girlfriend, Pam. Pam, with her perennial and largely treatment-resistant fungal infections perpetuated within the low cost panties she buys from the store's affordable nylon lingerie range. Pam's idea of high living is a night out at the dog circuit on a Thursday to wager the odd quid on spavined greyhounds with names like Antiperistalsis Lady. Then she'll try and get off with one of the trainers who skulk around the edge of the track after the races. They invariably wear Mata-lan jogging bottoms and XL vests, forearms dense with a verdigris of misjudged tattoos and are frankly welcome to buy her a Smirnoff Ice and try to get their chapped, pikey hands on her muggy pubis.

Rory's brother got out of Invidisham-next-the-sea. He got as far down the coast as Great Yarmouth where he does regular stand-up in the comedy clubs, got a bit of glamour in his life. He sent Rory one of his reviews, cut out of the local paper: *Some people burn with an incandescent blaze of talent. Mick Reeks smoulders like a tyre-dump fire: slow and remorseless, giving off low-slung clouds of bitter, toxic fumes.* Rory wishes he had talent.

He doesn't even get respect from his staff. Last week one of them wrote: Rory is a big stroker and lesbian and impotent and has nostral (sic) hair big twat on his office door in permanent marker. And the other day, when Derek asked him to sign his timesheet, he did his usual elegant flourish and distinctly heard Derek mutter, "I said sign it, not colour it *in.*"

Rory zipped up and made his way back out to the bar. He was probably going to have to help Dean back to his flat and he had made his mind up to do it sooner rather than later.

As he re-entered the bar, Rory looked up and suddenly felt the world tip a little further out of kilter than usual. He could still hear Dean, who was informing others in fond tones of his little step-daughter: "She's made a hole up between her Cindy doll's legs with a ballpoint and's using my roll-up filters as *tampons*. Growing up so fast these days." And right behind him, outside and visible through the plate glass window which overlooked the car park, Rory could see Milton coming towards the pub.

Rory frowned and narrowed his eyes. He reached out a hand and took hold of a brass rail that ran along the edge of a trough of artificial plants embedded in what looked like artificial chips of bark. On the wall to his left was a notice board advertising LOCAL IMFO. He took a couple of steps further into the bar, his entire concentration focused on the strangely distorted shape of Milton making its way between two rows of vehicles. No one else seemed to have noticed. Dean was foaming on to a dull-eyed Julie. Derek was sitting on a stool at the end of the bar, his head moving in an almost imperceptible figure of eight as he watched the fruit machine repeat its endless rapid cycle of illuminations.

Milton was now standing directly outside the Mace-bearer. His head switched back and forth as though try-ing to locate something elusive, and then looked straight in through the window and directly at Rory.

Rory shrieked. Everyone in the bar turned and looked at him. Dean's patter dried up and the last thing he said was, "…and got a dose off her," before there was the sound of gunshots, and Rory was the one person in perfect position to observe his brother and his brother-in-law, Frank, come edging round the side of the Macebearer, both of them pumping bullets into the side of Milton's head.

Milton's top half atomized. The force of the bullets threw him four feet to the right. He hit the window and remained leaning against the glass as though left propped up there by someone inside having a drink. Frank stuck his gun into the waistband of his pants and went over to the body. He nudged it with his boot then stepped nimbly back as it toppled sideways and hit the concrete, leaving a thick, gory arc on the glass.

Rory stumbled across to the door and hauled it open. It was beginning to get dark and the sodium lights were coming on. Everything was taking on a thin, tangerine patina. The roofs of the remaining parked cars glowed as though made from a fragile, alien metal.

Mick and Frank came through the open door. Rory followed them as they went over to the bar. Mick was pale, his eyes were wide and he looked pretty elated. Frank looked like he'd remembered his training. Mick leaned against the bar.

"Scotch, no ice. Frank, champagne? Rory? What you having?"

"A breakdown?" Rory said weakly.

"Don't be so fucking *camp*, Rors. Have a drink. Oh, and barricade all the doors and windows."

Everyone was staring at the new arrivals. Mick lit a cigarette and blew smoke towards the optics. "What's occurring?" enquired Dean. His voice was shaking. He kept darting glances through the window, his gaze dwelling on that swoop of *claret* in the corner of the glass.

Rory looked around. He felt perplexed and dizzy. The paramedics had put an oxygen mask over Milton's face and connected him to an array of monitors before whisking him away to hospital on blues and twos. He had been ashen and sweaty and his face had looked like a crumpled *dim sum* wrapped in cling film. One of the paramedics had mildly bollocked Rory for giving Milton a glass of water while they waited for the ambulance to arrive. Everyone had been standing about. Like now, everyone standing about in the pub, looking blank, vacant, outwardly devoid of even basic metabolism. Somebody breathed; Rory realized it was the sound of his own respiration. He drew in a gasp. Everyone looked at him. Mick turned, raised an eyebrow.

"What's going on?" said Rory. "What's happening?"

"I'll explain," Mick said.

The barmaid brought Mick's order over. "I drink from the bottle," growled Frank.

Earlier today I got a phone call from my agent. His name is Jon Index. You can't find him in the phone book, if you know what I mean. He finds you.

He told me he had a special job for me. Not a gig; this was all about my *other* job. My *Paladin* job. This is weird, telling you about it, but now I have to, so this is it.

When Rory and I were little boys, our father beat us. He drank, he gambled, he lost; he was unable to contain his disappointment, so he beat us. He terrified us, he roared and thundered at us, he broke my ribs and my arm in three places, Rory spent two nights in hospital. We both lost teeth. But he was remorseful, so our love for him – the fraught, troubled, fragile tenderness hurt and bewildered children feel toward their impaired and haphazardly damaging parents – never quite died. Which I think is a good thing. You can't see humour in the world if your soul is distorted by hatred.

We got older and the beatings stopped. He was verbal and punchy, but we rolled with it and finally, one night, he didn't come home at all. I was fourteen, Rory was twelve; Dad had stepped out in front of a Triumph Dolomite and his long losing streak was over.

Rory got bullied a lot at school. He coped by developing an interest in old movies. He had posters of Jean Harlow all over his side of the bedroom. Something about her just enthralled him. Most of us were frantically pulling ourselves off over Victoria Principal around this time, but not old Rors. He just gazed up at Jean, hands respectfully behind his head, and reflected peacefully on her jaded, silver-screen glamour and alcohol-fuelled demise.

I got round the bullying by using humour. Coarse, cutting, scorning stuff developed over time to protect me from the witless tossers and ingratiate me with the older lads.

Then I made a career of it.

And that was when Index found me.

"You're quite amusing," he said. I was sitting at the bar after my regular ten-minute Friday night slot at the club. "Bittersweet yet callous. You've built a repertoire up from a lifetime of genuine hurt. That's admirable."

"You've summed me up," I said. "I can die now."

Index laughed. He looked about fifty. He was average height, average build. He wore blue jeans and a white T-shirt with a V-neck pullover. When he laughed, something glinted in his mouth. His tongue was pierced.

"You one of those violent queers?" I asked.

Index laughed again. He appeared genuinely delighted by my charm. "No, not at all," he said. "Just a fan. And a businessman with an offer."

I raised my eyebrows in a gesture of cool offhanded-ness. Index offered to refill my glass, an offer I was disin-clined to refuse.

"There's just not enough laughter in the world, is there, Mick?" he said. His eyes shone with an everlasting bright good humour. I nodded, I think a little spellbound, and he continued. He just sort of spilled it all out, and he had such a look in his eye that there was no way I was going to dis-believe *this* pitch.

"There are *comedians,* yes, *funny* men, but where are the real geniuses: the Bruces, the Pryors, the Cooks? Where are the sufferers, the tormented few who get their material from anguish, injustice and fury? The ones who watch over us?

"You see, Mick, there are more destructive powers in the world than there are constructive ones. Entropy is a dark, ever-widening eye that never ceases in its function to see all and disassemble it. So we have to close that eye a little, we have to throw a little salt in it, shine a little light in it; temporarily *blind* it, if you like. To give us a chance.

"And that's what you do. Life tried to cripple you and it failed and now you're laughing back at it, mocking it, getting under its skin. You stop things from falling apart. You are at war against despair.

"I can give you success if you work for me, great success. Because you're rare, Mick. Precious. And in return, you watch over us. Stirring stuff?"

"Stirring as bagpipes, motherfucker." I saluted him with my whisky glass, spilling a little. Index just laughed that jolly laugh, and I saw then, just for a second, that the stud in his tongue was in the form of a tiny little silver strawberry.

"Entropy has followers, Mick. The Autoscopes. So named because we see ourselves in them and despair. They turn their skills to dismantling creation. They are entropy and we have always fought them and we will always fight them until creation can be remade. Unless we fail; and there are so few of us left now.

"So we use what we can. We use people like you to keep them at bay. You are our Paladins. And we search for our own kind, reborn Firmament Surgeons, and try to find them before the Autoscopes can kill them.

"There are perhaps only one or two per twenty million people and somehow the Autoscopes seem able to detect them before we can. Children disappear, Mick. Now you know why.

"So. You work for me and I'll give you success. And in return, when we locate a child, you find it and bring it to us before the Autoscopes can destroy it."

"And together we'll save the world," I said. "You're not a nonce, are you?"

Index virtually fell off his stool laughing at this one.

"They're not going to be able to touch you, Mick!" he roared. "You're too sharp."

I thought for a moment.

"These *Paladins*," I said. "Don't they all die futile, friendless deaths?"

Index composed his features into such a serious expression, that for a moment I almost regretted my facetious remarks.

"Only if they forget what they do best. If *they* start to despair, well, we're in terrible trouble, aren't we?"

I bought it. Don't ask me to describe the moment I went over, but I did. What combination of predisposing factors, persuasion, timing and delivery converted me? When you've grown up the way I have, you can smell bullshit from space, and Index just didn't give off that aroma. So I agreed. On a trial basis. He'd make me a success and in return, well, I'd go rescue his little reborn *Firmament Surgeons* with a gun in my hand and a bitter repudiation of life's antic bliss on my lips.

This isn't my first job. Three months ago we rescued a little girl called Lesley from an empty house on the Arbury estate in Cambridge. She's with Index at a safe house in East London. We haven't been able to locate her sister yet but we have some good men working on it Quayside.

There is a company of Autoscopes trying to get to Invidisham-next-the-Sea because there is a very special child there, a reborn Firmament Surgeon, and they intend to kill him. They are using the power of despair to fuel their incursion; they have tapped a rich vein here on this estate and are using the energy to turn the population into monsters and force a Gantry open from one of the Quays. Quays are places of safety, but recently this vastly powerful group of Autoscopes has decimated a number of them in their search for this child. They seem extremely agitated about the whereabouts of this child, and Index feels this might be because he has been reborn with the power to open up all the remaining Quays and bring about the Recreation.

They are hoping the monsters will cause disruption and leave the child vulnerable as he sleeps, easy pickings when they come through.

There is a wondrous symmetry to this job; Index tells me it's the reason I was chosen.

When we arrived on the estate, the first thing we saw was the ambulance. It was on its side, lights still pulsing. Frank had slowed the Chevy and we'd seen the remains of the technicians spread around the cab. We'd followed the road and seen that little bloke swaying across the car park. The entire top of his head was lifting up and down with teeth. Looks like he was the first to turn.

I looked at Frank and shrugged. He gave me a reassuring grin and nodded. Everyone else was looking at me with blank, frowning, headachy looks. Well, they needed to know.

"So, we need more guns," said Frank, in vigorous and wholehearted support of my story. "Estates like this have got more guns than *prams.*"

Julie had moved to the vacant stool next to Frank. She was eyeing his Magnum. "My boyfriend—well he's not really my *boy*friend—Jimmy's a drug dealer. I *think* he's got a gun." She smiled loosely at Frank. Frank turned and stared at her. He tipped the champagne bottle to his lips. It looked like he was inflating some sort of horrible, heavy balloon. Julie paled and closed her legs.

"Phone him, get him here," said Frank. "Anyone else?"

Rory stepped forward. He made a conscious effort to stop wringing his hands. "There's an old boy living above me, an Afghan asylum seeker who moved in a couple of months ago. He's a member of a sort of gun club that meets in a lock-up beneath one of the flyovers somewhere on the estate. I think they just sit round a gas fire and drink, but there might be a few rifles lying about. If he's in he could get them for us."

Frank nodded. "That's your job, Rors. Appropriate the rifles." He turned to Julie, who was talking into her mobile. She looked up and nodded. "I've told him to meet me in the car park. I told him someone from Thetford was up here trying to sell me crack."

Rory and Dean left the Macebearer by the back door, which led directly out onto the plaza. All the shops were closed and had their metal security screens pulled down. Only the Fish 'n' Chick'n was open for business over on the left, its window steamed up and streaming with condensation. Rory could make out the vague shape of Gavin Runs moving desultorily about behind the fryers. There were a couple of concrete tubs filled with vitiated soil and litter in the centre of the square. Everything was coated with that ominous rusty sodium-glow endowed by the square's single streetlamp. Dean was actually holding onto the back of Rory's coat.

"How pissed *are* you?" whispered Rory.

"Not enough," said Dean. "What are we *doing*?"

"You heard what Mick said. We need to arm ourselves."

They crossed the square and ducked into a stairwell. As they started up, they heard a sound from behind them. They clutched at each other and froze. They peered through a gap in the banister railings, their breath caught in their throats. "Oh, fuckin' *hell*," Dean moaned.

What sloped into the square had once been a man, surely; one could tell by the tracksuit bottoms. It came reeling in under the archway from the car park. It scraped the soles of its feet against the concrete in a lame, pigeon-toed shuffle. What had become of it above the waist was unendurable. Rory gagged.

They watched as the creature stepped into the amber light. It stood for a moment, swaying slightly, then seemed to sense activity to its left. It quivered. Slowly, it began to edge across the square towards the chip shop.

"We've got to do something, Rory!" Dean said. Rory was already on it. He had his mobile out and was punching in the phone number printed next to the sign above the chippy. The creature was picking up speed. Its feet scraped and dragged. It was navigating the concrete tubs.

"Come on, come *on,*" Rory hissed. The creature paused. Something on its head turned in Rory's direction.

"Hello, Fish 'n' Chick'n?"

Rory and Dean froze. From where they squatted they could see the misty outline of Gavin talking into the telephone next to the counter.

"Hello?"

The creature began to move off again.

"Bye, wanker."

Rory's phone was cut off. He squeezed his eyes shut. Dialed again. No reply. He looked up and saw that Gavin had resumed his activities at the fryers. He was ignoring the ringing. "Ah, come on you fat twat, answer your fucking *phone!*"

The creature had reached the chip shop's glass door. Rory was holding his phone so tightly he heard the casing crack. Dean grabbed his arm, pulling the phone away from his ear.

"It's too late," he said.

The door was pushed inwards then swung shut behind the creature. They saw sudden movement and a muffled voice registering shock that swiftly modulated up the scale into terror. More movement as the creature launched itself over the counter. The condensation was able to mask the specifics, allowing only a glimpse of the encounter, however it did nothing to smother the sound of Gavin's final scream and the horrible thick splash and monstrous sizzling as he was upended and plunged head first into the open fryer.

"My *Christ!*" Dean put a hand over his mouth. His eyes bulged above his blanched, trembling fingers. Rory slowly lowered his phone. He stood, pulling Dean up with him.

"We've got to get Babur," he said, and started up the steps to the second floor walkway.

Nobody wanted to leave the Macebearer. I sat at the bar with Frank, smoking and drinking my Scotch. There were two young mums with a couple of kids sitting by the window. They had taken the news of our situation pretty well, considering the strangeness of it. Maybe growing up on an estate like this prepared you for the kind of knight's move that had just now come upon them. When threatened, make as small a target of yourself as possible and chain smoke. Textbook.

We'd put what furniture we could lift up against the doors and the window but it was pretty flimsy. Most of the place was nailed down.

We waited. Every now and then, something would shriek or bellow from somewhere within the depths of the estate. We heard the muffled thuds of distant explosions that sounded like a row of cars going up like a string of firecrackers. Something large ran across the far end of the car park, hopping and flapping great leathery wings in a fruitless attempt to get airborne. It hurtled into a rank of recycling bins and collapsed. A rectangular green bin trundled unhurriedly across the asphalt like an unconvincing assault vehicle sent on a reconnoitre. It nudged the bumper of a parked Fiesta, which gave a startled honk from its alarm then fell silent.

We heard the screech of tyres and headlights suddenly lit up the car park as a large white IVECO Transit van swung through the entrance. It bounced up a kerb and headed straight for the Macebearer on a diagonal course. Julie leapt from her stool. "It's Jimmy," she said, "open the door, quick!"

Frank and I pulled a fruit machine away from the door and stepped out. The van had stopped outside the pub. The driver's side door flew open and a young man dressed in casual sportswear and wearing a Burberry baseball cap, its peak fashioned into a steep arch down which a small, sallow, sadistic little face peered, jumped out and hurried around to the front of the vehicle.

"He's got a shooter," said Frank from out the corner of his mouth. "Good boy."

Julie pushed between us and ran to Jimmy, but Jimmy was in the mood to discuss territory and registered disinterest by straight-arming her in the throat. She collapsed to her knees, barking.

Jimmy brought up his piece. It was a sawn-off shotgun. He waved it at us like an aid to detection. "Which one you chavs been pushin' wash on my *bitch?*" Jimmy articulated.

Frank stepped forward as the gun swung back towards me. He closed a hand around Jimmy's wrist and wrenched it downwards. Jimmy screamed just loudly enough to cover up the sound of the bones splintering. He sagged, wide-eyed and breathing loudly through his mouth. Frank shook him by the wrist – causing Jimmy to black out – which allowed the gun to drop from his indigo fingers. Then Frank stepped forward, pressed the muzzle of his Magnum into Jimmy's armpit and pulled the trigger.

Rory and Dean went up to the third floor. They stepped out from the stairwell and Rory peered around the corner of the building and along the narrow walkway. There were three flats on this side, the middle one being Babur's. It was directly above Rory's flat.

They edged around the corner and slid along the wall until they reached Babur's front door. Rory held his breath, listening. Was the old benefit fraud still up here or had he already left to meet with the other immigrants that congregated outside the Albion Hotel on the front? All of them casting their famished eyes about with guarded opportunism, blue-chinned and illegal, with a lift-groper's pallor and a history of psychiatric assessments to bolster their applications. Further callous thoughts coasted through Rory's head as he lifted a hand and knocked.

As they stood together on the walkway waiting for a response from old Babur, Rory found himself thinking about his life. He was aware of Dean's mucid panting beside him and could discern the jabbing movement of his chin as he darted his head about in limitless agitation. Dean, who perpetrated all manner of indignities upon sundry birds he met in clubs, then recounted his exploits with indecorous tang to the nearest deaf ear. What stopped Dean from despairing? Utter lack of aspiration, perhaps. An almost immeasurable incapacity to allow the gloom and toxicity of his few blunted relationships to afford him a nugget of insight into the superficiality of his existence? Probably. *Cunt.*

I'm better than this, thought Rory, and knocked again.

Frank walked around to the back of the van. "What's in the van, Gurgles?" he asked.

Jimmy opened his mouth, closed it. He was lying on his back in the road. His eyes were wide, staring. His hat had flipped off his head. "Maaah*faaah*," he said, eyes rolling, fixing on Frank. His upper arm, shoulder, and I should think a fair portion of his back, were gone. His mouth opened and I glimpsed a saliva bubble form between his lips, which glimmered momentarily, diaphanous and bronzed by the streetlight; it trembled like a dragonfly's wing, then winked out of existence at the very same moment Jimmy did.

"He's gone, Frank," I said.

Frank hauled open the rear doors. "*Fuck*," he said.

And the monster was on him.

Babur came to the door wearing slacks and a dirty grey vest. His braces hung in frayed loops from his waistband. He was

barefooted and was carrying a box of Cornflakes. He eyed
Rory and Dean with unconcealed mistrust.

"What do you want?"

"Have you got any guns?" said Dean from behind
Rory's left shoulder.

The pitbull hit the doors so hard they almost flew out of
Frank's grip. He just had time to absorb the shock, and
reacted by pushing the doors back together, vicing the
dog's head between them. He stood nose to nose with it as
it fumed and thrashed, claws scrabbling on the metal bed
of the van, exerting itself with an unhinged fury to attack.
Its head was a blur, like some possessed angle-grinder
straining to gnaw away its operator's face. I'd watched
Frank prepare a joint of beef once by cutting slits in the
thick, bloody muscle and pressing a fistful of garlic cloves
into the gashes. That's what that dog's head looked like,
battering itself earless against the sharp steel edges of
the doors: like an enraged and gory joint, tumourous with
great yellow cloves of teeth, animate with a mindless longing to *chew*.

I picked up Jimmy's shotgun and stepped round to
where Frank was duelling with the dog. I could see that
Frank was starting to sweat. There was a heat coming off the
animal, like the inside of a tumble dryer halfway through its
cycle; somehow damp yet arid simultaneously: sweat oozing
beneath the short, greasy pelt and the offensive, dirt-grey
stink of dog drool.

I shoved the barrels up between Frank's arms and was fortunate to find the sweet spot beneath the pitbull's jawbone, where the flesh is puppy soft and pouchy, at the first try. I thrust upwards, jamming the back of the dog's bony head into the narrow gap between the doors. Frank turned his head away.

"All I hear is gunshots, gunshots," said Babur. "Gunshots and screaming. It's like fucking Kabul down there."

Rory, Dean and Babur were all startled by the partially muffled blast of a large weapon. "That sounded like a shotgun," said Dean.

They peered over the low brick parapet that walled off the drop into the square. As they looked down, the door to the chip shop flew open and the creature that had killed Gavin came slithering out. It stopped and seemed to be listening. It appeared to be trying to ascertain the direction of the gunshot.

"What the fuck is *that* bastard?" said Babur, horrified, and dropped his Cornflakes over the side. The box hit the ground and detonated in a spray of orange flakes.

The creature made a sound, the most unlikely sound Rory had ever heard. It was like someone plucking the ring pull on an empty can, a kind of hollow, glottal *ping,* which Rory found unimaginably disturbing. Then, with a shocking and quite horrible haste, the creature belted across the square and charged up the stairwell.

"Oh, fuck *me!*" said Rory.

Rory and Dean bundled Babur back into his flat. Dean slammed the door and switched off the hall light.

"In here," said Babur, and led them into the kitchen. Through the window Rory could see fires burning in at least five different parts of the estate.

Babur closed the kitchen door. There was a small, Formica-topped table in the middle of the room with a couple of unmatching chairs beneath it. There was a cup of black tea, a pudding bowl and a carton of UHT milk on the table with a copy of *The Independent* folded open at the cryptic crossword. Rory noticed that Babur had almost completed it. He looked up to see that Babur was watching him.

"We're not all scroungers and idiots, you know," he said, narrowing his eyes.

Dean had opened the kitchen door and was peering down the hall. "I think it's outside," he said, then shrieked as the creature instantly began flinging itself against the door, each shuddering crash accompanied by that unearthly, frantic *ping! ping! ping!*

"Shut the door, you prick," Babur said in a low tone. He opened a drawer beneath the worktop and pulled out a carving knife.

There was a great splintering crash. Babur picked up the carving knife. He held it up and squinted along the length of the blade. He turned and looked at Rory, then at Dean. "Stay here," he said. Then he went to the kitchen door, pulled it open and stepped out into the hall.

"Think we'd better get inside," Frank said. He was wiping his face and neck with a bar towel.

"It's empty, Frank," I said. "Apart from what's left of the dog."

"Not the van. The pub. We'd better get inside the pub."

I looked up and caught the expression on his face. He nodded towards the car park. I turned to look.

"Right," I said.

Coming towards us from all sides of the car park were dozens of the creatures. And as they drew closer I began to hear the unnatural cacophony of sounds they made; groans and thuds, tinkles and rumbling eructations. Something was shouting a baroque torrent of dead languages and something else, towards the back of the crowd and maybe as big as a cart-horse, made an explosive, splintering jangle with each step, like a lorry-load of harpsichords being unloaded over a balcony.

"Actually," Frank said, "*do* get in the van." He went round to the driver's side and climbed in. Jimmy had left the keys. Frank started the ignition while I climbed into the back. I was nearly thrown off my feet as Frank reversed the van in a tight semicircle. I held onto the back of the passenger seat as Frank steered the van beneath the narrow arched entrance to the square, effectively blocking it off. He switched off the ignition and pulled the handbrake high and tight. He indicated the rear doors with a jab of his thumb. I climbed out and walked into the square. Frank followed and we stood there for a moment, looking around.

"You sure the kid's here?" Frank asked. "That's what Index said on the phone," I said. "He couldn't pinpoint the flat but was ninety-nine percent sure it was in this block."

Frank shook his head. "And Rory never knew a thing," he said. Then he frowned; someone had just fallen from the balcony over on our left. A carving knife glittered as it cartwheeled across the concrete.

Rory and Dean were both huddled behind the kitchen door. They heard Babur shout something in his native tongue, an oath precursive to engagement, and then there was the sound of a swift and frenzied encounter. Babur's voice was drowned beneath a deafening volley of hysterical *pings* and an odd *slumping* sound as a batch of oily tentacles unrolled across the plasterboard walls. Rory and Dean could hear a great deal of thrashing and pounding, punctuated by a systematic, brawny chopping sound.

"He's getting a pasting," Dean said, his eyes wide and appalled.

Rory nodded. He looked around the gloomy kitchen. "Quick," he said, "grab one of these." He slid a chair from under the table and pushed it at Dean. He took the other, a flimsy thing with a paint-spotted blue vinyl seat cushion, and lifted it up in front of his chest. He looked like a disastrously unaccomplished lion-tamer.

"Come on, then," he said, a little wildly, pushed past Dean and threw open the kitchen door.

I looked up. A figure was peering over the side of the second floor balcony. He was wearing a vest and appeared to be covered in blood. He looked like he was about to say something, and then I saw my brother and his mate come piling out of the flat behind him carrying furniture.

"What were you going to do, sit and watch?" the old guy barked.

Rory, Dean and Babur came down to the plaza and they all stood looking down at the body. "How the fuck did you do that?" asked Dean, an incredulous look on his face.

Babur wiped his brow on a hairy forearm. He appeared totally unharmed. "Element of surprise," he said. He walked off and retrieved his knife. "I don't think there are any more guns," said Rory. He jumped as something threw itself against the front of the transit van, making it rock on its axles. He felt deflated, nervy and exhausted.

"Here," said Frank, and tossed him the shotgun. He took a box of shells from his pocket and lobbed them as well. "In the glove box," he said.

Rory caught the shotgun in his arms but fumbled the shells. He bent to pick them up and, as he did so, unintentionally discharged the second of the shotgun's barrels.

"Fuck me, Rory, mind what you're doing!" yelled Mick. There was a rambunctious, orotund sound, like a large glass bottle half-full of overripe matter rolling in an arc across a marble floor. Frank was looking at Dean with a sickened look on his face.

Rory turned slowly, his eyes wide, horrified at what he must have done.

"You've *shit* yourself!" said Frank.

Dean darted his eyes from one face to another. "No I haven't," he lied.

Babur and Frank went over to the transit. Frank opened the back doors and they both climbed in. From where I stood beneath the streetlamp I could see them both talking and looking out through the windscreen at what was happening in the car park. The van occasionally trembled or rocked but otherwise remained firm. Dean had crept gingerly back into the Macebearer.

I turned to Rory. "There's some more stuff I've got to tell you, Rors," I said. Rory looked shot to pieces but I had information he needed to hear. I thought he could probably take it. I mean, it was kind of *happy* news. He was looking around the square like he was trying to remember where he'd parked his bike. He turned to me.

"Not more weird shit, Mick. That other stuff, that Firmament Surgeon stuff, it makes my head ache."

"Not weird, Rory," I said. "*Surprising*. But not weird."

Frank climbed down from the back of the van. He looked unimpressed.

"They're not all that," he said. "There's a few big boys out there, but they're mostly blundering about. Some of the others have made a few cracks in the windscreen but they're pretty ineffectual. Must be Dupes."

I nodded. The creatures were spawned from a lousy stock; they weren't suddenly going to discover might and vitality just by being transformed into externalised versions of their own sleaze and fear. Their sole purpose was to frighten and distract. Nasty trick, but we were onto them.

It was what they heralded that bothered me.

Already the streetlamp was dimming and a quality of the air was making our voices sound flat and muffled. My ears felt full of wax.

"Right, Rory. Your place?"

Rory looked baffled, and then he seemed to come to a little. "Yeah," he said. "Come up."

We went up a flight of steps and along the walkway to Rory's flat. He opened the front door and we went in. We entered the lounge and the first thing I saw was a large black-and-white poster in a clip frame over the fireplace. Jean Harlow in all her brassy allure.

"Still digging that chick?" I said.

"Still digging that chick," Rory replied with a wan smile.

I stood in front of the poster, my hands behind my back. I pursed my lips and tilted my head to one side. "Never fancied her, myself," I said.

Rory shrugged.

"You've got a little boy, Rory," I told him. "He's three."

"My God," said Rory. "My God. I should have known. I mean, I should have *guessed*. I should at least have…" He sat down heavily on the sofa and raised his hands. "It was only once, but…"

"Once is sufficient, Rory," Mick said.

Rory felt numb. He thought this must be what it was like to be told you had cancer. No, he couldn't say that. That was a terrible thing to think. He looked around his living room trying to focus on something unthreatening, something to ground him. Little dots of light floated behind his eyes. Mick sat down next to him. "Breathe, Rory," he said.

Rory gasped and looked up at Jean Harlow. Somehow he expected something surreal to happen, something of the David Lynch stripe; the boundaries of the poster would begin to flow out from the edges of the clip frame like a dark aura and Jean would step out of her compressed limbo, all sun-fade and smoke, and begin to sing in a child's voice "Saratoga, Saratoga, Saratogaaaa-"

"Gaaaa," said Rory.

"That's it, Rory, you breathe now," said Mick.

Rory looked around and saw his brother sitting on the sofa next to him. His shoulders slumped and he closed his eyes. "She used to come into the shop. She was all tits and tops-of-the-arms. Brown, freckly, you know. She had these two awful kids with her, Brandon and Jordan. Both different colours. One evening she was hanging about by the trolleys and asked me to go for a drink. I thought why not, so we did and I ended up back at hers. I don't even remember giving her one, Mick, not really. Then she stops coming into the shop and blanks me on the stairs and then a while later I see her with a pram and those two kids and think, stupid tart's got herself up the stick again, how fucking irresponsible.

"I never thought for a minute. Are you sure, Mick? Really sure?"

Mick nodded. "Do they still live here?"

"They live opposite. Number eighteen. He's a lovely little boy, Mick. His name's Alex. He gets a terrible time off those brothers. He's going to be a wreck. The oldest one's got an Anti-Social Behavioural Order on him already." Rory looked up at his poster again with tearful eyes, and Mick thought he recognised that look from a long time ago.

"No, he's not, Rory. He's the child we've come for. He's the reborn Firmament Surgeon."

Rory shook his head. "What? Mick. *Mick*. I can't really believe that shit. Not really."

There was the sound of a scream and a gunshot from outside. Rory nearly leapt off the sofa. "Believe the rest of it, though, Rory. You believe what you've already seen. Just trust me on the rest."

Rory stared at the floor for a moment, then sighed. He stood up and picked up his shotgun. "You'd better show me how to load this," he said.

As they came out of Rory's flat they noticed immediately that the light was different. They looked down into the square and saw the cause.

Above the concrete tubs in the middle of the plaza, a thin golden thread had appeared in the air. The Gantry was being forced open.

"The Autoscopes are coming," said Mick.

He saw Frank drop to one knee and fire into the Gantry. Something bellowed and for a second the strip of cold, golden light pulsed and receded to a mere filament suspended in the air. Then it began to rend again, and Mick fancied he could hear the fragile fabric between the dimensions popping like bubble wrap as atoms split off on their exotic traceries.

He nudged Rory and they ducked along the walkway. They turned right at the end and skirted round until they came to number eighteen. Lights were on and they could both hear noises coming from inside. They looked at each other and nodded. Mick straightened up, lifted his gun and kicked the door off its hinges.

Frank fired again. Babur had climbed down from the back of the van and was standing at Frank's side, twirling the carving knife in his fingers by the tip of the blade. Golden light strobed off the stainless steel; Babur flipped the knife, snatched the handle and hurled it underarm towards the gap in the air. There was an unearthly howl of agony and something large and dark reared up, blocking the light, then fell backwards, taking Babur's knife with it, embedded in a great, glaring, murderous eye.

Something else was forcing its way through. Light was smoking upwards, lengthening the breach and a figure stepped out into the square. It stood like a gunslinger, arms by its side, face obscured by long, fair hair. It wore a black coat with tails cut to resemble the carapace of a beetle.

Frank turned to Babur. "The Coleopterist," he said. "Index mentioned him." He began to walk backwards towards the van. He raised his Magnum and pumped a couple of rounds into the figure. The creature jolted but remained standing. It lifted its head and peered out from beneath its fringe with a high bank of tiny, glittering eyes. It hissed and a green, venomous fluid frothed from pinhole ducts beneath the eyes. It pulled its shoulders back and shot its cuffs and at once a torrent of cockroaches poured from its sleeves and clattered to the concrete like a hellish conjuring trick. The insects fanned out; some took off on slick, papery wings and swirled around in the golden light, rattling and colliding with each other.

The insects continued to cascade from the Coleopterist's sleeves as if the creature standing in the middle of the square were nothing more than a bottomless tank of filth, siphoning these awful bugs up from some great swarming chasm within it.

And behind it, something else was pushing through the Gantry. Something vast.

Mick and Rory edged up the hallway of number eighteen. They could hear sounds coming from the bedrooms at the back of the flat. If Rory remembered correctly, the two boys bunked in one room. The little one must have been forced in with them. Rory felt an enervating surge of sudden and overwhelming concern course through him. He felt totally disarmed as the new emotions began to harden into anger. He began to like the feel of the shotgun in his hands. Those little mistreating shits. My son. *My* son. My *son*.

Rory walked into Mick and nearly dropped the shotgun. Mick rounded on him, glaring. "Keep it together Rors, yes?" he said. Rory nodded.

They reached the end of the hall. There were three doors. Mick turned and gave Rory a questioning look.

"I don't know," Rory said. "I think we did it on the settee."

Mick took hold of the door handle on his right. "Ready?" Rory nodded.

Mick opened the door.

They both recoiled as something horrible sluiced out at them on a thick, phlegmy tide of matter.

"Sharon?" Rory said.

Mick knelt down to have a closer look. He breathed in a mouthful of air that smelt of cloves and onions and grease. It lay in a pool of glossy liquid, sagging on its flank. Between his parted knees a large grey cylinder peered up at him with cloudy, baked-looking eyes. The torso was a slab from which vestigial limbs protruded. Mick looked up at Rory. "*Sharon*?" he said.

Rory was staring down at the monster. "She was a looker in her day," he said, then brayed a loud and uncontrollable volley of feral laughter. He clapped a hand over his mouth.

Something hit the door to their left hard enough to burst a screw out of the top hinge.

Mick stepped back in time to avoid being showered with chipboard fragments as the door exploded. He raised an arm to cover his face and when he lowered it something utterly fearsome was standing in the hall before him, billowing and shining like tarpaulin.

Mick bundled into Rory and they both fell backwards. Mick dropped his gun and watched with anguish as it came down on its muzzle and sprang rascally beneath the creature's trembling forelimbs. It lowered its head and bellowed a great blast of snot and steam down the hall at them.

The sitting room door opened behind them and they wheeled round. The muscles in Rory's face were trembling. "Oh, what's going down?" he said.

Another creature had emerged from the room behind them. It had no face, no features; it was a tremulous block of pinkish, rugose flesh, and as they watched, it unhinged a cruel fan of fitments from its flank and began to slide up the hall towards them.

Mick reached round and grabbed Rory's shotgun. He spun and faced the thing standing in front of the kitchen door. It fixed stalk-eyes on him and switched its mantis head to the side.

"Who am I killing?" Mick said over his shoulder, "I like to know."

Rory's voice was loud in Mick's ear. "I think that's Brandon. He was always a beady-eyed little fuck."

"Excellent," said Mick and gave Brandon both barrels.

The creature's head disintegrated in a fine spray, fanning the kitchen door with a coating of greenish muck. Its long neck bucked like a whipcord and the creature slumped forward onto its knees like a slaughterhouse steer. The stump of neck farted a thick bubble of air, thrashed once then lay still.

Mick and Rory ran past the body of the Brandon-creature and crashed into the kitchen.

"You'll always find me in the kitchen at carnage," sang Rory. He had that riotous look back in his eyes.

Suddenly a collection of lethal-looking biomechanical tines slid through between the door and its frame. Rory leapt backwards, narrowly avoiding being speared through the side.

Mick lifted the shotgun and brought the stock down onto the jabbing tines with enough force to bend them and actually snap a couple off. The creature made a quivering, wallowing sound and tried to withdraw the crooked spokes. Mick hit them again and effectively fastened the thing to the other side of the door.

"Bollocks to this," Mick said. He reloaded the shotgun and took a step back. He raised the shotgun to waist height and blasted the door from about two feet away.

Smoke hung about them like fog. Rory coughed and waved the smoke away with his hand. There was a hole in the door big enough to climb through. Splinters like scorched fangs rimmed the hole and both men went up to it and peered through.

The hall was coated in a lumpy pink layer of smouldering blancmange. "Jordan?" asked Mick.

"I imagine so," said Rory.

"Fat little bastard?"

"How'd you guess?"

They heard a sound behind them and both spun round. It had been a sob.

I let Rory investigate the sound. He went over to the corner of the room and squatted to look beneath the kitchen table.

"Oh, hi," he said, sounding a little choked, "Hi. Come on, it's OK. It's OK. Let me pick you up." He turned his head and looked at me, eyes full of sorrow. "They've got him sleeping in a *dog basket,* the bastards. Come on, now, Alex. It'll be all right."

He reached under the table and emerged with a small boy in his arms. The child was white-faced and hung in Rory's arms like a soft toy. He had dark smudges beneath his eyes. He was dressed in a grubby white T-shirt and knee-length orange shorts with green piping around the waist. His feet were black with grime. He stared into Rory's face with a strange, still serenity. Then he threw his arms around Rory's neck, hooked his legs around his middle and buried his head in his chest. Rory grunted and staggered back a step but hung on. He carried the child over to me. He was grinning.

"Mick, Alex. Alex, Mick."

I reached out and ruffled his hair a little in a way I imagined an uncle might.

Alex was already asleep.

We came back out onto the walkway and could see that the Gantry had widened considerably. It was now a blazing yellow fissure through which something colossal was attempting to pass. As we watched, more of the creature strained its way through the Gantry, and legs, segmented and bristling with hairs, slid through and came down onto the concrete with a scrabbling, scratching sound. The air around the Gantry was swarming with huge bugs and I could sense more of them milling and clicking in the darkness of the doorways and stairwells around the perimeter of the square. A figure in a long black coat stood in front of the Gantry and I saw hundreds of those bugs well up from out of its coat, pour over its collar and race down its back. The Coleopterist had arrived.

I could see Frank and Babur with their backs to the Transit van. Frank was trying to force a fresh clip into his gun.

We ran along the walkway and down the stairs. We came out on Frank's right, crushing dozens of roaches beneath our feet. They split like ice-cream cones and long buttery strings of innards clung to our shoes as we executed a series of squeamish leaps over them. Frank saw us and palmed the clip home. He gestured to us to stay back.

We were close, though, and I could see a vertical line of eyes glistening along the foremost lobe of the monster's torso; they were as golden as the light from the Gantry and blazed with a terrible alien wrath. It must have seen – or sensed – Rory's child, and it increased its efforts to come through. It moaned and whined with fury and exertion and behind it, still contained within the Gantry, I could hear the desperate cries of other Autoscopes as they too felt the proximity of the child.

"Take him inside, Rory," I said. Rory was rigid with fear but I elbowed him and he tottered into the Macebearer with an ailing expression on his face, Alex held tightly in his arms.

I was about to go over to Frank and Babur but before I could move something came out of the Gantry – some kind of thick, serrated appendage – and sideswiped Babur. It sent him sprawling across the plaza in a welter of blood. He pitched onto his side and rolled into the doorway of Hurrell's Bakers.

I stopped, stunned. Frank ducked as the tentacle swept back over his head. He fired off a couple of rounds and then sprang up into the back of the Transit van.

A moment later the engine roared. The Coleopterist jerked its head as if waking from a trance. It made to follow Frank into the back of the van but before it could reach the open doors, the vehicle reversed into it, hitting it just above the knees. It flew forwards and sprawled onto the floor of the van.

Frank kept reversing. The van shot backwards and I caught sight of him through the passenger side window, looking over his shoulder and steering with his right hand on the wheel, left arm over the back of the seat. I heard muffled gunshots and the legs that were hanging out of the back of the van began to tremble. One of its boots was shaken loose and a torrent of bugs poured out of it the second it hit the ground.

The creature emerging from the Gantry was thrashing violently, its awful insect legs flogging against the concrete. It rose up and I could see a pale, distended thorax pushing at the bottom of the slit in the air, pressing it wider, swelling with effort to be born. And then the van slammed into it and its entire head and upper body were driven through the open rear doors and right up into the cargo area. The creature roared and lifted the vehicle off the ground. Its legs beat against the side panels and one of those serrated tentacles writhed across the roof, peeling up coils of metal like a can-opener.

It smashed the van back down. The windscreen blew out with a sound like a shelf full of wineglasses collapsing. The passenger door sprang open.

Frank slid out and rolled. He came up and ran across the plaza. He reached me, snatched the shotgun out of my hands, winked – the fucker *winked* – and then ran back towards the van.

The creature was rearing up, half of it still wedged in the Gantry, the other half jammed into the back of the van. All four wheels were off the ground and the creature was shaking it like a dog trying to shake off a muzzle. The sides of the van buckled and gonged.

Frank lifted the shotgun. As the van rose up again, revealing the dark, channelled underside, he fired both

barrels into the fuel tank. Petrol burst from the ruptured
tank. Frank ducked beneath the van and ran towards the
opposite stairwell. I lost sight of him for a moment as the
van crashed down into the widening pool of petrol, then
he was visible again as the creature threw itself back against
the edge of the Gantry, taking the van up with it. Frank had
pulled out his Zippo. He flipped the lid, thumbed the wheel
and lobbed the lighter beneath the cascade of fuel.

The van exploded.

The concussion hurled Frank off his feet. It blew
out every window overlooking the square. The wide plate
glass pane at the front of the *VAL-YOU!* Bargain Mart
imploded, showering the checkouts with a gale of shards.
An oily brown fireball rolled up through the chimney made
by the four facing walls of the plaza. I threw myself into a
stairwell, kicking up a storm of those big, greasy bugs.

I looked around the corner and squinted through the
rippling, turbulent air.

The creature was thrashing in the silent heat of the
burning van. Its legs had been reduced to carbon stumps
and that jagged tentacle had shrivelled to a charred cable
that lashed like a downed powerline with the movement of
the creature's body. All I could hear was that blunt, baking
roar of the flames.

I saw movement through the haze at the entrance to the
square. I thought it was Frank but of course, now the van
was out of the way, the creatures from the car park were
venturing in.

Then I did see Frank. He was hobbling out of the smoke
on what looked like a broken leg. As he came around past
the entrance, something with a wide scarlet mouth came
bounding towards him. He swung the shotgun and batted it
away like a cricketer rolling his wrists down the leg side. The
creature folded up and tumbled into the flames. I ran over
to Frank and half carried him towards the Macebearer. His
face was scorched and most of his hair above the brow was
little more than stubble. His eyes were puffy and red and his
lips were dotted with large, taut-looking blisters.

He grunted and leaned against me. As we reached the
door to the Macebearer, we heard the van come down hard
against the concrete. We turned, Frank hop-shuffling round
in my arms.

The creature had collapsed. Half of it had broken off,
where it joined the Gantry like a chunk of hot ash slumping from the end of a huge cigar. What remained was still
encased within the blackened frame of the van. As we
watched, the Gantry began to narrow. A small amount of
that wintry golden light still flickered around its edges but it
was weakening. The Gantry was closing.

More of the creatures had come onto the plaza and
these seemed to be disorientated and mystified by the
waning Gantry. I saw one of them, an alarming-looking
thing with a bleary Cyclops eye the size of a bullseye window, just topple over onto its back in what was effectively
a dead faint.

I helped Frank to turn on his good leg and we went in.

We limped up the corridor and went through into the main bar. I could see Rory sitting in a booth, holding the sleeping child in his arms. Rory looked close to exhaustion. Everyone else was at the window, peering out over the makeshift barricade of chairs and benches. Dean had his forehead pressed to the glass. "They're leaving," he said, and a large, white nebula of condensed breath bloomed over his head like an empty thought bubble. How apt, I thought.

Frank propped himself against a bar stool. "Here," he said and tossed his keys to me. "Get the Chevy and we're out of here."

I caught the keys and went over to the doors. I shouldered the fruit machine out of the way again and stepped out into the car park. I took a deep breath and tasted engine oil and burning petrol. The monsters had all filed up through the entrance to the plaza, drawn there by what remained of the Gantry.

I turned right and jogged past the entrance. I glanced through the arch and saw that the van was just a smoking grey steel cage. The monsters surrounded it. Something with a throat like a bullfrog had gone too close and had fused its air sac to the side of the van. It bounded feverishly back and forth, connected to the superheated panel by an ever-lengthening rope of melting flesh.

I reached the Chevy and climbed in. I started her up and drove back across the car park until he was outside the Macebearer. Only then did I turn on the headlamps.

The Macebearer's doors swung open and Rory stumbled out. He opened the passenger side door and handed Alex to me. "Hang on," he said, and returned to the pub. He came back out a minute later with Frank leaning against him. They went around to the back of the flatbed and managed to get Frank over the tailgate and onto the floor. He looked up at me and grinned. Gave me a nod.

Rory came round and got in beside me. He took Alex from me and buckled up.

"No one else wanted to come," Rory said. He didn't look surprised.

"Looks like you got out, Rors," I said.

"Got a bit of glamour in my life," he said with a slight, not-quite-confident smile. He looked wonderingly down at the sleeping boy.

I knocked the Chevy into first and we drove away,

I used to say to audiences that I did comedy in order to explore my sociopathic tendencies within a legitimised framework. This is partly true.

However, I now have a greater commission. Index tells me to keep my stuff surreal and extraordinary. That way the dark energies behind everything can't get a grip and do their unmaking. They hate our laughter because laughter is light. And in it there is no darkness at all.

There may not be pandas in East Anglia, but everything else I've told you is true.

Rory was almost asleep.

For about the hundredth time he looked down at the child in his arms. The interior of the Chevy was warm and quiet, lit only by the glow from the dashboard instruments. Mick was holding the Chevy at a steady seventy all the way down the M11 to London.

Rory smiled. As his eyes closed, he whispered some words to Alex, words that sounded a little bit alike.

One of them was *Dartford*.

The others were Jean Harlow.

THE VAGUE

The last thing we did every evening was to go around the outside of the cottage and examine the silver cutlery. You can see the hackles of the werewolves above the garden fence as they pace about beneath the gawking moon. Every now and then one circles back and tries to nudge the garden gate open with its awful elongated muzzle, but the silver bread knife we'd jammed into the latch makes it impossible for them to get through. Along the top of the fence we'd fixed more silverware as protection from those milling, lambent dogs.

Likewise, the lawn all around the cottage was studded with knives and forks, antique and tarnished but sharpened against our wheel to provide an adequate deterrent should the werewolves breach our outer defences.

One night we were awakened by a terrible sound. Robin sat up in his bed beneath the eaves and shouted my name. I stumbled out of my bed and went over to the window. The moon was high and stark, bright as a lamp, and encircled by a cold spill of stars. There were no clouds. The trees surrounding the cottage glittered like tinsel beneath the moonlight.

There was a werewolf in the garden. Somehow it had managed to clear the fence and had landed on the lawn. It was impaled through its front paws by two sharp silver forks. It looked up at my window with great yellow eyes, opened its mouth and screamed.

I shuddered, and behind me Robin cried out again. I stood fast and reached out to open the window.

"Don't," Robin said, but I undid the latch and pushed open the window.

I could hear the harsh, agitated breath of the beast. Its tail was hooked beneath its back legs. It shot a sudden, steaming jet of urine onto the grass. Its shanks were quivering. It knew it had killed itself.

I put my head out. "Hey!" I shouted.

The werewolf lowered its head and licked at the bloodied tines of the fork sticking out of its right paw. I heard a hiss, and a puff of steam plumed from the werewolf's nostrils. It whined and its back legs collapsed. It fell onto its side and more of the knives and forks dug into it. Its tongue lolled and the yellow eyes flickered, became slits.

"Hey!" I shouted again.

"What are you doing?" Robin asked.

There was a small vase on the windowsill. I picked it up and lobbed it across the garden. It hit the werewolf in the ribs and bounced away beneath an oleander bush.

The werewolf opened its right eye and glared at me.

Then it spoke. "Who are you?" it said.

Its voice was soft but carried easily up to me on the still night air. It was the most unexpected thing I have ever experienced. Even here.

I gasped. Robin had lit a candle and I turned to him, my mouth wide and wordless. His face was pale in the trembling candlelight and the shadow of his head and shoulders lurched and shrugged against the wall behind his bedpost. I turned back to the window. The werewolf had closed its eyes and was motionless.

"I was going to ask you that," I said, but the werewolf had died.

Robin's dreams had been laden with tumultuous skies cross-hatched with rusty wires and vast iron towers. The towers were held together with bolts the size of tank turrets. Beasts with empty eye sockets crept and felt their way around the bases of the towers, across the great ranges of dirt between the stanchions, their shark mouths biting at their fists whenever a heavy dissonant bell rang from some staggering vault above them.

"I don't want this anymore," Robin said one morning. He'd woken up crying again.

I said, "Neither do I, Rob." I stood at our bedroom window as the sun came up above the forest and watched the werewolves begin to tremble and falter and slip with their agonies away into the pines. I wondered again whether now might be the best time to attack them, but I couldn't risk dying like that. I had to take care of Robin. I had to protect him until he could find the way back for us.

I lifted my friend into my arms and carried him down the narrow stairs into the kitchen. He was still in his light green cotton pyjamas. I thought he looked a bit like a surgeon, for some reason, and laughed as I eased him into his wheelchair. Robin smiled, "What?"

"Nothing," I said and wheeled him over to the sink. I'd already been down and set a fire in the stove, so there was plenty of hot water. I handed Robin his washcloth and went over to the stove to cook us a bit of breakfast. It was funny, because before we came here, I'd been the one in the wheelchair.

We've talked about it, of course, through the long evenings here, and Robin can't remember. He says he only ever remembers being like this. There's nothing wrong with him physically; I make sure I help him exercise his legs so they don't atrophy, but in truth there's no sign of weakness.

I think it's in his head. I think it's like this place. All in his head.

So, what we do after breakfast is we go into town. It's a ritual. It gets us out of the cottage. There's a path that cuts through the forest. It starts at our front gate and runs straight for about a mile through the trees. It's a lovely walk if the weather's fine.

The path comes out onto a small lane that takes you into town. Quay-Katavothron is quite big; a large proportion of it is built around the rim of an enormous sinkhole, from which the town gets its name. The houses and shops are narrow and old-fashioned, built from the same smoky grey wood and vanilla-coloured plaster, and they rise up in tiers, honeycombed by tiny, dark passageways and alleys the locals call senlaks.

Nobody knows why Quay-Katavothron grew up around such a precarious drop; after all, the forest at its back could have been cleared to allow for some expansion – why not just build inland a little more? Some people say that proximity to a vertiginous drop allows a certain humility to develop within the townsfolk, something prayerful and alert, which—when the storms come and the rainwater washes the earth from the forest to foam through the senlaks and beneath the boardwalks, and pours in a frothing cataract over the lip of the pit—becomes a species of euphoric anticipation closely resembling a spiritual transport.

The parson's clubfooted and crazy and he hollers sermons from the bell tower. During the months when the rains come, Quay-Katavothron is a place of religious dreamers; hot psalms and fitful prayers flitter like pieces of distant lightning through the lobes and ventricles of the going-to-sleep and the coming-awake.

We get to town and I push Robin through the streets until we get to the oldest part of Quay-Katavothron. It's a narrow street crowded with thumbnail cottages, inns and antique shops. Tiny gargoyles perch like ancient, petrified vermin on many of the chimneystacks and gables. We go in all the antique shops and scour them for silver cutlery. Fish knives and cheese knives will do, with their sharp serrated edges. Then we fill the bag that hangs from the handles of Robin's wheelchair with the cutlery and make our way out of the Old Town and down to the lip of the sinkhole.

Robin wheels himself right to the edge.

The hole is vast. It is probably over two hundred feet wide and the same across. Its depth is immeasurable. Robin spits over the side and watches as the saliva drops, twirls and is torn apart by a crosswind. It's customary for us to say a prayer, so we give thanks to Jesus for our continued deliverance. We ask for wisdom to fathom our circumstances and enough faith to remove us from them. We ask him if we can go home.

Then we go to the Black Estuary Tavern for lunch.

The estuary is more sepia than black, and dense with silt and vegetation. It is very wide and opens out onto the Sea of Kyrou. The forest encroaches right up to the banks and drapes canopies and loops of creeper into the slow tide. Silt stirs, clouding the shallows.

On the far bank, backing into the tree line, stands the Tavern. It is huge; it has broad, scowling eaves, paint-sealed and decaying dormers and a great, green iron cupola. There are many windows looking out from the hundred small rooms and narrow hallways which labyrinth the upper floors.

We get a good meal there and a couple of pints of Crusader, which is the sweetest and most refreshing beer I've ever tasted. It's golden, light and tastes like elderflowers. It's with an eccentric, poignant regret, I know should we ever get back, that I'll spend forever trying to find a beer like this again, insisting on its existence to people and never getting anything close to approximating its blissful tonic; that's the problem with dream beer. What a thing to be concerned about!

We sat in our dark booth by the fireplace, enfolded by the full-bodied fragrance of the cold apple wood ash heaped in the grate. It seems like the atmosphere of the Tavern has accreted to the surfaces of the wooden benches and trestles; you can pare off black rinds like wax with a fingernail.

Robin ordered plum pudding and loganberry ice cream and for some reason I got the Roquefort and red onion mash, buttery swede and a piece of sirloin an inch thick and pink as an albino's eye. I say for some reason, because I actually remember ordering a Spanish omelette. That's what happens here; you ask for one thing and you get another. It's all a bit of a gamble, but you can't complain about the quality of the food once it's arrived.

After lunch we took a seldom-used path back to the cottage for a bit of variety. The sirloin had been soft and juicy but I could feel the weight of it in my belly and the three pints of Crusader had titrated me to optimal efficacy so I fancied the longer, moderately winding walk the path offered.

It was midafternoon and stifling. The air smelt of loam and warm foliage and was hot and dusty in my mouth; it made me want to curl up in the shade of some cool tree roots and go to sleep. I looked down at the top of Robin's head as I pushed the chair over the dry, bumpy earth of the path and envied him the leisure of his condition and the cool of the ice cream he could no doubt still taste on his lips.

I didn't disturb him when we were walking, because that was when Robin did most of his thinking. He considered the higher things; I just drifted, worrying sometimes about the werewolves and the eyeless things and the towers. The werewolves had begun in Robin's dreams but had somehow found a way out and into this world. I was living in a constant dread of encountering his other demons and spent a lot of time trying to formulate plans for each eventuality.

I think further incursions are close. I haven't told Robin but a week ago I went out into the back garden with a basket full of washing and found that sometime in the night a great metal pylon had appeared, overarching the entire lawn. I craned my neck and stood looking up at its tapering frame, wide-eyed and bristling with an awful creeping sensation. It was the horrible size of it, the gravity that exerted an almost nauseating pull on me, and the impression of slyness that came with its silent arrival. It was equipped with flanks of those cruciform branches that seem to give pylons their mildly amusing aspect of haughty indignance.

There was nothing amusing about this structure; this dismal, skeletal tonnage hung over the house, emitting a tangible field of menace and brought with it a sense that something was coming close behind it. Something unremitting.

I went back into the kitchen and sat at the table with my hands clasped on the oilcloth, staring straight ahead with tears in my eyes, until I heard Robin begin to stir upstairs. I got up and went to the window above the sink and looked out, aware of the pounding of my heart. The pylon was gone. I dropped my chin onto my chest and closed my eyes. I said a prayer, more an exhalation of relief than anything articulate, and went up to get Robin.

I don't want to tell him because I know it will disturb him; he'll fret and it will interrupt his thinking. And he needs to keep thinking because he's so close to the answer. His theory will free us and then we can go back and apply it to the problem that brought us here.

We arrived back at the cottage at about four o'clock. It had cooled remarkably, and I could see a dark line of storm clouds gathering to the west, massing above the distant ends of the forest. There would be thunder and lightning tonight and another full moon somewhere high above the ferment. Always a full moon now.

And old John Brittle would be up in the chapel in Quay-Katavothron, the rain pouring down his face and saturating his robes, barking hell and claps of thunder, mad, crippled, dreadful, shambling and raving beneath the low, heavy, rocking bell.

The storm reached us an hour later, though we heard it coming well before. It came like a nightfall of wars. We sat out beneath the awning at the side of the cottage and drank tea, enjoying the cool breeze, and watched as the sky arrived, all rowdy voltage and blasts. And as it rolled over us, the rain came.

We hunched our shoulders and grinned at each other as the rain beat like a prison riot against the tin roof above us and hissed into the lawn. The cutlery glimmered and shone like light bulb filaments each time the lightning lit the clouds. This would keep the werewolves away tonight. I got up to get us another cup of tea and some of the lemon cake I'd bought in our favourite bakery in the Old Town, but I never made it into the kitchen.

A pylon had appeared behind us while we had been sitting staring out at the rain.

The sky lit again and again, a monstrous pinball of flashes and detonations, and a bolt of lightning suddenly struck the tower. Blue webs of electricity glittered and crawled amongst the stanchions and it was then, uplit by dazzling currents that I made out the shapes of those terrible sightless shark-mawed monsters descending in a swarm.

Robin heard me gasp and turned his head. "Oh, Adam, why didn't you tell me?" he said. I stood by our back door, open mouthed and frozen. "Come on!" he said.

I dragged myself away from the soft light of the kitchen, my only hope to barricade ourselves indoors, hopeless and knowing we were done for, but Robin had other ideas. He grabbed the wheels of his chair and spun himself around. "The forest!" he shouted as thunder blew another hole in the night. It was as though the sky was full of phenomenal mines and the heavy black clouds were ceaselessly rolling over them. He reached down and pulled two silver forks from the grass at the edge of the garden. He threw one at me. I caught it and stood staring dumbly at him as he rolled his chair towards the path. "We've got to get to the Quay," he said. "We'll be safe at the Tavern."

I took another look up at the pylon. It was thick with monsters. They were hanging from the struts, trying to find footholds, hindered by their sightlessness. As I grabbed the handles of Robin's chair, one of them lost its grip and plunged over a hundred feet to the ground. It bit its own face to tatters and flung a shocking palette of innards across the lawn on impact.

I shoved Robin onto the path and trundled down to the gate. As I reached for the latch, the clouds parted to reveal the full moon. We looked up at it, nailed by the rain, and I said, "You want us to go into the forest?"

Robin looked at me, his hair dark, wet, moonlit, his eyes bright. "Yes!" he said. He held up a hand. "At least in there, we've got some protection."

I looked down at the fork he was holding, mottled with tarnish like the tail of a diseased fish, and then peered out into the woods.

Everywhere, yellow eyes were opening.

"We can't go out there," I said. I thought about getting us back into the cottage, but even as I was contemplating this I heard a muffled thump and turned to see that three of the creatures had dropped onto the roof. Already they were seizing great clumps of thatch in their huge, lead-coloured fists, boring into the upper rooms.

"Just believe, Adam!" Robin said. He held the fork out in front of him as though he was about to engage in some ludicrous and luckless joust. "Open the gate and believe we'll make it," he said. "We have to test the theory!"

I took a last look back at the cottage. A creature had staggered in through the open kitchen door and could be seen in silhouette through the window, biting at things, biting anything.

"Okay," I said. "I believe!" and shoved the wheelchair through the gate and ran with it into the forest.

I veered onto the path we had taken back from the Tavern earlier that afternoon. Robin lowered his head and began to pray. I bounced the chair along over the dirt and tried to avoid spilling Robin out onto the ground. I believed, though. Whatever that meant to Robin, I know our lives depended on it. I just wasn't sure what it was I needed to believe! I believed in God, I believed in Robin, I believed in the theory, I believed we'd be safe.

Until I rounded a bend and we saw that the path was crowded with werewolves.

And I believed we were lost.

We faced each other in silence. There were at least eight werewolves on the path; their flanks slid against each other as they wove around, turning tight, sinuous circles. They were agitated. Robin was holding his fork out in front of his chest like a crucifix in an old vampire movie, but I didn't think it was this that was causing the agitation. Innumerable others moved in the undergrowth, dark, heavy shapes circling us. The werewolves on the path seemed suddenly to arrive at a collective decision. They stopped their weaving and began to move towards us. I stepped around to the front of Robin's chair and lifted my fork. They lowered their heads and flattened their ears and growled and all at once the undergrowth exploded as the rest of the pack burst out around us. I cried out and fell back against Robin. His fork jabbed into the back of my thigh and I cried out again and dropped my own. I raised my hands and turned away as they fell upon us.

"Adam!" gasped Robin. "Look!"

I opened my eyes. I lowered my trembling hands.

The werewolves were running past us, great heads with golden eyes and caramel coloured teeth bared at the height of my shoulders. One of them brushed past Robin's chair close enough for him to reach out and run his hand along its side. Its tail flicked his face and Robin laughed.

He turned his head and looked back along the path. I followed his gaze.

The shark-mouthed creatures had entered the woods and the werewolves were rushing towards them, chasing them down.

What noise would a shark make if a shark could scream? It would be a terrible, mindless sound, unfathomable, like base metal coming alive, like oceans shattering.

The forest shook to the sound as the werewolves tore the creatures apart.

The path came out at the edge of the estuary and we followed the arc of the flaking bank. It ran past the Black Estuary Tavern and I leant into the back of Robin's chair and shoved him up the cobbled slope that led to the door. We had left the sound of battle well behind us, and all along the dark forest path Robin had been laughing and hanging onto the arms of his chair as we juddered over roots and ruts. He was in some kind of epiphany, his voice hiccoughing with each jolt.

"They were never a threat. All – *urk* – along! They were there to protect us. I brought them here to prot-*urk* us and never realized it! We have to get to the Tavern, Adam. The ans-*urk*'s there, I know it!"

He was right. I felt elated, terrified, on the brink of something awesome. Robin had created this place; his power was incredible. But neither of us could figure out much of the symbolism. There was logic, there was continuity, but also a whole stack of anomalous flourishes probably generated by vague shadows from Robin's Unconscious and producing the sensation of being hunted, the creeping threat we both felt oppressed by.

I pushed open the door of the Black Estuary Tavern and wheeled Robin inside.

Up in Quay-Katavothron the great chapel bell began to peal. Slow, foundry beats of hollow entreaty, imprecations from a vacant lot, each backswing of silence filled with the sunless sound of old John Brittle's deadpan raving. Now the rains had come, Quay-Katovothron would be aswill with foaming runoff and white-knuckle prayer. It was no place for us tonight. There would be no faith to activate the quanta, just a recitation of parched equations.

I went over to the snug and slid onto the bench.

Robin smiled. It was enigmatic and introspective. I looked around the room. The walls were dark, elaborately carved wainscot, and seemed to ripple like fluid in the fire-light. The granite above the panelling was thick, with windows set in deep ledges. Rain battered against the glass and made the bulging bullseyes weep flaxen moonlit tears. "Tell me about your theory," I said.

Robin nodded. "Faith is the interaction mediator for miracles. It's inbuilt through all creation. If you consider faith as a force then you can imagine that the dry religion John Brittle preaches with its fear and dogma would bind the townsfolk and prevent them believing miracles are possible. If a miracle is evidence of the eternal being immanent in the present and causing one of any possible outcomes to happen in that instance it explains faith's relation to quantum theory. It provides the basis for an argument that says supernatural outcomes are essentially in line with current thought about the nature of matter."

"Is there an equation for it?"

But before Robin could answer we heard a man laugh and we looked up. He was standing in the entrance to the snug. "Faith is worse than smallpox!" he quoted and slid into the booth next to me. He was short and stocky with a round face and close-cropped gray hair. He was wearing a maroon V-neck pullover. He had a strange smell, a kind of bitter, ferric tang that reminded me of a butcher's block.

Robin looked angry. "You have an equation for *that*?" he said.

The man faced Robin and smiled. It was a vain smile, full of boastful conceit. "I am the mathematics of extinction. I know the mind of God, and I am elegant."

"Who are you?"

"I am Jack Feculent."

"I know you."

"I serve the devil-in-dreams, the ripper of hope. I walked Whitechapel when the bell rang and I walk the Katavothron now. There is no hope here, son."

Robin pushed his chair away from the edge of the bench and out of the snug. He was red-faced with fury. I stood up, but Feculent's bulk prevented me from following. I climbed up onto the table and jumped down to the flagstone floor of the Tavern. Feculent had begun to shake. And as he shook he perspired. Beads formed on his brow, in his hair, above his mouth and ran down his throat to soak into the neck of his sweater. I thought at first that he was laughing but then I saw the flesh beneath his chin begin to ripple and stretch. There was a loud snapping sound, like a bad bone break, and when he turned to look out at us, a brutal downturned mouth full of teeth like shards of flint hung open and appalling on his face. He brought his hands up from his lap and they held cruel blades, serrated and caked with blood. And then I saw the blood that ran down the backs of his hands, coating them, and had a moment to wonder where it was coming from, what injury was he carrying? But there was no injury; it was pouring from his sweater, giving off that cast-iron stench. It was dyed in blood and his profuse sweat was reconstituting it and making it flow, gloving his hands in gore.

Feculent got up and stepped out of the snug.

I took hold of the handles of Robin's chair and began to pull him away from danger. I was jarred as Robin reached down and gripped the wheels, braking himself. I staggered and stepped back, my hands raised. "Robin," I said.

"No, Adam," he said. "I want to know what he wants."

Feculent walked towards us. "I want you to give up, son. Call it a day. Stop embarrassing yourself!" He laughed, a high-quality, cheerful hoot and held up the blades. Blood dripped onto the flagstones between his feet. Suddenly he lifted his arms and brought the blades together above his head. A spark jumped from their clashing edges and every windowpane in the Tavern blew inwards.

We recoiled, covering our heads as the thick panes crashed to the ground around us. I heard Feculent laughing and the sound of the rain as it poured in through the shattered windows. I smelt the saturated forest and the peculiarly isolated scent of the Estuary. I heard howling.

And as I ducked away from the implosion, I remembered.

Howling. Screaming. Nothing.

8.45. Tavistock Square. It is the 7ᵗʰ of July. We are on our way into Town. Robin's got an interview with an engineering firm and I'm going along for the ride. Robin says we'll go to a museum or maybe the Tate Modern after lunch. I remember Robin pushing me onto the platform. It's very busy because it's rush hour. We've bought a couple of ham rolls for breakfast; Robin is trying to take bites out of his while negotiating the crowds. Crumbs land on my head. We feel the rush of air as the train barrels out of the tunnel and glides into the station. I see tiny, sooty mice darting beneath the rails like balls of dirty cotton blown by the pressure of the tube train's arrival. To my amused astonishment, people stand aside for us. The doors breeze open and Robin nods thanks as he tips my chair back and jolts me into the carriage. It's pretty full already and passengers have to arch their backs and press against each other to make enough space for my chair. I grin. I don't come to London very often so everything is pleasing me this morning. We settle into a niche between a tall man in a camelhair coat and a pretty young woman with red hair tied back in a loose ponytail. She is wearing a gray woollen skirt and I sit back, take a bite out of my roll and admire the backs of her legs. Robin reaches down to apply my brakes and I see that he is looking past me, peering along the length of the train. I look up at his expression and frown. He has a flake of crusty roll stuck to the side of his mouth and I am about to point this out, not wanting him to attend an interview looking like a prat with breakfast round his chops, when I hear somebody shout. The train is rocking, pulling into the tunnel. The lights flicker. I turn and look in the direction Robin is facing and see a young man standing in the middle of the aisle. He is sweating and looks both terrified and elated. He is fumbling beneath his jacket.

And then I feel Robin's arms around me and he is saying something and the world tips like I'm falling backwards out of my chair but it's not me, it's everything else going away down some kind of terrible, sudden slope in the world.

Screaming and detonation. Howling. Darkness. Nothing.

I gasped and opened my eyes. I felt like I had been doused in icy water.

Robin was looking up at me. His expression was comically quizzical. I shook my head. He can't remember, I thought. He brought us here, snatched us away at the moment the bomb went off and has kept us safe in this Quay by will and faith and he can't remember. He suddenly looked incredibly tired, worn and vulnerable and my heart clenched for him. It was up to me to save him now. We had to get out of the Tavern.

Feculent was chanting. His voice was low, thick, and the words fell from his revolting mouth like bits of muck. I covered my ears and Robin did the same. They were loathsome words.

As he spoke, the glass began to slide about on the Tavern floor. It gritted against the flags, moving towards a point in front of Feculent where it began to gather. The glass glittered in the firelight, rising up as it accumulated, interlocking in an attempt to find form. The centre of it began to glow like a fog lamp.

Feculent moved his hands amongst the rising column of fragments. The shards tumbled between his blades and continued to rise, organizing themselves into a dense, faceted column. Feculent continued to work, and as he worked the glass softened, began to bud and slowly distended into slender limbs that reached down towards the flagstones.

Robin and I watched mesmerized, horrified. As the glass took shape the light in its middle brightened. It gave off more heat than the Tavern's fire. Feculent was moulding it like lucent clay, now confecting smoky panes from its flanks, wings that lifted its tottering limbs off the floor. Where a head might be forming, it developed a ring of dark, embryonic eyes, like cigarette burns in agar. A mouth was opening.

I glanced down at Robin. It was time to go. His head had dropped and his mouth was open but unmoving. His fingers were trembling, still clamped to the wheels of his chair. His eyes had rolled up beneath their lids. "Robin!" I shouted, and yanked the chair backwards. Robin started, opened his eyes. "Ahh!" he said and lifted his hands. There were friction burns on his palms from the wheelchair tyres.

"Sorry," I said, and pulled him backwards, towards the door.

Feculent shrieked.

The creature was complete. It stood on glass canes, trembling like a foal, wings unfurled above it. It looked at us with those insectile dead-alive eyes, opened its mouth and gave out an awful, ear-splitting, splintering sound.

Feculent made a gesture and the creature rose off the ground. It tipped towards us like some kind of crystalline kite; its forelegs clipped the tavern floor and rang like wine glasses. I backed us away, towards the door. "Do you know what the hell that is?" I said. I had got us as far as the door. The creature was advancing; it seemed to be finding its equilibrium as it drifted about a foot above the flags.

"Yeah," said Robin. His voice was flat, weary. "I know what it is. I've seen them in dreams before. It's a vitreophim."

I threw open the door and dragged Robin outside. The creature uttered that crippling screech again and launched itself towards us. I slammed the door and heard the creature crash against the wood. Something broke off and fell to the floor. It made a sound like a fluorescent light strip shattering. Must have lost a leg, I thought, and shoved Robin down the cobbled path and onto the track that led up into the senlaks at the back of the Old Town of Quay-Katavothron.

I had no idea where we were heading. I thought we might find safety somewhere in town but had no real place of sanctuary in mind as I ran panting up the hill. I could see a yellow oblong of lamplight ahead, identifying the entrance to a narrow senlak, and bent my back into pushing Robin's chair towards it. I heard the vitreophim crashing through the forest somewhere behind us, scything through the undergrowth.

The trees thinned out and we emerged from the forest at the edge of town. I pushed Robin into the senlak. It was barely wide enough to fit his chair but I could see ahead to where the passage opened out into one of the many tiny gaslit squares that colonised the backs of the Old Town. We burst out from the senlak and crossed the square in five strides. Ahead were some steps leading up to another level. The steps curved and at the crest stood a small chapel no bigger than a garden shed. Candlelight ebbed and loomed like a golden cloth being fluttered against the leaded glass. The rain beat down into the square, rattling against the broad leaves of potted plants that stood outside the doors of cottages that walled the square. I skidded to a halt at the foot of the steps.

The vitreophim was at the entrance to the senlak, illuminated by misty yellow lamplight. It screeched and tried to squeeze into the gap but its wings were too wide and it jarred against the brick. It had lost one of its forelegs; nothing remained but a jagged stem about an inch long projecting from its body. If it kept lunging at the walls of the senlak it would damage its wings, an outcome I thought worth encouraging. I left Robin at the foot of the steps and walked back across the square. There were stones in the plant pots and I picked some good-sized ones out, liking the smooth, weighty feel of them in my hands. I went to the senlak and drew back my arm.

The vitreophim saw me and threw itself at the opening, wings glistening in the downpour, beating the rain to a fine spray. I launched a rock down the senlak. It flew past the creature's head. I took better aim and threw another. It sliced through the air and clouted the vitreophim at the base of the neck. I threw another. The vitreophim had pulled back and stood trembling in the mud between the senlak and the forest. I had one more stone left and I let it fly. It soared the length of the senlak and smashed into the vitreophim's chest. The glass beneath its throat starred and fractured. Light from within burst from the cracks in dazzling blades and the creature reared up screeching, those unhallowed beams blazing like smoking searchlights. Then it rocketed skywards, revolving like a lighthouse bulb, and disappeared over the canted and ancient roofs of the Old Town.

I ran back to Robin. He was saturated and shivering but grinning at me in delight. I grabbed the arms of his chair and began bumping him backwards up the steps. The rubber grips were slippery and the chair was heavy but I eventually got him to the top and started down another narrow alley.

"Go to the sinkhole," Robin said.

We shot through another square and came out onto a road I knew led down to the front. We barrelled down the hill towards the vast, tenebrous mouth of the pit. At the bottom of the hill on the corner stood John Brittle's chapel, unlit and dismal, unloading iron chunks of censure from both the bell and the parson's klaxon throat.

We rounded the corner and stopped at the edge of the sinkhole. A row of five-storey buildings rose up just a few meters from the edge, like seafront boardinghouses, with ironwork porticos and balconies and dark cyclopean attic room windows way up amongst the elaborate, cowled chimneystacks.

I looked out across the black rink and almost expected to see our reflection in a surface but there was nothing but depthless air.

Robin took my hand and, startled, I looked down at his upturned face.

"We have to jump," he said. "It's the way home."

I thought for a moment. Something that had been troubling me for some time now was worming its way back into my consciousness.

"The way home?" I said.

Robin nodded. "We have to open it. Somewhere down there is the gateway back."

"Gantry?"

"Gateway. But, yes, Gantry sounds right."

"Leap of faith," I said. Robin squeezed my hand. "Robin, there's something you need to know."

Robin's expression was open and expectant and suddenly my heart was breaking. I knelt down beside him.

"I can't come with you," I said. Robin opened his mouth, frowned. I put a hand on his shoulder. "You know I'm right. Something's been happening since we got here. I go to sleep at night and it's like I don't exist anymore. I don't dream. Nothing. Every day you bring me back. I think I died and you brought me here with you to keep me safe. If I go back with you I'll be gone forever."

Robin shook his head. "No. We can go home, Adam. Have faith."

I lowered my head and closed my eyes. The Katavothron bell, all clang and condemnation, was clouding my thoughts. I could hear the hectoring counterpoint of Brittle's bitter sermon.

"Faith I can find. Faith enough for both of us, Robin. But it can't be reckless. You're needed there. Something's trying to dehumanize our world. It tried to destroy you once and failed. Go back with your theory and challenge it."

Robin was crying. "I'll stay here with you," he said, and suddenly the bell seemed louder. My eardrums felt like they were being hit with hammers. John Brittle racked up his preaching and I fancied I could hear the muttered, bargaining prayers of the townsfolk rising like fog off the estuary around us.

"You want to stay?" I asked "You'd do that?"

Robin was nodding, tears sliding down his cheeks. He looked so cold. I reached out to embrace him and the vitreophim came out of the sky and hit us like a grenade.

I felt something rake down the side of my body as I was thrown across the path. I rolled and tried to sit up. I could see Robin's chair lying on its side, one buckled wheel still spinning. I couldn't see Robin.

The vitreophim was hovering above the lip of the chasm.

I stood up. I felt blood running down my leg. I squeezed my eyes shut to try and clear my vision. The vitreophim hissed and darted its head at something beyond the rim. I heard Robin shout.

I stumbled across the path and looked down. Robin was hanging from an outcrop five or six feet below. He saw me and shouted something. The vitreophim tipped towards me and glared at me with its ring of formless, hateful eyes. I ducked and pulled the chair towards me, thinking I might use it as protection. Robin shouted again and this time I thought he said, "Use the fork."

The vitreophim came at me and I pushed the chair at it, using it to batter the thing away. Use the fork?

I saw it, the slender, long-handled silver fork that Robin had pulled from the lawn to use against the werewolves. It was stuck between the arm of his chair and the seat cushion. I pulled it free and held it up.

The vitreophim reared back and cocked its head.

"Like a tuning fork!" Robin shouted. I could hear exhaustion and desperation in his voice.

The vitreophim lunged at me again and I caught it in the throat with the tubular metal of the armrest. The vitreophim screeched as the metal rang and a chunk of glass broke and fell onto the path. Light pulsed like arterial blood. And I knew what Robin was asking me to do.

I struck the tines of the fork against the handle of the chair. It rang sweetly and I felt the vibrations through my fingers. I held it loosely and as the vitreophim came at me again, I reached out and struck the fork against the side of its head. There was a brief resonation and I was thrown backwards as if electrocuted. The vitreophim spun away and circled out across the sinkhole. It was trembling and I could hear a high-pitched whine, the kind of sound a wine-glass makes when a fingertip is run around its lip.

I crawled to the edge of the sinkhole. Robin was still hanging from the outcrop but I could see that he wouldn't last much longer.

There was a sudden fracturing sound and a scream followed by a blinding flash of light as the vitreophim exploded. It burst like a firework and sent its smoking remains showering down into the depths of the sinkhole.

Robin was calling up to me. I got to my feet and stumbled over to him.

"I'm going to go now, Adam," he said. I didn't reply, but sat down with my feet hanging over the edge. "Believe for me?"

"No problem," I said and smiled. I felt incredibly tired. I became aware that the bell had stopped ringing and that Brittle had ceased his maundering. "How could I not?"

Robin smiled back and his expression was suddenly bright with joy.

Then he let go.

I kept my eyes fixed on a point at the far side of the sink-hole for a long time. Then I stood up and groaned. I'd have to look at that wound in my side when I got back to the cottage. It would do for now. I walked away from the edge of the sinkhole and put my hands in my pockets. I discovered that I had some money. I stood in the silence for a moment. The rain had eased to a fine, blowsy drizzle. I shrugged.

"I believe I'll have a pint of Crusader," I said. If I was going to stay here I might as well search out a new local.

I hunched my shoulders and began to walk back into town.

"I *believe* I've earned it."

ISLINGTON CROCODILES

Ray Cade was enjoying his favourite dream.

He was one of a large crowd of people thronging the wings of a medieval cloister. The clothes of those around him reflected the rustic pageantry of the age; Ray wasn't having any of it. He was in his Burton's whistle. Charcoal grey. Cream shirt, no tie. Good shoes. Ray looked up at the lush tapestries that hung on the walls. Nice touch, he thought.

A red carpet ran the length of the stone floor until it reached the throne at the back of the room. A ginger-haired, rarefied-looking young man sat on the throne. He was going 'mmmm' and 'ahhhh' as he perused a seemingly endless parade of naked young women who were presenting themselves to him. Utterly absorbed by this glossy harem, his eyes bugged out and his lower lip lolled away from his teeth, a damp, fleshy semi-circle revealing gum-recession and a faint, floury mottling of thrush.

Ray frowned. Look at that saucy ponce up there getting all the class bush. That's my taxes paying for all that,
he fumed with resentful proletarian ire (although, fair to
say, Ray and the Inland Revenue hadn't done any official
business in a long while).

Ray stepped out of the shadow of a marble column and
marched up the centre of the carpet. There was a hush; Ray
grinned and pulled his gun. He shot the king in the teeth.

The king's lower jaw atomized. The potted remains of
his head popped up like a butterfly bomb. The crown lifted
and fell. The king's perished head dropped back and sat at
a quizzical angle on the stump of his neck. The big watery
blue eyes regarded Ray with utter disbelief. Ray wondered
whether the king's actual brain was still *going* in there. He
grinned savagely and waggled the muzzle of his gun at it.
He looked around at the adoring faces of the birds. Some
of them were quite famous, he observed. '*I'm* the fucking
King now!' he bellowed. The crowd roared.

Ray loved this dream. When he awoke from it, sweaty
and hard, he couldn't get it out of his head all day. Ray
dwelled on it.

In this dream, Ray Cade had arrived

'Yes, Ma,' said Steve Iden as he listened to his little Dutch
mother niggle him about all the things she felt he ought
to be doing with his life. This did not include, among
other things, working for a gangster and smuggling buk-
kake DVDs into London from a lockup on the outskirts of

Amsterdam. Steve could see where she was coming from, although when you make a point of visiting your mother after a five month hiatus to make sure the old girl's doing all right, intending to catch up on family business and maybe leave her a couple of hundred under your tea cup to help her out until next time, you don't expect her to go through your bag the moment your back's turned; she might have been looking for dirty shirts but Steve thought he would never forget the feeling, on walking out of the bathroom, to find his ma staring at the cover of a DVD depicting a woman getting *that* done to her. Shame, Steve felt. It was, even Steve had to admit, *disgraceful* material.

Steve made sure he was on the three` o'clock ferry early. He went straight to the bar and took a seat at the counter. He ordered a pint of Guinness and three packets of Bovril crisps. He had a good view out across the harbour and spent the next hour watching Holland recede as the ferry chugged into the North Sea. He was aware of an unsettled feeling, a free-floating cloud of anxiety churning in his belly. It was a constant distraction and he knew it would not abate until he had seen Ray and confronted him with his news. He picked at his crisps.

Eight hours later Steve strolled down the canopied walk-way and out onto a dark, wet Harwich jetty. He tossed his bag over his shoulder, having negotiated customs with the insouciant ease of someone who has backpacked through Asia financing the trip by way of prankish near-death drug runs.

Dawlish and Gadd were hovering at the rear of their dark blue transit, sharing a cigarette. Dawlish was about fifty, Gadd younger but enfeebled by drink. They both regarded Steve's approach with suspicion. Dawlish let out a heavy curtain of smoke through his nose so that it drifted up and concealed his coarse, narrow face and tiny, stoat eyes. He was so imbued with practiced malevolence that he seemed to transcend real menace and now merely did a good impersonation of himself twenty years ago. He ground his cigarette out, oblivious to Gadd's outstretched hand and subsequent look of dumb disappointment.

Dawlish brandished a guarded, sideways expression at Steve and held out a hand knuckled like a bag of new potatoes.

Steve shrugged and slouched the bag off his shoulder. He swung it into Dawlish's grabbing fist. Dawlish shoved the bag at Gadd, scowled at Steve and walked off round to the driver side. Gadd stood blinking, clutching the bag against his chest and stared at Steve over the handles.

"No peeking, Brian," Steve said. "You'll go blind."

Gadd snorted, possibly with disdain, although Steve thought probably not; disdain was too sophisticated an emotion for Brian Gadd. His repertoire didn't extend much beyond a species of sly spite; it was probably just a cold.

Steve went to the back of the transit, opened the rear door and climbed in. Gadd got into the passenger seat and buckled up. Dawlish glanced at Steve in the rearview mirror and as he did so the entire cab lit up.

"Arsehole!" Dawlish spat, turning his head away from the glare of the high beams. Steve leant forwards and squinted through the windscreen but could see nothing beyond but bright light. *Customs?* he thought, rather more curious than alarmed. After all, Gadd had the bag. Job done in Steve's opinion.

Steve slid-waddled to the back of the van and opened the doors. He stepped out into the cold and drizzling night.

"Where are you fucking going?" Dawlish said.

Off on my toes, Steve thought. "I'll get a B&B," Steve said. "I'll take a raincheck on the lift. Thanks anyway, boys." And flicked the bill of his baseball cap in a farewell salute.

"Get back in here, you cheeky little cunt," Dawlish hissed.

"Yeah, *you cunt*," Gadd contributed, emboldened with reflected bravery. He was still mindlessly clutching the bag of porn beneath his chins like a nosebag full of ordure.

Steve turned, a big grin on his face, "Give my regards to Ray," he said and made to set off across the car park.

"Now where would you be going in such a hurry, young man?" a deep voice said, and a large and heavy hand came down on his shoulder.

Steve spun around, loosening the grip. He stumbled and slipped on the tarmac, lost his balance, and even as he was falling to his arse on the wet ground, he recognized the voice and was laughing as rainwater soaked into the seat of his pants.

"Who are you?" Ray asked with customary disrespect for formalities. He was addressing a pair of Doctor Marten's sticking out from beneath the sink.

"Plummer," the boots replied in a deep voice with a complete deficiency of irony.

"I asked you your name, not your fucking trade," Ray said in a tone he was developing to address menials with both economy and weight.

The long legs attached to the burgundy boots unhinged and a torso slid from beneath the sink. Muscular arms reached up and huge hands gripped the underside of the sink unit, pulling a pair of shoulders equipped with a close-cropped and unsmiling head out of the recess. The man sat on the lino looking up at Ray.

"My *name's* Plummer," he said. He held a wrench between his fingers like a small steel bone. There was a scar running from the corner of his left eye to the dark comma of his flared left nostril.

To give him his due, Ray stood firm.

"And I'd bet my minimum wage that you're the troublesome little fucker they call Ray Cade," Plummer said.

"Now, you didn't hear that in ward round?" Ray said. He extended his hand.

Plummer spent a moment appraising the young man standing in the kitchen before him. Tall for his age. Far too much time spent on his hair. Imbued with a load of charisma and self-assurance. An untreatable little shit bound for either great things or chaotic self-destruction. He'd seen them come through here before: arrogant, conceited, full of embryonic magnetism but never with anything coming close to this level of poise and authority. Plummer smiled.

Matty bounded into the kitchen. "Come on, Ray! Meeting!" Ray held his tongue. He winked at Plummer. "I could use you," he said.

They shook. And the rest, as they say...

"Plummer, you nearly made me shit myself," Steve said, laughing.

"I'm not responsible for your feelings," Plummer said. He reached down to help Steve up off the wet ground.

"I don't *feel* like shitting," Steve said. "You're responsible for setting off an autonomic reaction. I've *got* a fucking mobile."

"Switch it on, then, Mr. Missed-fucking-messages."

"Ah," Steve said. "Never have it on going through customs."

"Right. Ray's got a job for you."

Steve wiped his hands over the sodden denim covering his backside. He flicked grit and water from his palms. "I've just got back," he said. "Can't someone else go?"

Plummer grinned. "It's a London job. You get the night off. Then it's on."

Steve looked up at Plummer's grinning face and sighed. If Ray had sent Plummer, there was little point in playing the overworked card.

"What's the job?" Steve asked.

Plummer's grin grew wider. "We're going to do the Bank of China," he said.

Steve stood on the kerb outside the Bank of China on Cannon Street. He was cold and tired and was having trouble believing they were actually going to do this.

He watched with something like amazement as a bright yellow digger trundled its way through the morning traffic, orange bubble flashing on the cab roof. Be conspicuous, Ray had said, and no fucker will take any notice of you. Plummer nudged him and handed Steve a yellow hard hat.

"Put this on," he said.

Plummer turned and unfolded a low three-sided metal barrier, which he propped up on the pavement against the wall of the bank. There was a grille set in the wall and behind it a recess containing what looked like a large piece of gray, porous rock. Plummer was setting out a few Men Working triangles and a couple of cones for good measure.

He looked up and saw that the digger had arrived. It sat at the side of the road, chugging idly. Jason Spicer sat in the cab. He lit a cigarette and nodded to Plummer and Steve. He looked pretty wired.

A stream of pedestrians wound around them, intent on other business, heads full of pressures real and imagined, eyes not seeing details, just scanning for proximity, speed, predators, a kind of primitive visual processing that would enable them to reach their destinations without the need to flesh out the world around them; they were passing through a pencil sketch of lines and angles and little else. Steve felt oddly displaced: subjectively more substantial because of his involvement in this brazen operation, yet consequently transparent to the masses because of it. He shook his head. The yellowness of the hard hat felt like a beacon howling for attention. He sank back into a species of watchful self-possession, which he hoped would allow the bald-faced deception to continue without triggering a 'What the fuck are *you* doing?' response from any moderately alert passer-by. It was like he was trying to keep a plane in the air just by thinking hard enough about it. Or perhaps it was more than that; Steve felt he was currently solely responsible for keeping the Earth from breaking orbit and swivelling off into the sun.

Plummer took him by the elbow and led him a few steps away from the barrier.

"Steve," he said. "We're going to do it now, right. Once it's out you and Spicer take it and go. You go to the station and get on the first tube out of here. Two or three stops and then get out onto the street. Get a cab to Ray's and we'll see you there."

Steve nodded. It was a thoughtful nod. "What about the digger?" he asked.

"We leave it," Plummer said. "I'll disappear. See you at Ray's. Like I said."

Steve spent a second scrutinizing Plummer's expression. There was no indication on this configuration of features that what he was asking was as absurd as it sounded. In fact, Steve found himself thinking, with something close to wonder, that the expression on Plummer's face could most closely be defined as serene.

Plummer smiled and the digger started to grumble into action. Steve turned and saw that Jason Spicer was grappling with the levers in an attempt to swing the toothed scoop around so that it could hang over the pavement in preparation to take a crack at the wall of the bank.

"This is never going to work," Steve said mostly to himself. "We'll never get away with it."

Plummer squeezed his arm. "Listen," he said. "Once Ray's got it, it won't matter what we leave behind. We won't have to worry about anything. Nobody's going to be able to touch us."

Steve felt sucked in, stuck trembling against the mouth of something far out of his control. He thought that this might be the most ill-advised thing he had ever agreed to take part in. He tried to focus. Think about it, Steve, he groped. The worst you can get is wanton vandalism on a surreal scale. Two years, with your record? Maybe six months. You can do that again. He squared his shoulders and watched as Spicer threw the levers and the digger butted its jagged head into the side of the bank.

Steve winced. The digger smashed through the grille. Spicer manipulated the levers, an expression of one in the throes of creating high art on his face. The grille screamed and pulled free from the wall in a cloud of concrete. The grille was dragged down against the pavement and sprang free from the digger's teeth. It clattered to the ground. A group of pedestrians had stopped to watch, Steve noticed, snapped out of their blind passage.

The digger reared back and thrust forward into the recess. It came away in a cloud of rock dust. It shot forward again and this time the stone came out with it.

"Go!" said Plummer. Steve felt himself propelled towards the digger's scoop. He stumbled across the pavement, dimly aware that the cab door was open and Spicer was climbing out, carrying a large Hessian sack.

"Shut up, or the next voice you hear is gonna be your physiotherapist's."

A pause.

"Shut up, or the next voice you hear is gonna be your *speech* therapist's."

Ray Cade was practising his menaces. They were out in the smoking area. Ray was pacing about with his fists clenched. Steve was rolling a cigarette.

"What do you think?" Ray asked. "Which one?"

Steve lit his roll-up. "You could vary them," he suggested.

Ray considered this.

"You don't want to sound like a cunt," Ray said. "You've got to get this stuff right or they'll just laugh at you. Then you're finished."

Ray was getting pumped up. His face was as tight and pink as a phimosis.

Steve found himself wondering why Ray was so bothered by etymology; his expression alone was sufficient to induce panic.

Matty sprang genially onto the patio. "Meeting!" he said.

Ray rounded on him. He smiled. "Shut up," he said, "or…"

They sat in a circle in the Meeting Room. Thirteen chairs supported twelve Adolescent Unit inpatients and a staff nurse. Ten of the allocated thirty minutes had elapsed in silence. Ray sighed and looked around at his fellow patients. Opposite sat a couple of girls with their knees up and their faces hidden behind lank curtains of hair. Next to them a fifteen-year-old boy with white face make-up and rings of black eyeliner sat staring at his boots.

"Look at that poor cunt," Ray contributed to the group. "If you could sell shit, he wouldn't have an arsehole!" He brayed a coarse bout of laughter, sat back and stared at the ceiling. "Dear oh fucking dear."

"It sounds like you're quite angry, Ray," Matty facilitated, ashen-faced.

Ray blinked. He turned his head minimally in Matty's direction. "Angry?" he said, "I fear you may be projecting. I've never been happier in my fucking life!"

Steve helped Spicer lift the chunk of stone out of the scoop. Spicer had put the sack on the ground with the neck wide open. They placed the stone into the sack and pulled the material up and over it.

"Can you manage?" Spicer asked.

Steve shrugged. He felt lightheaded. He looked around for Plummer, but he had disappeared. It was just the two of them, standing outside the Bank of China and by now people were starting to emerge from the bank with questioning expressions on their faces.

Steve took the neck of the sack and twisted it into his fists. He straightened and lifted the sack. It was heavy but he reckoned he could make it down the road to the tube station as long as he wasn't in a chase. He turned, flipped the hard hat off his head and began staggering down Cannon Street.

Spicer kept alongside him, throwing glances back towards the gathering crowd outside the bank. People were pointing at them.

"Fuckin' hell, Steve," Spicer moaned. "We're going to get stitched."

Steve grimaced, "Get hold of this sack and help me."

They had reached the entrance to the underground. Ahead were a short concourse and a set of stairs. The sound of an inexpertly handled penny whistle piped up from the stairwell, emanating from the pitch of a busker presumptuously assuming that a few tootled notes connoted sought after and rewardable street entertainment.

Steve and Spicer staggered to the top of the steps. Behind them came the sudden and diuretic whoop of a police siren. Steve swung round just as Spicer ran into him.

"Shit!" said Steve, and lost his balance. He felt the momentum of the stone swing out into the stairwell and pull him helplessly towards the drop. The sirens were multiplying. Steve's knees buckled. Spicer clutched at him but succeeded only in swiping him round the back of the neck. Steve grunted and let go of the sack.

Tostig Kemp heard the sirens and paused with the tin whistle to his lips. He looked up and saw two men arseing about at the top of the steps. He was sitting cross-legged on a woollen blanket with a small cardboard box in front of him. A sign was propped up against his knees: *Homeless and hungary*. There was the grand total of eight pence and a piece of chewing gum in the box. He was wearing a little red hat with a bell on it and had a threadbare shawl around his shoulders.

"Damn filth," he thought, which just about amounted to his last experience of conscious neuronal activity because a second later a large Hessian sack containing a lethal amount of mass flew from the hands of one of the men, hit the bottom step and bounded up into his face.

Tostig Kemp's final musical output consisted of a harsh and bubbling *poot!* as the whistle was rammed between his teeth and out of the back of his head. The stone dropped into his lap, fractured his pelvis and ruptured his testicles. Had he been alive, the pain would probably have been sufficient enough to kill him.

Tostig's head lolled forward and a glut of dark blood slid from the end of the pipe like oil from the nozzle of a can. It splashed onto the exposed and channelled chunk of stone lodged between his knees.

Steve stood over the slumped body. Around him commuters were milling. Someone had screamed, which was a bit of a pisser. It drew attention.

Steve reached down and pulled the sack off the busker's dislocated lap. He looked around and appraised the gathering crowd.

"Has anyone phoned an ambulance?" he asked the group of white and uncertain faces gathered around the body. Galvanized by Steve's trick authority, mobile phones were fumbled into activity.

Steve looked down at the corpse. The weight of the stone was becoming unsupportable. The muscles in his shoulders were burning. He hoisted it into a clumsy hug and began to back away from the crowd. Jason Spicer appeared at Steve's side.

"Is he…?"

"He most certainly is," Steve said. He felt sick. He could see the mouthpiece of the tin whistle projecting from the base of the busker's skull.

"It was an accident, wasn't it?" Jason said.

"Yeah. An accident," Steve said. His mouth was filling with saliva. "Let's get out of here."

They stumbled away from the crowd and headed down the green-tiled corridor. Steve could hear the hiss and vibration of a train arriving at the platform ahead and tried to double their speed. They had to make this train.

They lurched onto the platform. Steve heard the warning beep as the doors prepared to close and threw himself at the carriage. They piled in just as the doors slid together. The train shuddered and pulled away.

Steve hated tubes. He hated the cold fireplace smell of the platforms and the thundering insanity of the train's mindless, rocking pelt through the decaying London substructure. It was a sensation more akin to dropping down a shaft than travelling horizontally; he felt hemmed and jolted, a cheek bite away from panic.

He dumped the sack between his feet and leaned back against a partition, breathing hard. Spicer was staring down at the stone.

"What is it, Steve?" he asked, his expression quaintly fearful. "What's Ray want with a piece of old rock?"

Steve shook his head. The neck of the bag had collapsed around the stone and Steve could see the dark bloodstain soaked into the top of the porous rock. He bent and tugged the Hessian back over it, grimacing. "I don't know," he said, "perhaps he's finally gone insane."

"What you want to avoid is a forensic history. At our age. You got any forensic and people get twitchy. You need to go down the Mental Health route. Get a trick cyclist involved;

get a Social Worker, lovely! Blame your inclinations on trau-
matic past experiences. Learn the language; my behaviour
is a maladaptive coping mechanism perpetuated and maintained by my inability to regulate my emotional responses
to fuckin' *blah blah blah*. You should hear the pony that little wanker trots out during our *individual time."* Ray made
a rapid onanist gesture with a loosely clenched fist. "Total
bollocks."

They were in Ray's room, the biggest of the twelve
inpatient rooms along the main corridor of the Adolescent
Unit. Plummer was leaning against the sink, ostensibly there
to empty the bin should a member of staff put their head
in, but actually attending Ray's every utterance with the joy
of the newly enfolded acolyte. He was spending more and
more time with Ray, sharing a fag outside now and then,
whispered conversations in the kitchen; Ray was grooming
him. Steve sat in a chair beneath a large black-and-white
poster of the Kray twins. He was far less credulous, having
recovered well from a nasty little drug induced psychosis
that had necessitated this particular three-month admission.
No Section, fortunately. He'd been only too glad to get away
from the mealworms and all the little black bubbles, thanks
very much.

He did find Ray's antics entertaining, though, and had
struck up a kind of sidekick relationship with him over the
last month since Ray had arrived on the unit. It was more
a tribute to Steve's easygoing and personable charm that he
had attained some sort of unobtrusive equality with Ray,

which suited him just fine, and which he had no intention of pushing too hard. Steve knew he was smarter than Ray, knew it pretty soon into the relationship, but was also canny enough to recognize someone with enough power to create a dark and intriguing wake in which to follow and observe.

And then there was Claire, Ray's sister.

They could endure no more than two stops along the line, both expecting hordes of police to come pouring onto the train and arrest them at each station, or for the train to stop at the platform with the doors mechanically secured until reinforcements arrived, the driver having been informed over the radio that there were inept felons aboard his train. But nothing happened, and they both alighted at Blackfriars without being apprehended and made it out of the station and into an overcast London street that was not teeming with police cars, coppers with guns and megaphones and cordoned off television crews.

Steve heard Jason mutter, "Fucking Radio *Rental*!" and then he saw a taxi idling in a rank and they made their way over to it.

"Islington Green, mate," Steve said as they slid into the back. The stone sat between them, wrapped in its sack.

"What you got, there, mate?" the driver asked, eyeing the bundle. He looked Greek, or Turkish, and smelled of something congruently ethnic.

"A dead horse with a hat on," Steve said through clenched teeth. "Can we go? *Please*?"

And thought, as the driver pulled out into heavy rush hour traffic, *Why the fuck have we just nicked the Stone of London?*

Ray's flat was a large two-bed apartment above an antiques and bric-a-brac shop called Buy Curios on the Islington Green high street owned by a couple of *Tchaikovskys* in matching purple pullovers named Trev and Vince. The theme of the flat was minimalist; a low table, two auburn leather sofas and a Bang & Olafson stereo were the only objects in the room. Ray was standing with his back to the window. Steve, Spicer, Dawlish and Gadd were sitting on the sofas while Plummer made tea in the kitchen off the hall. Steve could hear him whistling.

Ray walked across to the table. The stone sat in its centre. Ray regarded it with an expression that Steve thought was possibly one of the most disturbing he had ever seen on Ray's face; it was a base combination of greed and desire, hinting at a kind of possessiveness which might cause him to lash out and kill anyone mad enough to try and take the Stone from him.

"'Scuse me," Steve said and got up. He went into the kitchen and leaned against the worktop. Plummer lifted a couple of tea bags out of the pot with a spoon and lobbed them into a bin beneath the sink. He was still whistling.

"We'll be on the news by now," Steve said. Plummer grinned.

"No matter," he said. He went to the fridge to fetch milk.

Steve was beginning to feel a little downcast. The adrenaline rush was long gone and he was finding this whole scenario mildly upsetting. "Do you actually know what's going on?"

Plummer splashed milk into an assortment of mugs. "Yes, I do," he said.

"Plummer," Steve said, "we've known each other for a long time. Will you stop being so enigmatic and tell me why Ray got us to steal an artefact of historical interest and why he's so fucking entranced by it?"

Plummer said, "Ray's been doing a bit of research. He's discovered an interest in his family tree. It's enlightened him somewhat. Given him big ideas."

"Ray doesn't read," Steve said. "Do you see anything other than DVDs on his bookcase? He's interested in petty crime and coercion. Not particularly improving pastimes."

"Not reading, Steve. *Research*. Talking to people, listening. Gathering information."

Steve frowned. Ever since he had met him at the Adolescent unit, he had known that Ray harboured dreams of criminal magnitude. Unfortunately, perhaps his lack of genuine imagination or his poor choice in cronies, sidekicks, gofers and allies—or a combination of both—had perpetuated a career of relatively small time operations. Enough to get by on, but not enough to make much of a ripple in the underworld and assure him his place in the pantheon of gangland giants. At this rate there would be no garish paperback biography of Ray's life for sale in the supermarkets, full of tabloid literacy and exclamation marks, and illustrated with black-and-white photos of Ray giving it large in a diversity of resorts and bars, arms around darts players and waning comedians and enjoying a glass of wine with the lovely wife. No, Ray needed to get cracking if he was going to start enjoying the big time.

"That stone is the London Stone. It contains the life force of the City itself. It's said that whoever owns it has the power of the entire City at their disposal. It has not escaped me that it found its way into the wall of a bank, finance being at the heart of London's strength."

"What's this got to do with Ray?" Steve lowered his voice. He could hear Ray talking in the lounge, his voice urgent and excited. He was asking Gadd to fetch something.

"It's his name and his destiny," Plummer said, "I've always been intrigued by it. Cade and the Stone are connected. Do you know your history, Steve?"

Steve shrugged. "I never applied myself," he said.

"Have you heard of Jack Cade and his rebellion in 1450?" Plummer asked. Steve shook his head.

"Well, you should look it up," Plummer said. "*So long as the stone of Brutus is safe, so long shall London flourish.*"

"Where'd you get this sword from, Ray?" Gadd asked.

Steve started. "What the fuck?" he said, and leaned his head out of the kitchen.

Steve could see Ray standing by the table. He was holding what looked like a broadsword in both hands. Steve walked down the hall and went into the lounge.

He was dimly aware that Plummer had followed him up the hall and was standing just behind him, sipping his cup of tea, and then Ray lifted the sword – an ancient looking, pitted and rusty weapon – over his head and brought it down onto the stone like an executioner practising a beheading.

"I'm the Lord of London!" Ray shouted.

Jason Spicer let out a jumpy giggle. Dawlish and Gadd sat next to each other on the sofa. Gadd looked like he wanted to hold someone's hand.

"Ray?" Steve said, but felt Plummer lay a hand on his shoulder. He half turned. Plummer put a finger to his lips, and then pointed at Ray.

Steve looked.

"*I'm* the fucking King now!" Ray roared.

2

Claire visited every Saturday although it was clear that Ray despised her.

Ray's father would drop her off outside the unit and then drive off down the pub for an hour while Claire went in, announced herself to the nurse in charge and then went to spend some time with her brother. She brought cigarettes, magazines, drinks, posters, CDs, sweets. Ray took it all, and then blanked her for the duration of her stay. She'd follow him around, chatting, encouraging, trying to touch him, but Ray just stalked off and sat in the smoking area until she left. She only brought him a book once, Steve recalled, and this had induced a dreadful rage, giving Claire grounds to run for cover as he ripped it up and threw it at her: "*How to Kill a Mocking Bird?* What do I want a fucking book for, you stupid little cow? Fuck off. Don't bring me fucking books again or I'll pull your tiny *tits* off!"

Even Steve was mortified by Ray's reaction and followed Claire to the door as she left. She was crying again.

Steve looked at her as she fumbled with the door handle. She was tall and slender, with long, slim legs which seemed to pole forever from beneath a short denim skirt. She had a shoulder-length bob that framed her pretty, gentle face. Her hair was thick and glossy and Steve found himself wondering what it would feel like to run his fingers through it.

"Are you OK?" Steve asked, knowing immediately that many other, less cuntish, openers might have been employed. He offered her a slack grin by way of apology.

Claire looked up and nodded. She had large gray-blue eyes. "I'm OK," she said, sounding extremely resigned, and sighed.

"Do you want a Coke?" Steve offered, growing in sophistication. "Or a biscuit?" *Oh you cock!*

Claire smiled and her eyes shone with sudden good humour. "No thanks, Steve. I gotta go. See you next week." She pushed open the door and left Steve thinking two things: Steve. She called me Steve. She knows who I am. And: Next week? How am I going to wait that long?

The week dragged. Steve tried every trick he knew to get Ray to tell him about Claire but Ray would only become morose or abusive. Steve didn't want to raise his suspicions, so eventually he dropped the subject. By the end of the week he knew three things about Claire: She was nearly fifteen, three years younger than Ray, she had killed their mother, and Steve was crazy about her.

That was also the week Ray twatted Matty.

Matty had challenged Ray about his relationships during their weekly individual time. Something innocuous, like *how do you feel about losing your mother?* and Ray had gone over the desk at him. It was decided in ward round that Ray wasn't really addressing his issues and was becoming a toxic influence on the Unit. His behaviour was becoming problematic; he was disrespectful, arrogant and was swanning around like he ran the place. Matty was still off sick and considering pressing charges for assault. Ray's Consultant vacillated; Ray was still talking about vague suicidal ideation during their meetings and she felt he continued to pose a significant risk. His depressive symptoms seemed to have cleared up quite quickly but there was still this nagging self-harm. She decided it would be best to review it next week and in the meantime chase up the referral to the Therapeutic Community in Brighton and allocate him a Social Worker.

Ray was laughing. This was one system he knew how to play.

"Why does he hate you?" Steve asked. Ray had snatched the *Viz, GQ* and Marlboro lights from his sister and had gone off to the coffee shop in town where he would meet up with an off-duty Plummer and get his weekly cannabis supply. Claire was sitting in the lounge with Steve. She was wearing a pink, strappy T-shirt which showed off her pale shoulders and the intriguing indentations above her collar-bones, blue jeans and a pair of sandals with large, black, sharp-looking plastic daisies on the insteps.

Claire shrugged. She looked pale and tired today. "He hates me because Mum died giving birth and he hates Dad because he told the surgeons to prioritise my survival over hers. Simple really. Don't blame him, he was only little and he lost his Mum. 'I needed Mum, not a sister!' he'd say. He still says it. It's fucked him up royally."

Steve stared at her. "It wasn't your fault," he said. *Biscuit?* he thought, feeling lame.

"Yeah, it was," Claire said. "It was absolutely my fault. You can say I didn't mean to do it, but it *was* my fault. Ray's always blamed me and probably always will, but he's my brother and I love him."

"He's been here a while," Steve said, "Maybe he'll come to terms with it."

Claire shook her head. Her hair rocked softly against her shoulders. Steve squinted. "He's a psychopath," she said.

Steve sat back, moderately aghast. "That's a bit harsh," he said.

"Not really," Claire said. "He's got a personality disorder connected to a developmental trauma following the
death of his mother. Classic. I've done a bit of reading. You
don't think I'd put up with his shit without understanding
him, do you?"

"No," Steve said, "I guess not." Claire was smiling.

A car honked its horn in the car park.

"There's Dad," Claire said and stood up.

"Er," said Steve.

"Er what?" asked Claire. She slung her pink handbag
over her shoulder. She smiled at him. Steve was convinced
he was cherry red; he felt hot and congested.

"Next week, if Ray doesn't want to see you, perhaps
you and I could go into town for a Coke and a bite to eat,"
Steve didn't actually say. He said instead, "Next week. See
you next week, then. Claire."

"Sure," she said, and stepped past him. The soft skin
of her forearm brushed against Steve's bicep. Steve felt
his pupils dilate. "You can take me out for a cup of tea
or something, if you like," She added as she opened the
door.

"Give me your mobile number!" Steve blurted.

"No way!" Claire said, laughing, and left the building.

"Don't talk to my fucking sister!" Ray said.

This caught Steve off balance. "What?"

"You heard me, I don't want you talking to that little
bitch, all right? Leave her alone."

Steve decided to play it cautious. This was the first time Ray had turned on him; up until now he had enjoyed a favourable measure of immunity from Ray's capricious wrath. He didn't want that to change.

"OK," he said, and felt like a dismal coward. "Only trying to be friendly."

Ray glared at him across the pool table. He stroked in an easy red. "Well, don't be fucking friendly, OK?"

Steve saluted him with his cue. "Consider it done," he said. "I won't talk to her on the ward again." Which was easy to say, now that he had Claire's mobile number.

A fortnight later, Ray went down to Brighton to be assessed for admission to a Therapeutic Community. To the relief of the Adolescent Unit staff, Ray was accepted and swift transfer of care was arranged.

On the morning of Ray's departure, he and Steve were sharing a last cigarette out in the smoking area.

"This is going to be a fucking holiday," Ray said.

Steve blew a couple of smoke rings. "Hope you're right," he said. Ray had come back from the assessment full of ideas. He was going to lie low, play the game and start building his empire. "You'll be out of here in a few weeks yourself," Ray said. "I'll keep in touch and give you the nod when I've got something for you. Come down to the coast for a while and we'll see what happens."

Steve, seventeen years old and not much looking forward to the prospect of gainful employment, said, "Like a shot, Ray."

Ray flicked his cigarette across the lawn. "Right," he said and went inside to fetch his bags. Steve followed him down the corridor. The walls were decorated with posters of Kurt Cobain, Teletubbies and a selection of pitiful collages. Steve shook his head; this was one weird place to be perfectly honest.

Ray's walls were stripped of posters and his stereo was packed up in boxes. He picked up his bag and looked around. Steve leaned against the sink.

"Going to be quiet without you, Ray." Steve said. *And mildly less menacing,* he thought.

Ray pursed his lips. He seemed distracted, perhaps merely by the prospect of moving on, but Steve thought it was probably nothing to do with anything sentimental, more likely a brief and almost unconscious evaluation of the progress of his plans to date.

They went out into the car park at the front of the building and Steve helped load Ray's gear into the back of a taxi. A nurse escort was already sitting in the front seat with a thick folder full of Ray's notes on his lap. Ray stuck out a hand.

"I'll be in touch," he said.

Steve shook Ray's hand. "Great. Good luck."

Ray climbed into the back of the taxi. Before he closed the door, he said, "And keep away from my fucking sister." He grinned and slammed the door.

Steve swallowed and made his features grin back.

Steve watched the car pull away, then turned and began to walk back around the side of the building into the garden.

He got out his mobile and called Claire.

"Hi, baby. Yeah, just now. Where do you want to meet?"

Steve stopped and looked around. He had the distinct feeling that he was being spied on. "Hang on," he said and walked back towards the smoking area. There was a small window giving into the old sluice room, where Plummer kept his buckets and tools. Steve stood on tip-toes and peered in.

"Shit!" he said, and stumbled backwards as Plummer's long, pale face loomed up before him. Grinning, Plummer pressed his nose against the window, his breath fogging the glass. Steve stood panting on the lawn. His heart was racing. He could hear Claire's voice saying, "Steve? Are you all right?"

Steve looked up at the sluice room window. Plummer was gone. A faint nebula of condensation was drawing in on itself as it evaporated from the glass.

Steve lifted the mobile back to his ear. "I'm OK," he said. "Just Plummer fucking about. Let's meet up."

The next day, Steve was only mildly curious to find out that Plummer hadn't turned up for work. By the end of the week he was baffled by his continued absence. The following Monday a small man with alopecia and waxy ears called Lawrence was pushing a mop up the corridor and Steve asked a nurse where Plummer was.

"The agency haven't heard from him for over a week," she said. "They've sent us a new chap. People don't stay in this job very long, Steve."

Steve pondered the small domestic as he walked back down the corridor to his room. Lawrence grinned. "All right?" he said.

"Yeah, I'm all right," Steve replied and went into his room. He shut the door and sat on his bed. Time to go, he thought. He could hear the mop slapping about outside his door accompanied by the sound of Lawrence's whistling. He felt restless. He got up and put his coat on, checked for cigarettes, then went back out into the corridor.

"Off out?" asked Lawrence, from behind Steve. Steve jumped.

He frowned. *Definitely* time to go.

Steve was discharged a fortnight later and got straight on a train to Sussex. His parents were divorced and his mum had moved back to Holland. His father was living in a Housing Association flat on an estate in Kent, subsisting on sausage and chips and chemical cider. Steve was supposed to be staying with his dad but reneged on that part of the discharge plan because the thought of sitting in a roomful of busted furniture with walls and ceiling the same colour as his father's fingers and nicotine-rinsed quiff for any length of time filled him with a horror verging on the atavistic.

Ray had called earlier the previous week to fill Steve in. He was having the time of his life. Three meals a day, gentle therapy, trips to the pub in the evenings and a Sunday carvery, vulnerable birds and a few *tender* blokes to lean on. Ray was playing the game.

Steve's mother had put some money in a Building Society for him. It wasn't much, but enough to keep him going for a while if he was economical. Steve knew his mum wanted him to join her in Holland eventually, but he doubted that would figure in his plans. He needed to move around.

As the train approached Brighton, Steve looked out of the window. He was sitting next to a young woman in a business suit. She was pretty and smelt of expensive perfume. Perhaps it was just the motion of the train, but Steve had spent a large part of the journey with his sports bag on his lap to conceal a wearisome and resolute boner.

He was about to have a rummage for some chocolate when his attention was drawn to something carved into the steep slope of a chalk hill beyond the passing fields. It was four o'clock in the afternoon and the carving shone as though illuminated in the low autumn sun. Even from a distance, Steve could see how tall the figure was. It was a faceless outline of a towering man holding two staves, one either side of his body.

"I go past him nearly every day and I never fail to get a little shiver."

"What?" said Steve.

The young woman pointed at the chalk figure. "The Long Man," she said. "There's something benign about him, isn't there? Something *protective*."Steve looked back at the figure. The train had passed it and the angle of the hillside was turning the Long Man away, seeming to make the staves draw together like a curtain.

"I guess," Steve said. "Kind of imposing, isn't he?"

The woman smiled and went back to her book.

Five minutes later the train drew into Lewes and the woman stood to get a bag down from the overhead rack. The sun was very low now, about to fall behind the surrounding hills, and the carriage was filled with a sudden soft luminescence. Steve squinted up at the silhouette of the woman standing in the aisle. She appeared to be surrounded by a penumbra; her teardrop earrings gleamed like molten metal. Steve blinked and suddenly felt as though the rest of the world had been dashed from him in a bright and eerie faint. He felt weak and inexplicably fragile. *Flashback*, he thought, and felt panic rise in his chest. He looked down at his hands, expecting them to be gloved in black foam, *the* black foam, but they were unblemished.

Frightened now, Steve peered back up at the woman.

He saw her raise her arms and hold them out at her sides. She spoke, and her voice rang like a cluster of tiny bells.

"When the Great Instrument is found, the Long Man will come down from the hills."

There was a sharp squealing sound and Steve thought the woman was shrieking, but then the train jolted and he realised it was the brakes halting the train at the platform's edge. The sun disappeared behind the station building and the carriage abruptly lost its uncanny, suspended radiance. Steve moaned.

"Are you okay?"

"Huh?" Steve said. His ears were ringing.

The woman bent down and looked at Steve with an expression of concern. She held her leather briefcase in one hand and a hefty looking holdall in the other. "You looked like you were about to pass out," she said.

Steve stared at her as other passengers began to press past. She grunted as a man in a bright red puffer jacket elbowed her into the gap between the seats. He was jabbering into a mobile phone.

"Yeah, I'm okay," Steve said and gave her a patented mild grin to reassure her. His heart was pounding in his chest and his throat felt constricted.

"Cool," she said and stepped out into the flow of disembarking commuters. She looked back, though, once, as she reached the doors and smiled. She moved her lips and was gone.

Steve slumped back into his seat, frowning.

It had looked like she had mouthed, "So long, man." And at the time that's what he chose to believe.

Twenty minutes later the train rumbled over a viaduct and Steve got his first view of Brighton. He could see rows of narrow terraces and corner pubs, churches and winding lanes. It was choked with traffic. Everything was funnelling through the back roads towards the main drag on the front. There was a long promenade populated by huts and strings of lights; there were two piers, one dilapidated and neglected, the other vibrant as a fruit machine. Everything looked shabby and rakish.

Steve smiled. He could see the sea.

Ray met Steve at the station. A jumpy-looking little wretch whom Ray introduced as Jason Spicer accompanied him. Steve shook hands; Ray's grip was firm, but when Spicer put his hand in Steve's it felt like grabbing a handful of cigar butts out of an ashtray. Dry, brittle and unclean.

Ray had finished with therapy against professional advice and had set himself up in a bedsit at the back of the North Lanes. It had never been about recovery for Ray.

"I've discharged myself," Ray said. "We're staying with Jason's brother."

Jason's brother was a stallholder in the Lanes. They strolled through the Lanes as everyone was packing up for the day. Steve crunched through market-stall debris and litter. People were loading trucks with wardrobes, Africana, ceramic tiles, memorabilia, Art Deco. They reached an arcade filled with books, records. Spicer twitched, "I'll get the keys, Ray." He disappeared into the arcade, leaving Steve and Ray standing in the middle of the road.

"Where'd you find that?" asked Steve.

"He's a contact," said Ray. "He's useful."

"As a draught excluder?"

Ray grunted. "While you've been on your back with your hands in your boxers I've been circulating. Hasn't taken me long to meet a few people. We're having a get-together tonight. You're going to be interested, Steve. Very fucking interested."

"No doubt about that," said Steve.

Spicer reappeared carrying a bunch of keys on a grimy yellow smile-face fob. He rattled them under Ray's nose. "We're in!" he said.

Steve followed Ray and Jason through the Lanes until they reached a door at the side of a clothes shop. Spicer fumbled a Yale key from the bunch and slid it into the lock.

"Up we go," he said and pushed open the door.

They climbed a staircase that led to an unlit landing. Spicer performed the palsied, metallic shuffle again, cupping the bunch in his fragile fists and rattling them like dice, until he brought forth another key.

They went into the flat.

"It's a shithole, babe," Steve laughed. "There's damp like armpits in all the corners and it smells like a hamster's crotch. You know, I found a cockroach rattling around in the bath the size of an *otter!*"

"An otter?" Claire said. She was creasing up.

"It was so fucking *big,* Claire. I had to wrap it up in bog roll. Two hands full. It struggled. As I chucked it out of the window it hissed, 'I know people!'"

"God, it sounds like Ray."

"Aw fuck! Do you think I just caught Ray having a bath in his natural state and dumped him in an alley?"

"How embarrassing!"

"Yeah, what a *faux pas*. What a way to thank his hospitality!"

Steve was standing at the end of the pier. He'd excused himself on the pretext of getting a packet of cigarettes and had found himself walking towards the front. It was almost dark and the lights were enticing. He wandered through the Lanes and came out by the Pavilion. He walked up to the entrance to the Palace Pier. It was chilly and the sea roared and crashed against the beach. There were still a lot of people about and the bars and restaurants were getting full. Steve went onto the pier, looking down through the gappy planks at the foaming water. He could smell doughnuts and spicy food and the all-pervading bitterness of the sea. Gulls floated like smuts. Above the faded and speckled blue roofs of the amusement arcades starlings shoaled and folded like a dark rendering of coordinated longing.

He walked past the arcades and booths until he reached the end of the pier. He leaned against the flaking railings. There was a small jetty below and a stack of eroded machinery. A worn sign advertised seasonal fishing trips. Steve looked out across the bay. The lights of the hotels and boarding houses glimmered like garlands all along the front.

Steve felt good. This was the new start he needed. Wherever things led from now on, he was in control. He took out his mobile and phoned Claire.

Steve walked back to the flat in a first-rate mood. He'd arranged to see Claire at the weekend and the plan was to try and get up to London at least once a week to spend an evening with her. He was desperate to see more of her but he also needed to keep Ray sweet and take on a few jobs, so he knew that, at least in the short term, they would be apart for much of the time.

He let himself in through the street door and climbed the stairs. Ray had promised a get-together of sorts, just an initial meeting of the gang over a few drinks and some smokes, but, judging by first impressions, there didn't appear to be a whole lot to get excited about. The idea of Jason Spicer holding his bladder over anything bigger than selling weed to a school boy made Steve chuckle to himself in a most hearty way. He knocked on the landing door.

Spicer answered. "Where have you been?" he asked. "Ray's waiting."

Steve frowned and stepped into the flat. He followed Spicer down a narrow hallway. He could hear Ray's voice coming from the living room at the front of the flat, then a low, sardonic laugh that made the hairs on the back of his neck prickle.

"Well, stone me," Steve said as he entered the room.

Ray was standing smoking a joint by the door to the kitchen. He blew out a dense sinusful of smoke and handed the joint to the man sitting in an armchair to his left.

"Hello, Steve," said Plummer. "Nice of you to join us."

Jason's brother, Ginger Lee, turned up an hour later with a paunchy Goth called Bambi – which was about the least

Transylvanian moniker Steve had ever heard – and a greasy brown paper bag full of Chinese food. Bambi deflated into a tatty recliner and sat with her solid thighs apart revealing a taut, black Lycra gusset beneath the crumpled hem of her mini skirt. She sported a pale sebaceous node in the corner of her left eye about the size of a butterbean.

"Come on, lover, let's get out of the way," Lee said from the bedroom door. "I'm knackered. These boys want to get to know each other."

"Aw, I wanted some chinky," Bambi said, eyeing the brown paper bag. It was semi-translucent from the grease. She ran a fat tongue across her black lip-sticked chops.

"Save her some," Lee said to the rest of the room. "You can have it tomorrow, babe. I'll heat it up for breakfast. Come and have a nosh on my pork pagoda."

"OK," Bambi mumbled, an acquiescence that was virtually lost in the immense, effortful expulsion of air she emitted as she heaved herself out of the recliner.

She must have a diaphragm like a fucking *dinghy*, Steve thought as he watched her sway across the sitting room and disappear into Lee's bedroom.

He returned his attention to the others. The room was full of smoke; it hung like a ghostly hammock halfway between floor and ceiling. Steve had refused to partake so soon after his admission, and the others were cordial enough to respect this.

Ray was talking.

"So Plummer goes up to London and gets us digs on his old manor. Puts us in touch with a few people with a little bit more on their plates than they can handle and we take over a small operation. Nothing too flash to start off, just some easy money."

"When can we start, Ray?" Spicer asked. He was engulfed in a lumpy coffee-coloured beanbag. He looked like someone had stubbed him out in a rotten tangerine.

"Give me two weeks," Plummer answered.

Two weeks, thought Steve. That's pretty quick work. He thought about Claire. Both of them in London would be great. Things were progressing well.

"Two weeks," said Ray.

Six years later, Claire said, "Steve, if you tell him, he'll kill you."

"He's going to find out," Steve said. "It's better if it comes from me."

Claire shook her head. Her eyes blazed. "He hasn't seen me since he came back from Brighton. I don't want that to change."

Steve paced back and forth across the dining room of his flat. "I should stop working for him," he said. "I should get a proper job."

"That's something we both agree on," Claire said. "What this hold is he has on people, I'll never know."

"It's just easy," Steve said, "he makes it *easy* to stay on board. There's always a job to do. Trips abroad."

"It's exciting?"

"Yeah. It's exciting. And easy. God, I sound like a moron. I'll get a job."

Claire sat back and laced her fingers over her belly. "My man," she said. "In a suit."

Steve raised his eyebrows. "Fuck that, I was thinking more along the lines of lorry driving."

"Really?" said Claire. "You can't drive."

"I'll think of something. Lighthouse keeper, ambassador, weapons inspector."

Clair stood up and went over to him. She put her arms round his waist and kissed him.

"You do whatever you like," she said, smiling. "Just be a great dad, OK!"

3

Ray stood looking down at the stone. He was breathing heavily and had a sheen of perspiration on his brow. He held the handle of the sword in his right hand, the tip of the long blade resting on the carpet between Gadd's feet. A lock of hair had fallen into his right eye. Spicer coughed, sat forward and peered at the stone. The sword had virtually split it in half; there was a large chunk out of it and a crack that jagged down to its base.

Steve looked around the room and tried to gauge the feelings betrayed on the faces of the men. Dawlish was sitting back on the sofa in the way someone with an aversion to dogs might had a large and aggressive-looking Alsatian just trotted in: body turned away, knees drawn up, expression hypervigilant, thin lips pursed with distaste. Gadd looked embarrassed. Spicer remained with his elbows propped on his knees, eyes darting from the stone to Ray and back to the stone and giving the impression he was restraining the urge to say something he would mortally regret in order to break the tumescent silence. It was a strange tableau depicting dwindling expectation and what might just prove to be bathos of career-ending magnitude.

Then the doorbell rang.

Plummer stepped past Steve and went downstairs to answer the door.

As swiftly as it had developed, the tension was broken; the peculiar, muffled quality of the atmosphere cleared and Steve realized he could hear the traffic again, as though his ears had popped. Everything zoomed back in. Spicer twitched and said, "Now what, Ray?"

Ray Cade turned slowly, and the tip of the sword lifted until it was pointing an inch away from Spicer's left eye.

"Kneel before your King," Ray said, glaring. "In all fucking seriousness."

Steve edged towards the stairwell. He could hear footsteps ascending and the sound of the street door slamming. Dawlish was standing up. He looked like he might try and restrain Ray, but before he could step around the coffee table, Ray roared, "*Kneel!*" and jabbed the sword forward into Spicer's eye.

Spicer squealed and threw himself backwards, clutching at his face. The tip of the sword was blunt and rounded but the force of the blow had split Spicer's brow and no doubt bruised, scratched and deposited rust in his eyeball. Blood flowed between his fingers. "Fuck, *Ray!*" Dawlish said and stepped around the table, his huge hands raised.

Ray spun and brought the sword round in a high arc. Dawlish watched it coming but was too amazed to react. The flat part of the blade whacked into the side of his head and Dawlish went down as if his legs had been kicked from under him. Ray hefted the sword and took it in both hands. His expression was serene and Steve saw in that moment that Ray had almost surely gone insane. He stood over Gadd and said again, this time in an even, almost reasonable tone, "Kneel."

Gadd was trembling, his big, bland, doltish face a mask of confusion and shock, but he moved his backside to the edge of the sofa and slid onto the floor and knelt there looking up at Ray.

And as he did, two men entered the room.

It was Trev and Vince, the proprietors of the antique shop beneath the flat. They were both wearing their trademark purple sweaters, cream linen trousers and fawn loafers. They ignored Steve and went over to Ray. They arranged themselves on either side of him and looked down at the stone. Ray stood a good six inches taller than them both.

Trev appeared delighted. He clasped his hands together beneath his pelican chin and sighed.

"You used it, Raymond. Good *boy!*"

Vince was nodding, his eyes wide and excited, "We've waited so long! Look at it, all broken, all *spent!*"

Ray looked suddenly perplexed, "You said use the sword on it. You said it was the key."

"Yes, yes, you did *fine*, Ray, just fine," said Vince and clapped Ray on the back.

"You said it would give me power," Ray was starting to frown, his expression darkening. "You told me it would be *limitless.*"

Vince laughed, a high girlish sound, and said, "We needed you to open it, Ray. Only you could do that," and as he spoke, it seemed that the quality of the light in the room changed, slipped down to a crude gloom, and his voice became low, polluted, capable somehow of imparting solely *disreputable* things: "*We had to tell you a load of old shit so you'd believe us, you greedy fucking moron.*" And he laughed again and this time it was the sound of a murderer's bathwater taking chunks of meat down an already clogged and rusty drain hole.

There was a sharp crack, like a pane of glass fracturing, and Steve felt suddenly sick with fear.

He was in the doorway and hadn't heard Plummer come back up. Steve assumed he had left at the same time he had let these two creatures in off the street. Steve decided it would be a very good idea to join him and began to creep away down the stairs

He reached the door and managed to open it, but the descent had been in the sludge of a nightmare, and the skin had almost been crawling off his back with cold, petrified gooseflesh, and his eyes were wide and his jaw was clenched as if wired, because what Steve had seen at the last moment, as he started down towards the street, was enough to drive the sense from anyone sane.

Those men, that Trev and Vince, shopkeepers, vague acquaintances of Ray's for the last six years, a couple of innocuous but slightly shadowy fairies, were starting to alter. Ray had looked up and for a second caught Steve's eye, and his expression had been a horrible combination of cruelly dawning insight and incalculable fury.

Then Steve was gone, slipping away with the image of those two *Tchaikovskys* with great and terrible jaws hanging off their faces dropping to all fours and falling on the man to whom they had promised the world and left standing mystified and shattered with nothing but a blunted medieval weapon with which to defend himself.

Steve stepped onto the pavement. He paused for a moment to look up at the window above the shop. He strained his ears above the unending roar of the traffic and thought, or maybe imagined, that he could hear Ray shouting and the sound of wet, exhilarated snarling. Steve shuddered.

He felt disorientated and shaken, and was already doubting what he had seen just before he'd started down the stairs, reframing it, coping with it by rationalizing it away on the old flashbacks when a dark blue Ford Escort pulled up at the kerb in front of him.

The passenger side window rolled down and Plummer leaned across and put his head out.

"Get in, Steve. Fast!"

Steve stepped up and opened the door. He took a last look up at the window above the shop and could make out movement, frantic and cartoon-like, in silhouette behind the sunlit glass. There was a clang as something hefty and metallic ricocheted against the radiator beneath the windowsill.

Steve climbed in.

As they pulled out into the traffic, Steve thought he saw the street door fly open. It might have been an accident of shadow and the movement of the car, but Steve said, "Stop!"

Plummer continued to accelerate up the Islington Road.

"Wait, Plummer!" Steve shouted, rounding on the driver. It had been no illusion; as they were speeding away, Steve saw Jason Spicer stagger out from under the porch and collapse on the pavement, still clutching his face.

Plummer glanced at the rearview mirror. His expression was impassive, highly concentrated. "Fuck them," he said mildly.

Steve reached into his jacket pocket. He was not surprised to discover his hand was shaking. He pulled out a packet of Bensons and lit up, holding his lighter steady in both hands. He exhaled smoke and sat back in the seat. He closed his eyes.

"What do you mean, 'fuck them', Plummer? They're our friends."

Plummer's eyes remained fixed on the road. "They're not my friends," he said. "And they're not yours."

"What?"

"Never have been." Plummer said.

They drove past the Angel tube station and turned left onto City Road.

Steve kept his eyes on the road. Through clenched teeth, he said, "They're the only friends I've ever had."

Plummer laughed. "I'm the only friend you've ever had, Steve. Give me a smoke."

Steve tossed the packet of Bensons into Plummer's lap. Plummer scooped it up and put the box to his mouth, pulled out a cigarette in his teeth.

"Light?"

Steve handed Plummer his lighter.

"Thanks," Plummer lit up and blew smoke through his nose.

They drove in silence through the heavy traffic. "You shouldn't be afraid of your friends," Plummer said eventually.

Steve shrugged. "What do you mean?"

"You were afraid to tell Ray that Claire was pregnant. You were afraid to tell him you wanted to stop working for him."

Steve felt his heart sink, felt oddly embarrassed as if caught lying with no decent excuse for it. But he had good reason. Good reason to be afraid.

"OK," he said. "How the hell do you know that?"

Plummer glanced across at his passenger. He smiled. Steve was startled by the unexpected gentleness in that smile, a depth of feeling he had never before seen on this strange, hard man's face. To Steve it looked as though Plummer had suddenly conceptualized the notion of grace and undergone some sort of astonishing conversion.

"I know so many things, Steve," Plummer said, and the gentleness was there in his voice, too. "I'll tell you what I can."

"Where are we going?" Steve asked.

Plummer returned his attention to the road.

"We're going to get Claire," he said. His fists were gripping the steering wheel tightly; his knuckles were white, Steve noticed. It was the first sign of tension Plummer had betrayed.

"Claire?" he said. "Why?"

Plummer grunted and stepped on the brakes as a bus pulled out in front of them.

"Because she's in danger, Steve," he said and swung the Escort into the oncoming traffic. A horn blared and Plummer cursed. He cut back into the eastbound lane, left the bus chugging in his wake.

Then he was standing on the brakes again, this time stopping the car completely as the traffic ahead ground to a halt. "Fuck it!" he said.

Steve looked up and saw the snarl up.

And saw what had caused it.

He turned to stare at Plummer with a fierce and unknowable terror rising in his chest. Fear for Claire and fear for the baby. But also a sudden and unruly fear for his sanity that was undeniably real and unfeasible to put down to anything so pedestrian as a *flashback*. This time there were no excuses.

Why? he had asked. And now that seemed rhetorical, because something so alien and disquieting had materialized, straddling the road ahead and plunging immense iron legs through the roofs of buildings and crushing the vehicles fateful enough to be beneath them, that he was filled with a sense of approaching threat so extreme it exercised an almost gravitational compulsion on him.

Plummer craned his neck and looked up through the windscreen. Steve leaned forward and followed his gaze.

There was a cyclopean structure spanning the road, a pylon of immense size, bolted and plated with battleship sized flanks of metal. It reached up and up, tapering away into the low London afternoon sunlight.

Plummer sat back in his seat and frowned, as if calculating their next move. He put the Escort in first and edged forward.

He spoke then, steering the car out of the jam and edging it across the oncoming lane. They pulled out and slipped down a side street that remained partially negotiable and pulled away. It made little sense to Steve, but it was enough to fill him with an incomprehensible dread made somehow worse by the fact that his companion seemed both calm in the face of it and singularly aware of its intention.

"What did you say?" Steve asked.

"The Autoscopes are coming," said Plummer.

"What the hell is that thing?"

Plummer steered the Escort with skill through the dense traffic.

"It's an Ingress Gantry," he said. "Or I-Gantry, if you want to sound cool. I don't give much of a fuck either way myself."

Steve was half-turned in his seat, looking back through the rear window. He could see the massive structure towering over London and was witnessing the effect it was having on the City's people. Traffic was grinding to a standstill. Vehicles were pulling over, the drivers climbing out to stand, craning their necks to peer up at the Gantry. Some were talking into mobile phones or holding them up to take photos; others were engaging with each other, pointing, and looking more disbelieving than alarmed. Steve could hear the mounting intrusion of sirens. A group of young men raced past the Escort, shouting, and headed away towards the Gantry.

Steve was about to say something, but Plummer's mobile phone went off. Plummer hooked it out of his jacket pocket and said, "Yeah?"

Plummer made some acknowledging grunts and a minute later hung up. They came up to an intersection and Plummer braked. He looked out of the driver side window. "There it is," he said.

"What?" asked Steve, and ducked his head to follow Plummer's gaze. "Oh, shit," he said.

"The Mile End Gantry," Plummer said. "They're appearing faster than we predicted. That's a problem. We have to get Claire and leave London before it seizes up completely."

Steve rubbed his eyes. He took out his Bensons, lit one for himself and one for Plummer. "Here," he said.

"Thanks." Plummer took the cigarette and plugged it into the corner of his mouth.

"So, tell me about this problem, Plummer," Steve said. "Please."

Plummer nodded, but Steve wasn't expecting any of it, especially when Plummer started talking about God.

"There are two realities, Steve, the material world and the unconscious world. God upholds the material by his Word; we uphold the unconscious with our dreams. Only the unconscious is infinite."

Steve shook his head, blew smoke out of the window. "Right," he said.

Plummer went on, "It's our practice ground; it's where we work miracles now that we've lost confidence in our waking reality. It's where we walk on water, where we *fly*. When Man fell, God gave us the Unconscious as a reminder that we were once gods ourselves so that when the time came for the re-creation of the material world some of us would be ready and remember our destiny."

Plummer drove them out onto the A13, where traffic was still moving. Steve could see the Mile End Gantry in the distance to their right. He frowned, and tried to focus on what Plummer was saying.

"With the Fall of Man came entropy, disease and death. God created a race of beings called Firmament

Surgeons, engineers of Creation, to hold back the decay.
But they saw what Man was capable of and used their own
free will to choose obedience or rebellion; many fell. They
became Autoscopes and sought to hasten the destruction
of creation. Cigarette?"

"Uh, yeah," Steve said and handed Plummer another
smoke. He felt as though the interior of the car had become
something terrifying, a racing cubicle filled with smoke and
bad light, a trap in which he was to receive some kind of
appalling revelation that would drive him mad. He was a
smart guy, a sceptic and until now had considered himself
to be a reluctant agnostic, but he had never expected God to
stick his head in and start roaring out of Plummer's mouth.
"Plummer, is this bullshit?"

Plummer shook his head and glanced over at Steve. "Of
course not," he said. "In a while there's going to be Gantries
all over London and they're going to open and things are
going to come out. Terrible things. And they're going to be
searching for us. For you and Claire. Mainly Claire."

Steve shut his eyes and put his hands to his temples.
"Because of the baby?"

"Yes," said Plummer. "The child Claire is carrying is a
reborn Firmament Surgeon. And we think she's one of the
children who can bring about the recreation."

"We? Who's *we*, for fucks sake?"

"The good guys." Plummer smiled and Steve saw that
incongruous tenderness beatify his expression once more.
He felt a sudden inrush of calm, and it was welcome.

"There have been so many battles," he said. "We've lost so many to the Autoscopes, to the devil-in-dreams, and they are so powerful now. We've fought them for nearly four thousand years and we've held them back, but it's time for us to face them for the final time. We have to save your child and get her to a safe place or it will have been for nothing."

"Are you a *Firmament Surgeon?*" Steve asked.

Plummer laughed, "Nah," he said.

Steve sat back in his chair. He suddenly felt conned. This *was* a fucking joke. "Plummer-"

"I'm a Paladin," Plummer said.

"A-"

"A Paladin. The Firmament Surgeons are supernatural beings but they've used men like me throughout history to do their work on the ground, to orchestrate and keep a weather eye out. I was never there for Ray. I was sent to the Unit to make sure certain things happened, to ensure your destiny unfolded along the right lines. This is the culmination of *history* we're talking about!"

"But Ray had all the ideas," Steve said.

"Who put them in his head?" asked Plummer, and winked. "Listen, the Autoscopes use bad men, psychopaths, shitheads to do their dirty work. The *Toyceivers*. Trev and Vince thought they were controlling things when they gave Ray the sword and told him about the Stone. But it was me that introduced them, me that gave Ray the historical spin I knew would appeal to his conceits. It was what I left out that mattered."

Plummer's phone rang, and Steve jumped, heart hammering. As Plummer lifted it to his ear, Steve looked out of the window and said, "Don't tell me."

Two more Gantries had appeared.

"Cheapside and Whitechapel," Plummer said. "Yeah, we're nearly there." He hung up.

"Who are you talking to?" Steve asked.

"Jon Index," Plummer said. "A real live Firmament Surgeon. He's at a safe house in Dartford keeping three very powerful children from harm."

"Are we taking Claire there?"

"Not wise. We need to get out of London. Once we have Claire, Index and his Paladin will meet us and we'll travel together with the children. Somehow we're going to have to open an Egress Gantry and get away."

"Where to?"

"One of the Quays," Plummer said. "Another place of safety, but this is sustained by the unconscious of one of the children. A little girl called Lesley."

"Fucking hell," Steve said, "my head hurts."

Plummer laughed, and his phone rang again.

Two more Gantries had materialized, one in Southwark, the other at Blackheath. But this time Plummer stayed on the phone. His expression darkened and he swore. "Okay," he said and pocketed the phone.

He turned to Steve, and Steve discovered that his brief and comforting calm was a fragile misapprehension.

"They're opening," Plummer said, and for the first time, for a terrible, bleak instant, there was fear in that man's eyes, like a flicker of lightning on the horizon of a dark, flat sea. "Dear God, not yet."

Steve craned his neck as a formation of fighter jets tore overhead. They were low and fuming, aiming towards the Islington Gantry with howling combatant purpose. Steve watched as they banked then disappeared into the distance.

"Backup," he said.

"They'll be no fucking use," said Plummer.

"Oh," said Steve. "That's a shame."

4

Claire was watching the news, her hands linked over her belly. Reporters were talking about some kind of phenomena appearing all over London; cameras showed footage of the immense pylons and the buildup of Army vehicles and troops which were congregating around them. There was a cut away as a jet fighter roared past and another showing an American reconnaissance AWAX plane circling in the distance, its sinister radar slowly revolving.

Claire stood up and went over to the window. She pulled the net curtain aside and peered out. From the tenth floor of the flats she could just make out the slender, tapering frame of what must be the Mile End Pylon stretching up into the cloud base.

She shuddered and let the curtain fall back. She went to the sofa and paused, feeling restless. She thought about going next door to see if Maureen was catching this. Claire thought that everybody within reach of a TV would be glued to their screens, awestruck and childlike with apprehension. She remembered how she had felt watching the Twin Towers collapse, a kind of watery trepidation, a wonderment that had nothing to do with delight and an excitement that had nothing to do with pleasure, yet it had been thrilling in a purely breathtaking way. She'd been sitting there on the sofa, she recalled, eating lunch as the planes hit. And it had been an immediate instinct to connect with someone and share the news that had led her to go and knock on Maureen's door. Maureen had answered, attired in housecoat and slippers and, a little wild-eyed, had virtually dragged Claire into her flat where they had stood watching the news on Maureen's little TV/video player combination portable, and Maureen had said, intoxicated by events, "It's amazing, Claire. Do you think there'll be any more?" Claire had realised that Maureen could probably contentedly watch planes crashing into tall buildings all day.

A rapid knocking on the front door startled her. Claire went down the hall and called, "Hang on." She stepped into the kitchen where her phone was charging. She picked it up off the worktop, switched it on and saw

1 missed call displayed on the screen. Claire remembered
the reporters saying that the first pylon had appeared
in Islington and she reckoned that Steve was probably
trying to get hold of her to tell her he was OK. She
unplugged the charger and carried the phone out into
the hall, thumbing the dial button as she went. There was
another barrage of knocking. Claire looked through the
spyhole above the letterbox and could see the distorted
figure of Maureen standing in the passage. She undid the
latch and opened the door.

"Come in, Maur," Claire said, and stepped aside.

She looked up from the phone just as a long, serrated
blade slid into the side of Maureen's head, went all the way
through and emerged in a red jet. There was a moment, as
Claire staggered back down the hall, dropping her phone
and tripping on the nap of the worn kilim runner, when
Maureen's pupils glittered with a bright, reflective silver lus-
tre, like fish scales floating on the surface of her eyes, and
Claire had time to understand that it was light reflecting off
the blade that had passed through her sinuses and divided
her eyeballs. And then she felt herself falling backwards,
falling, just as Maureen was collapsing, brimming with news
and suddenly just too dead to impart it.

The hand holding the knife tensed and wrenched the
blade free. Maureen's head was tipped against her left shoulder as the blade tore against her skull and for a moment
she looked too animated, too terribly quizzical to be dead,
but then the blade was out and she fell on her face in the

doorway, small slippered feet plumping soundlessly on the tiles as she twitched.

Then the killer stepped over her body and came into the flat. Claire looked up, numb with fear and shock, and saw the man walking towards her. He was a very strange look-ing killer. He was average height and stocky with a round, cheerful face and short, cropped grey hair. He wore slacks and a purple pullover. He smiled and Claire saw that he was carrying a blade in both of his fat, pale hands.

"Hello, Mary," he said, and at last, Claire screamed.

Claire tried to get up off the floor, but the man was stand-ing over her and had a foot on either side of her hips. "For God's sake," Claire gasped, "I'm pregnant."

The man smiled again, an engaging kind of look similar to the expression one might see on the face of a man sud-denly remembering a happy event from the past, something to give him a warm glow. "Oh, I *know*," he said, and held the blades out above Claire's stomach.

Instinctively, Claire curled up and rolled onto her side. She caught the man off balance and he stumbled. Claire tried to push herself away, but as she thrust out her legs the man fell onto her and she felt something slide into her, a coldness so wrong and loathsome and *sharp* that she bit her lip and felt her eyes roll up into her head. She said, "Uhh," and tried to push the man away but there was no strength left in her. Somewhere in the distance she could hear conversation and realized it was the TV. Despite her pain she heard the raised voice of a reporter remarking on the fact that something was happening, some new development. There were lights. Strange, dazzling rills of light crawling over the brackets and bolted stanchions of the Islington Pylon.

Claire turned her head and the face of her assailant was an inch away, the same enigmatic smile playing about his lips. The blade, which had entered beneath her ribs and punctured her lung, had been meant for her baby. Claire experienced a rush of fury and lifted her head off the floor, butting the man on the bridge of his nose.

There was a splintering crunch and the man roared. He threw himself away, leaving the knife still protruding from Claire's side. Kneeling, goateed with blood, he glared at Claire and raised the other blade. "I'm going to cut that pup out of you and *peel* it alive while it's still dangling from the cord," he said and staggered to his feet.

Claire groaned and pushed herself up on her elbows.

The man stepped towards her.

Claire looked down at the knife and the blood that was soaking through her shirt. She felt tears welling in the corners of her eyes. And then something moved in her belly. A kick. It was the first physical indication of movement she had felt from the child, and she thought, oh, *baby*, and then she was no longer lying on the floor in the hall of her flat, no longer suffering the brutal agony of a stab wound and punctured lung. She was somewhere else, and was watching *a child standing beneath the overhanging branches of the willows that grew around the bank of a peculiar eye-shaped pool. A flat-bottomed punt was moored to a trunk and threads of shadow slid like ripples across its sand-coloured planks. There was a picnic hamper sitting on a checkered cloth on the near bank. The child knelt and started unpacking the hamper. She sang to herself as she placed the cakes and bottles of drink on the cloth. She was a very beautiful child, with delicate hands and an unselfish, gentle face. She dipped her hands into the hamper and lifted out a large, heavy-looking cogwheel. She held it up and put her eye to the threaded hole bored through its middle. It had large, angular teeth and looked like a slice of hard, brass sun. The child placed the cog on the cloth and smiled. She wiped her oily hands on the grass and sat back on her haunches.*

There was movement in the trees behind her, and as she turned, someone came into the clearing.

The man stopped for a moment as she looked at him and appeared to be attempting to work out the meaning of her expression. The child looked surprised to see him, but curiously off-guard as though she had been expecting someone else.

He crossed the clearing smiling, because her expression had suddenly changed into something altogether more gratifying.

She had seen what he was carrying.

Panting, he reached her. He snatched her up by the front of her dress and lifted her by one hand. He trod through the cakes she had laid out, smearing them beneath his shoes. He laughed thunderously into her pale, terrified face, breakneck eyes shot through with unseemly light.

He had come through centuries for this moment; he had been the Ripper once, and had walked Whitechapel in search of the pregnant whore carrying the child. He had killed Mary Kelly and cut the reborn pup out of her while she rolled her eyes in the appalling moment of her death. Now this! His masters were generous with their opportunities, that couldn't be denied.

With his free hand he lifted the serrated blade before her.

She made no sound. The blade gleamed, chopped the air.

He took a moment to look around before rendering her carrion, and had that moment to see the great creature come thundering out of the trees towards him. He had a single moment to see it in its full beauty, before its tusks bore into him and threw him from the child.

Bleeding, trembling, he rose, blade gone, and saw the creature bulking over the girl.

Tusks gory, it faced him again, and bellowing, rushed him.

Glorifying once more into something of light and terrible pressure, this time it rent him in half.

Plummer and Steve pulled up outside the flats and got out of the Escort. There was a big red four-wheel drive Frontera at the curb in front of the entrance. There was a man sitting in the passenger seat and a teenage boy in the back. As they walked past, Steve glanced in and saw another two children asleep on the back seat. A young boy of about three was cuddling a worn-looking soft toy. Steve thought it looked like a llama. Cute. Beside him and curled up against the teenage boy was a little blonde girl of about seven.

When Steve saw the face of the man in the front, he stopped. He experienced a moment of disorientation and then realized with a jolt where he had seen him before. The man turned and looked at Steve and Steve knew for sure. He remembered perusing Ray's DVD collection in the bedroom of Ray's Islington apartment. Most of them Ray had got from his own pirating operations and there were very few that had come with a receipt and guarantee. Steve had pulled one out. Mick Reeks' Perrier Award winning stand up show, *Cats Cause Cancer*. Steve had heard of this guy, had seen some of his stuff and enjoyed it in fact, but was surprised it was to Ray's taste. Reeks was mordant and bleak, surreal and uncompromising. Ray was more a *Jackass* kind of guy.

Ray had come over. "That bloke does me up!" he'd said. "Does me *right* up!"

"You think he's funny?" Steve had asked. There was a photo of Reeks on the back of the box, onstage with a radio mike and a cigarette. Short, curly haired, restless-looking.

"He does this bit about pandas in Norfolk, Steve. Fucking *pandas*. Never laughed so much in my life."

Steve shrugged. Pandas didn't strike him as particularly sidesplitting.

Ray had taken the box from Steve and held it up, gazing at the picture on the back. "Strange what happened to him."

Steve had raised his eyebrows. "What?"

"Disappeared last year. Just like that. *Pffft.*"

And now Steve was standing outside Claire's flat looking in on Mick Reeks and Reeks was smiling.

"Oh, fuck," said Plummer.

Steve turned, and saw that what remained of his world had fallen apart.

A man was coming out of the entrance to the flats carrying his girl. Steve ran over and helped him place Claire on the grass verge by the pavement. She was pale and covered in blood.

"She's alive," the man said, kneeling by her side.

"What happened?" Steve asked. He was crying, and looked up as Plummer walked over, searching his expression for some kind of understanding.

"Jon," said Plummer. "We have to get her out of here."

Index nodded. He looked worn. "The child is incredible," he said. "Somehow she managed to open a Quay and take me in. It was Feculent. I've been after that bastard for a long time." He shook his head. "Incredible power. Not even reborn yet and she can do this."

There was the sound of a car door opening and Mick Reeks said, "Guys, if we're going, we'd better do it sooner than later. Look over there."

The men looked west, towards the Mile End Gantry, and saw what was coming.

Something had detached itself from the Gantry. There was a pillar of light contained within the frame of the structure, like a vast silver filament. Dark specks were dropping from the stanchions and descending on the city. Something was staying in the air, though, and making progress towards them. It was still too distant for Steve to make out what it was, but he heard Plummer hiss, "You, too, you bitch? You're *mine.*" Steve looked up and saw Plummer step away from the group and walk slowly across the road, never taking his eyes away from the dipping, swaying thing flying towards them. He pulled something from his jacket.

And then a low-slung and elegantly wasted grey Saab 900 convertible screamed around the corner of the flats and drove straight at him.

Plummer threw himself out of the way. The Saab braked, mounted the kerb and stopped. The driver's side door flew open and Ray Cade stepped out. He was carrying what remained of the sword in his left hand. The blade had snapped, leaving about a foot of jagged, rusty metal protruding from the handle. He came around the back of the car and walked towards Plummer.

"You *cunts,*" he said. Ray was dishevelled and bloody. He had a deep gash running across the bridge of his nose and it looked like something had bitten his left cheek. His hair was sticking up at the back in a spiny dovetail and his suit was ripped, filthy and covered in thick shining patches of what appeared to be saliva or some sort of mucus.

Plummer faced Ray. He pointed the gun he had taken from his jacket at Ray's head. Ray stopped advancing and stood glaring at Plummer. "You wouldn't fucking *dare!*" he hissed. "After everything I've done for you."

Plummer remained impassive. He had assumed his true role now and there was nothing about Ray that could elicit any sense of subordination. "Get back in the car and drive away," Plummer said.

Ray was *quaking* with rage.

As Ray and Plummer stood in the road, Steve felt a hand on his shoulder. He looked up and saw Index standing over him. "Look after Claire," he said and walked over to Plummer.

"I'm supposed to be the Lord of London," Ray said in a tone that was both truculent and grossly disenchanted.

Index said, "You've fulfilled your destiny, Ray. Now you're finished. Get out of here or you'll die by the side of the road."

Ray blinked, stared at Index. "Who the fuck are *you*?"

"The stone was the Great Instrument, Ray. You used your ancestor's sword to operate it. It allows all the Gantries to be opened."

"Jack Cade didn't open any *Gantries*," Ray said.

"He failed, Ray. He wasn't careless of the feelings of others enough to be used by the Autoscopes. And the time wasn't right for the children to be born and brought together. We have all four now and the prophecy can be fulfilled. Get out of here, Ray. You've been used. Don't die for it like Jack Cade."

Steve was startled by what he heard. He suddenly remembered the train journey to Brighton six years ago at the start of all this. He recalled the woman in the carriage transfixed for a moment in slow twilit dapples, arms raised at her sides, saying *'When the Great Instrument is found, the Long Man will come down from the hills.'*

And as he remembered this, he heard something else. It was the low chugging of a small motor, a distant chopping, puttering sound, and he squinted and saw how close the thing in the air was. It was quite clearly a person riding some kind of outlandish flying machine. It was about three hundred feet up and less than a quarter of a mile away.

While Index was engaging Ray, Plummer stepped aside and walked over to Steve. The gun remained at his hip, pointing at Ray. Ray glowered, but the fight seemed to have gone out of him; the remnant of the sword hung from his fingers, the shards of the blade dangling a foot above the asphalt.

"How is she?" Plummer asked.

"I don't know," Steve said. "She's breathing. She's unconscious. She's stuck with a fucking *carving* knife, man. What are we going to do?"

And then Steve was startled as the little dark-haired boy, carrying his worn stuffed toy, came between him and Plummer and placed a hand on Claire's belly. Steve looked up and saw the Frontera's rear door open, with Reeks standing still holding the handle. Inside, Steve could see the teenage boy sitting with his head lowered and his lips moving. He looked like he was praying, or chanting something. The little girl was still curled up with her head on his lap, but now she seemed to be breathing more quickly, as if having a nightmare. The little boy, who must only have been about four, looked up at Steve and smiled. It was a beautiful grin, full of reassuring and unspoilt hope, and his soft brown eyes shone with infectious optimism. Steve's eyes were tired and teary, but he managed a grin back. "Hey," he said. "You okay?"

"Okay," the boy said. "Chloe looks like you. Blue eyes." Then he knelt down by Claire's side and closed his eyes, hand still placed on her belly.

Steve looked up at Plummer with a puzzled expression, but Plummer nodded and returned his attention to the flying creature that was nearly upon them. "Nurse Melt," he said. "On her Uproar Contraption. She wants Lesley, but she's not having her." He raised the gun and fired.

The machine, a misshapen frame of junkyard parts, lurched and wheeled away, taking it and its operator on a trajectory over the roof of the flats. Steve could hear the engine clattering as it came around again. He looked down. The little boy was talking, but Steve couldn't hear what he was saying. In the car, Lesley was thrashing and the older boy was holding her, soothing her, as he prayed.

Mick came over. "They're working together," he said. His eyes were wide and he seemed awestruck. "This is wonderful."

Steve stroked Claire's brow. Her eyes were moving beneath their lids; she was dreaming.

He flinched as Plummer fired again. Steve looked up and saw the flying machine come around and aim for them.

He saw the crazed thing in its saddle, a huge, pale woman with a tattered flag of orange hair flying out behind her like a child's depiction of a rocket's flame. He heard her screech, and as she took the bullet high in the pallid meat of her right thigh, Steve saw that her face was ripped, her lips flapping like rinds.

She screeched again and twisted the cow horn handlebars of her ride. The Uproar Contraption tore away, engine wailing, the huge, filthy sheets of the wings thrumming and rippling. It flew back towards the Mile End Gantry and as Steve watched, he could make out the shapes of things coming to meet it.

There were more airborne silhouettes, and things that leaped from building to building. There was something tall and thin, nodding like a vast, black stick of burnt cartilage. And something pressed between the buildings, a monstrous slab, extruding tentacles with the supple reflex of a snail's eyes. What came in its wake, or led on with roars and merciless deeds at street level was unknowable, but Steve had seen enough to know that they were all dead in less than about fifteen minutes.

Plummer was standing next to Index. Ray was gone.

Steve stood up, left Mick standing over Claire and the boy, and went over to them. "Where's Ray?" he asked.

"We let him go," Index said. "Five hundred years ago, your ancestor, Alexander Iden, followed Jack Cade to Heathfield near the South coast and killed him. You've got a choice. You can try and follow Ray, chase him down and kill him. Or you can leave him and come with us."

"Why would I want to kill him?" Steve asked. Until this morning, despite the fear he had felt, Steve had always *loved* Ray.

"It's your destiny," Index said. "Now or later."

Steve shook his head. "No way," he said. "Let him go."

Plummer nodded. "Then let's get out of here," he said.

The four men stood together, Steve, Index, Plummer and Reeks, and watched the children work. Alex, the dark-haired boy, Lesley—dreaming a fractal dream of her complex terrain – and Robin, in congress with the unborn one, their Chloe, fulfilling the prophecy, bringing the Long Man down from the hill.

There was a change in the air, the atmospheric precursor to an electric storm. Steve squinted as the rising wind blew grit across the car park. He felt the hairs on his arms furring up. He watched as a line of light appeared in the air ten feet away, widened to become a narrow, golden doorway, and allowed ingress to the largest man Steve had ever seen. The light faded, but Steve was sure he caught the impression of a second figure, a smaller man, remaining inside the Gantry, and behind him a place of staggering magnitude populated by rank upon rank of vast, complicated brass machinery, like the very clockworks that wound up to power the sun.

The Gantry closed, and the man stood before them. In each hand he held a metal rod equipped at their tops with a lever of some sort. Steve looked into his face, the great, bearded, suffering-eyed face, and felt a wave of compassion almost drown him.

Plummer stepped forward. No small man himself, Plummer had to look up to make eye contact. Then he embraced him.

"I thought you were lost," Plummer said. "Old friend."

The man closed his eyes, nodded. *I was*, his expression said. *For so long.*

Index carried Claire. Mick had Lesley, sleeping still, in his arms and Alex stood between Steve and Robin, holding their hands. The llama was tucked beneath his right armpit.

The Long Man, as Steve thought of him, was standing by the verge. He held one of his levers out over the grass. Plummer said something to him and the man plunged the lever into the ground. He squeezed the mechanism at the top and almost instantly a Gantry opened behind him.

"Come on," said Index and they walked up to it. Without looking back, Index carried Claire through and Mick followed. Robin paused. Alex looked up at him, then at Steve. "Go on," Steve said.

Robin frowned, but entered the Gantry with Alex.

Steve turned to Plummer.

"What are you going to do?"

Plummer looked at the giant. "We'll stay." He turned and pointed towards the Mile End Gantry and the monsters that swarmed from it. "We have things to take care of."

Steve looked at the ground, closed his eyes. He was thinking about Ray. He said, "You want me to stay?"

"No," Plummer said. "Claire needs you and so does the baby. You go now. Take care, Steve."

Steve put out a hand. Plummer took it and they shook.

Then Steve turned and he went through.

JUNCTION CREATURE

Towards the end of May, the surrounding fields become luminous. Beneath the wide, unsettled skies, the soil at the edge of the fens and beyond brings forth, for some dark spring days, brief dazzling ingots of yellow, stinking rape. And then, almost overnight, the crop is harvested, the lights go out, and profusions of poppies emerge like beads of blood welling from the raw, grazed earth.

The countryside is flat, littered with machine parts and the shells of outbuildings, windmills, pump houses, and neglected railway lines. There are plenty of working farms, stables, boat-builders, but it is the dereliction that seems to give the landscape an age. It leaves its history lying around like discarded rind.

Other abundant features are the water towers, great structures that bestride the fields and roadsides. The variety of their architecture is striking; some look like follies, with their turrets and fancy brickwork, others like alien war machines bristling with panels and aerials, others still look like colossal viruses, built from diagrammatic specifications in textbooks, their elevated reservoirs like stylised concrete capsids.

This land: inert, dreary, interminable to some; an inspiration to artists, horsemen, travellers, preservers of Tudor architecture, bucolic, antique and primal, keeps secrets and legends tight in the dark back rooms of drowsy pubs, the fire-lit tiled parlours of isolated farmhouses and the intricate quarters of the tithe cottages lining the drives of the ubiquitous studs.

It is seldom fragrant. In fact it often stinks. The air carries the heavy odours of silage and ordure. Miles of churned manure; huge slumbering pigs, lethargic and deliberate, outside their ranks of half-cylinder tin shelters; the scorched beetroot stench of the sugar factories and the miasma of hops fermenting in the breweries; that sudden, bright, dirty incandescence of rape.

And there are brutes at large in the fens, the fields, and the night-lone back streets of dark and secluded villages: Black Dogs and Big Cats, phantom beasts, elusive monsters. They have always been amongst us here, their burning eyes glimpsed across a yard, through dark windows, watching from a remote horizon.

This is Old England and these are its legends, its Hob-footed thugs.

But now there is a new unease, a slow paranoia creeping through this old, measured shire. There is talk of a new beast.

And its name is Junction Creature.

A young boy cycles to school on a cold spring morning. He has a new red sports bag slung over his shoulder. It's filled with books, trainers to change into at playtime and his lunch - chicken sandwiches with pickle, a Penguin biscuit, and an apple, a bottle of water, and a Hartley's lemon jelly. When it's time, he will attempt to eat the jelly in secret because if the other boys see him with a jelly, he gets teased, but he loves them and he eats them in defiance of their opinions.

His name is Alex and he is ten years old. He lives on a farm with his uncle and aunt. It's not a working farm any-more. His uncle sold off most of the land and converted the barn so that he could concentrate on being a sculptor. Alex is fascinated by his uncle's work. He makes things from metal and glass, and they look alive as they arch, stretch, and climb towards the timber roof of the barn. The light strik-ing from his uncle's arc welder will illuminate the barn with electric flashes long into the night.

Alex is just as fascinated by the man, his uncle Sandy. He is a large man, completely bald with an untamed black beard, and a moustache he teases out and waxes into two long, twitching stilettos of hair. His eyes are dark and his mood is often reflected likewise within them and beneath the intense crush of his brow. When he wears his weld-er's mask, the top of his hairless, shining head rises like a dome above it and his beard and the tips of his moustache protrude from underneath it and from its sides like wild weeds struggling from beneath a cloche.

His aunt, Jean, is a different matter. She is beautiful. Like an actress, a starlet, as his uncle calls her. She has long, curling, silvery-blonde hair and a face that expresses an abundance of exciting knowledge and experience. She doesn't do much except lounge about the farmhouse drinking gin and looking gorgeous in her antique gowns and dresses, but she is kind, in a detached and mysterious way, full of her own enshrined passions which express themselves internally and are only occasionally evident in a rosy flush or a deep satisfied sigh. Sandy is devoted to his wife. He is fiercely overly protective and frustrates the life out of her with his constant fussing. For a big man, Sandy is gentle as a lamb. He adores Jean.

Alex smiles, thinking of them both, and pushes down on his pedals as he heads down the lane. He is looking forward to a brisk kick-about in the playground before the bell. They're 26 - 12 up from yesterday's match. He can almost feel the tennis ball flying from the toe of his trainer with that satisfying and mildly painful hollow crack it makes when you catch it just right off your toes.

Today, though, Alex doesn't make it to school.

A couple of monsters see to it that he doesn't.

As he cycled, from across the fields came a cry. Hearing this, he skidded the bike to a stop and stood with it tilted between his knees. He looked around. The sound continued, off to his left. He grimaced. It began as a low note and Alex felt it blanket his bones with a chill. It began to rise in pitch, gaining in volume and it was the most awful sound he had ever heard, a sound, he thought, that wanted to hurt you.

The birds for miles rose up out of the distant woods and filled the sky with wheeling black static. They flocked in great pulsing blotches against the low white cloud. Alex shielded his eyes with the palm of his hand and squinted through the low morning sunlight. He gasped.

The birds were flocking as one, regardless of species. They wheeled towards where he stood. Crows and doves, woodpigeons, starlings and magpies, all turned and shoaled together in total formation. It looked as if the sky was folding and unfolding itself. They swarmed overhead and Alex saw nightjars and wrens; herons, ducks, kingfishers and owls, all in a profusion above him. But the thing that shook him, which made the whole spectacle truly upsetting rather than just bizarre - owls, flocking? - was how they all looked. Up close, they all appeared terrified, as if this whole thing was out of their control. Their beaks gaped and their little eyes bulged. And throughout it all, that sound driving them on, welling up out of the woods.

Alex turned his bike around and started to pedal home. He needed Sandy to see this, to hear the cry.

As Alex reached the end of the lane and cut along a path worn into the earth at the outskirts of the farm, the weather changed and snow began to fall, great flakes swirling down from the darkening clouds. Soon he was riding through a dense and thickening blizzard, aware that the snow was settling quickly on the hard, churned earth and budding branches around him. There had been snow here before in early spring. But the end of May? And this sudden? This storm? Alex skidded his bike onto the driveway leading up to the farmhouse, the wheels slipping on a thickening mat of snow. He reached the farmhouse just as the front door opened.

He climbed off his bike and kicked the stand down. He stopped for a moment and peered through the snow. The sky was white, the birds had gone. Whatever had terrified them could not keep them airborne in this blizzard and they had taken roost against it. The screaming had stopped, too. Alex breathed deeply, snowflakes landing on his head the size of moths.

He turned to go inside, but as he was about to push the door open he glimpsed something move in the field behind him. He paused and looked back down the path and as he did so two beasts charged out from the cover of the hedgerow that edged the property and flew towards the farmhouse.

One of the beasts was low to the ground and scaly. It had a human face and outrageous curly blonde hair, as if someone had stuck a dolls head on a Gila monster. It walked on all fours, although all four limbs were arms with long fingered hands. It had spines like knitting needles in a ring around its neck.

The other creature had left the path and was circling; a cluster of eyes, like a spider's, high on its forehead, glittered with malice as it stalked. It walked upright but with a stiff caution as if it had recently recovered from a near-fatal accident. It had a face as round and pale as a pudding bowl, and was featureless apart from that handful of eyes. It wore a dark pinstriped suit, which was smothered in mud and blotchy with mould. For an awful moment of stillness it stopped and stood there, swaying slightly in the snowfall, when it marked Alex. It reached out an arm and pointed at him. It made a gesture with its thumb and index finger like a pistol and mimed a shot at him. Alex felt a rush of air along his cheek and a small hole appeared in the doorframe behind his head.

Alex cried out and ducked. It only got off one good shot.

From out of the farmhouse charged Sandy. He threw himself at the creature. It made to fire on him but didn't get a chance because Sandy seized its wrist and was wrenching at it like the leg of a stubborn Christmas turkey. The creature shrieked and made a desperate imploring gesture to its companion. Sandy punched it in the gut, collapsing it like a clothes airer. The doll-faced thing blubbered, rolled its haunting blue eyes towards the brawl and scuttled across the grass to assist. The three fought in the snow, Pinstripe on his back with Sandy savaging its gun hand, the lizard-thing circling, slapping and whining. And all the time the snow continued to fall.

Then, from behind Alex: "Sandy!"

Aunt Jean put one hand on Alex's shoulder. In the other she held a slender glass full of gin and tonic with ice and lemon. The ice clinked as she leaned forward and yelled across the yard.

Sandy was up, his broad, muscular back heaving from the exertion as he stood over the injured brutes. His fists were clenched and he was trembling with fury. He booted the lizard-thing in the face and turned and stalked back to the farmhouse, his barrel chest heaving.

The thing in the pinstripe suit lay on its back in the snow, arms and legs splayed out; it appeared dead. The other creature ran around it, flakes of snow caught in its blond curls. Lying there, its hands were blue with the cold but it didn't seem to notice. Then, suddenly, pinstripe sat up. It fixed Sandy with its tiny cluster of beady eyes and something unzipped beneath its chin. Fluid dribbled down its tatty shirtfront and then two huge fangs slid out; it lifted its gun hand.

"Inside!" shouted Jean, as she shut the door behind them.

Alex was too shocked to say anything and went running through to the sitting room. He went over to the window which faced onto the yard and looked out.

There were no more shots though, only a shriek of fury. The creature was on its feet again and was holding its shattered wrist in its good hand. It flapped it and tried to point it at the cottage, but it was useless. Sandy, standing beside

Alex, murmured something contented, and patted Alex's head. They watched as the two beasts turned and stalked away. They disappeared back into the hedgerow.

Sandy gave Alex a hug. He patted Alex's back and Alex could smell the good smell of paint and varnish on his clothes from his work in the barn.

"I'm okay," he said.

Sandy ruffled Alex's hair and stepped over to the window. The snow was falling more thinly now and had yet to cover up the scuffed tracks in the grass where he had seen the beasts.

"What are they?" Alex asked.

Sandy was silent for a moment, behind them the fire roared. Alex could hear the clink of ice being added to the makings of another gin and tonic.

"Toyceivers," Sandy said.

Alex didn't know what to make of the word, but before he could say anything else there was a sudden explosion of noise from outside. It sounded like a circus load of animals blundering around tearing up trees and bushes.

Sandy snarled. "Right," he said. "This is it. Let's get to the barn."

Sandy and Alex went through the cottage, locking up and fixing the shutters in place. Aunt Jean sprawled on the sofa in the living room with her drink. Sandy worried over her but she shooed him away and blew him a kiss, saying she'd be fine.

Upstairs Alex took a moment to look out of a window but all he could see was the snow-covered yard which appeared as smooth and mysterious as the wide white screen of the picture house he loved to visit in town. And then, like grotesque images projected onto that screen, the creatures began to come, edging onto the whiteness from the border of the farm.

Alex banged the shutters closed and locked them. He then returned to the top of the stairs, his heart hammering in his chest. He paused in the stairwell and looked down; Sandy was by the front door pulling on a pair of boots. He was speaking soothingly to Jean, who was telling him to stop it and get the boy to the barn.

Alex ran down the rest of the stairs and stood with Sandy by the door. Sandy reached for the handle, but before his fingers closed around it, something hit the front door with enough force to splinter the frame.

"Out the back," Sandy said. His voice was calm and steady but there was a different look in his eyes now. Anger and regret together, and with that the all-consuming protectiveness. It made him look stronger than ever.

Above Alex could make out a sound, there was something on the roof, battering at the tiles.

Again something crashed against the front door, popping it open off its latch. Cold air blew in and something was out there on the porch craning in at them. It had a thick grey neck and a tiny head. It was all teeth, studded with fangs. It made a sound unlike anything Alex had ever heard before, like paper tearing endlessly.

Outside there came the sounds of growling and roaring, of things slithering and purposeful. Something the size and shape of a marrow waddled across the yard carrying blades.

Sandy shouted and kicked at the thing jammed in the doorway. It swung its small, lethal head but missed and clocked itself on the doorframe. It slumped away from the opening and Sandy was able to dodge the thing beyond it as it slung a blade at him. It flew past his face as he leaped aside, and embedded itself in the banister rail.

Sandy shoved what remained of the door shut and latched and double bolted it, top and bottom. Then he took off down the hall and through to the kitchen, with Alex following. Uncle Sandy threw open the back door and checked outside. So far nothing had ventured around the back. The barn stood high and wide across the back yard, its large, heavy wooden doors slightly ajar.

"Come on," he said, and they ran full tilt across the yard and into the barn. Sandy pulled the doors shut and secured them with heavy timber. They stood, breathless and wired. Sandy took a look around.

The barn was Sandy's workshop. In the middle of the floor was a workbench made of an ancient pine tree. It was littered with bits of wood and metal, cogs and clockworks, oilcans, drill bits, engine parts and electronic circuits. There were tiny motors, resistors, amplifiers, canisters and beakers. Against the wall he had installed a lathe, a sanding belt and an angle grinder. The walls were hidden behind cabinets and shelves full of tools and equipment and the whole room was sweet with the smell of varnishes, linseed oil and paint. His welding equipment stood beside the bench, a spot welder and an arc welder, both with red steel housings and side ventilators like gills. The floor around them was scattered with welding tips that looked like a spill of bullet casings. Everywhere else, arrayed around the barn and lurking back in the storage area, stood his sculptures.

Alex could hear the racket outside; things barging around and battering at the farmhouse and the walls and doors of the barn.

"Uncle Sandy," he said. "What about Aunt Jean?"

Sandy was at the back of the barn amongst his sculptures. He was yanking leads and plugging them into sockets built into the floor.

Still working, he said, "She'll be fine, son. Nothing's going to harm your auntie Jean."

Something battered against the barn door. It made a low drumming sound and then the tip of a tentacle pushed beneath the gap between the ground and the bottom of the door and probed about.

"How do you know?" Alex said, a little desperation creeping into his voice. The tentacle flattened beneath the door, leechlike, and tried to push further inside. Alex considered stamping on it but it looked clammy and repellent.

Sandy went over to the wall and pulled a switch. There was a flash and a crackle and Alex felt all the hairs on his head rise in an invisible caul of static; he looked around, his eyes wild. Sandy was standing with his hands on his hips,

looking up at his array of sculptures. Electricity was crawling across the floor in a rippling blue tide. Sandy was wearing rubber boots but Alex was still wearing his school shoes.

"Uncle Sandy!" he said, his expression stupefied, his
arms out at his sides, hands spread wide.

"Oh, jump up on that bench, son. It's wood. It'll insu-
late you."

Alex climbed up onto Sandy's workbench, scattering
tools and detritus.

The electricity had reached the sculptures and was
climbing up their struts and along their spars like tinsel.
Alex could see bulbs alight in their heads and within rib
cages made from the hollow chassis of reclaimed cars and
trucks. Sandy was watching, his eyes narrowed against the
blazing currents. He lifted his welding mask off the bench
and put it on. He glared at Alex from behind the green Perspex rectangle set in the face. He was probably grinning. He
pointed at the monumental figures craning against the roof
beams.

"I haven't just been making art, Alex!" he shouted. The
noise outside had increased, as though most of the efforts
of the creatures were now solely directed at the barn. The
doors and the walls shuddered and dust sifted down from
the roof. "I've been creating an army!"

Behind him, something moved. It made a grinding,
groaning sound, like hollow cylinders of bronze being bent
beneath a great weight. It was an unusually antique sound,
of something old filling with a very new life. Alex thought

of a giant squid in a storybook squeezing the body of an iron ship somewhere far out to sea, crimping its hull like a pipe cutter.

Alex squinted. Long bluish shadows rocked on the walls and against the roof beams. Sandy went over to the barn doors, undid the bolts and lifted the timber.

As Sandy pushed open the doors, revealing a scene of slush-churned riot, the creatures jostling in the yard to surround the barn, his sculptures lifted their craning bodies on their metal-glass limbs and marched, beneath their jagged, orchestrating shadows, out to meet the madness.

Alex stared in wonder. He edged down from the bench and followed the energised creations as they ducked beneath the lintel above the thrown-wide barn doors and emerged onto the snow. Flecks of snow still glanced through the air, blown on a light breeze. There were a dozen sculptures, all lit from within. Bladed arms flung out to greet the monsters, mouths that had been the grilles of cars, and the insides of presses and trashed machines, opened and bit at the air.

They steamed and glowed, and they attacked.

Alex watched the rout.

The sculptures advanced, limbs and jaws scything, scattering the monsters across the dirt-churned snow. From around the barn and from the roof they came, absurd, grotesque things, deformed by malice, shrieking with wrath, to join their falling, gored, splintered comrades, but they, too, fell in great numbers, and as fast, beneath the sculptures' assault. The sculptures pincered, legs scissoring, blades flashing, impaling, chopping, until they had marshalled the monsters into a huddle off towards the entrance to the farm. There they dipped their steaming faces and slashed the remaining monsters to ribbons.

Alex stood, pale and shivering, just outside the barn door. Sandy stood beside him, a sledgehammer in his fists, his breath steaming from beneath the welding mask, his eyes glittering like the mean eyes of a pike glimpsed rising from the dark emerald water of a lake. As the sculptures returned to their hangar, Alex stood unmoving while they trooped past, ducking beneath the lintel, re-taking their places at the back of the barn. Sandy pushed the doors shut. He turned and looked at Alex. Alex felt the shock of the morning's events begin to do its cold work on him and he shuddered, tears filled his eyes. Sandy bent down and soothed him.

"It's okay son," he said. "It's okay."

How was this okay?

"Who… who are you, Uncle Sandy?" He asked, his voice muffled against his uncle's overalls. "Who are you?"

"Come on," Sandy said. "I've got something I want to show you."

"I've seen plenty already," Alex said. He was staring at the ground, at the gouges and impressions left in the dirt and slush, and at the blood, and the bits.

"They're not human, none of them are," Sandy said. "At least, not anymore. Don't fret over them. Think of them like characters in a cartoon. Just, you know, from a really nasty cartoon. Anime, that sort of thing."

He leaned the sledgehammer against the side of the barn and walked off towards the gate at the end of the drive. There he pulled off his welding mask and dropped it in the mud. Alex followed, stepping over lumps and chunks with his eyes half-shut. He reached the gate where a heap lay steaming. He could see the bodies were already rotting.

"It stinks," he said.

"They don't last long once they're dispatched," Sandy said. "Won't be anything here in an hour. Just in time for Jean's late-morning drink. Come along now."

Alex followed Sandy across the lane and they pushed through a hedge at the side of the facing field. There Sandy led Alex across the field. It was fading yellow, a great sea of wilting rape. Alex wrinkled his nose, everything smelt bad today – off. The sky was white as a label. He looked around for the promise of poppies, but they remained discrete, the field bloodless. When they came to the bottom of the field, Sandy said, "This is the place."

Alex stood next to him and peered down. There was a cutting, and a railway line running through it, it was just a single narrow gauge.

"What now?" Alex asked.

"We wait for our ride," Sandy said. "And while we wait, I'll tell you more about Quay-Endula."

During some quiet evenings, when they were sitting by the fire in the living room, or playing cards or board games at the kitchen table, Uncle Sandy would tell Alex stories about the glorious town of Quay-Endula.

Quay-Endula is a town spread throughout the steep hills surrounding a great blue bay. It is a place of turrets and spires and fabulous follies, rambling pavilions, markets full of billowing pastel tents and gazebos. Quay-Endula has fountains like cathedrals; it has plazas and parks, open-air theatres, carnivals, trams, funicular railways, cable cars strung between great glittering pylons and a pier like no other could compare. The pier of Quay-Endula is a mile long, so they say, stretching out into the sea. It has its own fairground with a Ferris wheel the height of a skyscraper. It has helter-skelters and rocket ships that fly round on gleaming metal arms. It has arcades full of pin-ball machines and shooting galleries. All this is built on a wooden raft held up on fragile, barnacle-brittle iron legs.

Quay-Endula is also populated with monsters. Not the bad kind, not like those that had come to attack the farm, or those in books and films that terrorise and dismay, or lie concealed under beds or hide in closets, or creep with black hearts and burning eyes; but of the mighty kind. Epic things, creatures of renown, which live amongst the men and women of the Quays and are reminders to them of unfathomable wonders and the responsibilities that come with their apprehension.

Alex really wanted to go to Quay-Endula.

It was a place you could go to in your dreams, Sandy had told him. It was a safe place. There were people, he said, like angels, who looked after the Quays. There had once been countless numbers of Quays, all unique, all lovely. But something had wanted to destroy them. Something that hated their existence and the hope and love they gave.

That thing was the devil-in-dreams.

The devil-in-dreams was implacably opposed to the keepers of the Quays. The keepers were called Firmament Surgeons, and they had been trained as engineers, to keep the mechanisms of Creation running against the entropy arising from the fall of man. It was a great task and one which would be superseded at the Re-Creation, but for now, while eternal events took their course, and wars raged on Earth and in Heaven, the Firmament Surgeons worked and fought and wove their Quays and upheld the dreams of man.

But having free will and being able to choose, over time the devil-in-dreams exerted his influence on the Firmament Surgeons as he had on man and angels before them, and many fell. They became Autoscopes and they began their onslaught of the Quays and their struggle for command of Dark Time, the eternal, fluid chronology of dreams.

It is the Autosomachy, this war, and it is raging to an end.

"You want to know who I am?" Sandy said as they sat together on the bank leading down to the tracks. "Well, I'm your uncle Sandy. But I'm something else, too. Something I could only reveal to you when the time was right, and now that time has come upon us early, but that's okay. I've been preparing for it, ever since you were sent to live with us. You were sent to me to be kept safe because you are to be a Firmament Surgeon and you're a very rare and important boy. I'm your Paladin, Alex. I've always looked out for you."

Sandy was watching Alex carefully. Alex hugged his knees and peered down at the rails.

"You've seen enough today to know I'm not making things up. I never was. Quay-Endula is real, as real as all this, but I wasn't being completely honest when I told you it's a place you can only visit in dreams. Everyone dreams about it, everyone knows about it, somewhere in his or her subconscious. Firmament Surgeons can take people there and keep them safe, refresh them, give them hope. But there's another way to get there for people like you. It's called a Gantry and you can open one and we can go there."

Alex nodded, still staring off into the distance.

"You always said you'd love to go there," Sandy said as he nudged Alex with his elbow.

"That was different," Alex replied. "Like wanting to go in a rocket to Mars. I didn't think it was real."

"It is! Isn't that great? Only thing is, the war's reaching its conclusion and Quay-Endula is now about to come under attack by everything the Autoscopes can throw at it. That will affect this world very badly. If they get in and they gain ground, then people will stop dreaming, and they'll stop caring. We have to help save the Quay and warn people here."

"You seem very confident, Uncle Sandy."

"Once we get there, you'll see things the same way, lad. You'll be in your element. Hah! I've been so looking forward to this moment!"

Alex shook his head. He was about to say more, ask more questions, but then, coming from about a mile down the track, he heard something approaching.

He looked up at Sandy and saw that he was smiling.

The sound grew closer, building and thrumming. He felt the ground beneath them tremble with its approach. Breathless, Alex waited, and then he saw it rumble into the cutting.

It drove a great caul of sparks before it, firefly debris from its shearing wheels. It was an iron bulk, a locomotive salvaged from a crusher. It was a square-backed, steam-driven thing of ancient industry. Driverless it thundered, following its route through the forest and the fields surrounding the farms. It had no lights, just the blazing cloak of molten swarf, which cooled and twinkled over its channelled flanks.

It was called Railgrinder, and it groaned past them, a dreadful, beautiful machine, and as it travelled, it reaped the rails of rust.

"Come, on," Sandy shouted over Railgrinder's noise. They slid down the cutting and onto the tracks, following the stately rocking of the locomotive's back end.

Moving slowly enough, Sandy lifted Alex up and swung him into the open engine cab. He trotted along beside Railgrinder, grinning, and then grabbed a rail and jumped aboard. Together they stood there, rocking and bathed in firebox heat, the whole world full of clangs and ferment and turbulent row. Everything stank of coal dust and old black oil, hot pistons and sparks.

Sandy laughed, at the noise, at the furious rocking of the machine, at the absurdity of it. Alex was filled with a strange, drifting relief. It was good. He hugged his uncle.

"Enjoy it, Alex," Sandy shouted over the noise. "This is yours. It's your Instrument."

"My what?" Alex yelled, now laughing as well.

"It's your Instrument. It only takes you to the Quays. Only you can use it for that. It's engineered for you, for now."

Alex leaned out and looked up the line. Railgrinder swayed and ground its way with cumbersome utility.

"What do I do?"

"Wait. There's a tunnel coming up ahead. We can use it as an ingress point."

As they came around a bend, Alex saw the tunnel mouth. It was cut into a low hill, a mouldering redbrick arch. Railgrinder took them in.

Alex looked up at his uncle. "You okay, Uncle Sandy?"

Sandy said nothing, his eyes were fixed straight ahead, his fists clenched and a sheen of sweat had broken out on his face. The sweat beaded the dome of his bald head; he looked like he had been caught out in a light shower.

"Don't like tunnels much," he said through gritted teeth. "Never have."

Alex patted Sandy's arm. He hadn't ever considered his uncle to be the phobic type, but he looked like he was struggling now, really hanging on.

"We'll be out soon," Alex said, his voice bright and echoing in the tunnel above the rumble and clatter of the train. Railgrinder's sparks threw light around them like a cauldron of molten ore. Sandy's sweat gleamed golden.

"One way or another," Sandy said. And then: "There. Up ahead."

Alex looked through the porthole above the firebox.

Less than a hundred yards ahead, a circle of light hung suspended in the darkness. It looked no bigger than a wedding ring.

"Is that the end of the tunnel?"

"No," Sandy said. "There's more than a mile to go. That there's your Gantry."

"It's tiny."

"Railgrinder's yours, remember. Here, take the throttle."

Alex slid past Sandy and took hold of the long, brass lever. He looked up at Sandy, who nodded, and then Alex, knowing exactly what to do, pushed the lever forward. Smoke blew from the engine's stack and rolled in a low, gritty storm above their heads. Railgrinder lurched forward and gathered speed. As they accelerated, so too did the circle of light begin to grow. It expanded of its own volition, not merely owing to the decreasing distance between them. Its edges rippled outward and as Railgrinder approached, it spanned the tunnel with an opaque, luminous disc. Alex held tight to the throttle and closed his eyes.

Both he and Sandy bellowed with a thrill of terror as Railgrinder roared in through the Gantry.

Alex opened his eyes. He pulled back off the throttle and Railgrinder slowed to a crawl. Alex looked at Sandy; he was beaming, the weathered skin around his eyes and nose was black with soot. In contrast his teeth looked very white. Alex rubbed a hand over his own face and the palm came away begrimed, smelling of cinders.

"I can't believe I'm finally here," Sandy said. "Outside of a dream."

They had emerged from the Gantry into a different world. The sky was clear, unclouded, cooling to twilight blue. The tracks followed a ridge, and beneath on both sides, fields of purple flowers set off into the distance.

"Lavender," Sandy said. "It's so beautiful."

Beyond that were the mountains, a barricade of low, red rocks against the sky. Farther on, there was a stand of forest, where the tracks headed through it. Sandy breathed it all in deeply. Alex leaned against the side of the cab and looked out across the lavender fields; he could smell the dense, blessed perfume of it.

"It's later here," Sandy said. "It'll be nightfall soon."

"Is this Quay-Endula?" asked Alex.

Sandy shook his head. "This is your Quay. This is Quay-Fomalhaut. We need to get to Quay-Endula as fast as possible."

"Aren't we safe here?"

"Not like we would have been once. There have been incursions, Alex. Parts of this Quay have already been taken."

Alex watched the fields roll by, silent, breathing their scent. After a moment, he turned back to the Railgrinder's controls and thrust down on the throttle again. Their speed increased and they headed into the distant forest.

They travelled on through the darkening stands of trees. For a while, the track followed the curves of a stream and Alex watched the sparks from beneath the grinding wheels casting out in a continuous wave and alight in the shady water, brightening for the briefest of moments the gleaming pebbles just beneath the surface. Soon the stream meandered away and he could see where it ran off into a channel built into the hillside. He could hear it frothing and chopping against the stone walls at the channel mouth. Sandy stood up and stretched. Railgrinder drove on, riding its flickering waves of embers. Ahead more obscurity beckoned.

"Can you hear the mines?" Sandy asked. "The Fomalhaut mines are working again."

Alex stood still and listened. Above the continuous chafing of Railgrinder's plates and the incendiary crackle of its firebox, he could just make out the sound of something distant and industrial; it was like the clanging of dull iron bells and the muscular hiss of great plunging pistons. The more he attuned his ears, the clearer it became. They were approaching a place of heavy engineering.

"We'd better hide ourselves," Sandy said. He gestured for them to crouch down behind the low sides of the cab.

After a mile or so Railgrinder swept around a bend and they came into a clearing. They kept their heads down as Sandy peered over the side of the cab. The noise was immense here, an endless clatter and thunder of machinery. Alex peered past Sandy's shoulder and saw that they had entered an enormous yard. Railgrinder took a route around the outskirts and he could see that they were passing through a mining plant. There were pitheads and pylons, ranks of fat hoppers, rumbling conveyor belts and low, dark single-storey factories. Flashes of cold, blue light illuminated the grimy windows, which Alex recognised as the spitting radiance of arc welders. Railgrinder rumbled over a set of points and Alex could see that more rails ran off towards the middle of the yard where rows of trucks full of coal waited in a siding. Everything was moonlit and coated in a thick, grey dust. As Railgrinder took them behind a row of sheds, Sandy stood up and went to a lever by the firebox. He grasped the handle and wrenched it down. Railgrinder's wheels screeched and Alex staggered as it came to a halt.

"Don't worry," said Sandy. "Just going to make a bit of trouble here, then we're off." He jumped down out of the cab.

"What are you doing?"

Sandy pointed to the closest pithead, a tall pylon supporting a drilling rig. It looked ancient, and it creaked and groaned as it worked.

"Sabotage," he said. "These mines have been abandoned for years. Now the Autoscopes have their Toyceivers working them again, mining for materials for the war. I'm going to inconvenience them and buy us a little more time."

Sandy disappeared around the side of the shed. Alex climbed down and peered around the corner. He watched Sandy walk over to a heap of large wooden reels. There he crouched down and inspected them, then pushed one over onto its side. It was the size of a barrel and tightly wound with steel cable. He rolled it across the yard until he reached the pithead then took hold of the end of the cable and unravelled about ten feet of it. It looked heavy and very strong but Sandy managed to loop it around the foot of one of the supporting stanchions. He reached into an overall pocket and took something out; it was one of the many tools he had designed and made to fashion his sculptures, and he began working on the end of the cable. The yard was lit by intermittent bursts of blue light from the arc welders. A conveyor belt tipped a load of ore into a hopper with a sound like a brief, localized landslide.

Alex kept watch while Sandy finished fashioning a hook onto the end of the cable and used it to fix the loop like a noose around the stanchion. He gave it a tug and it held firm. Sandy pushed the reel back across the yard and up to the rear of Railgrinder. He unravelled the remaining cable and kicked the empty spool away. It rolled in an arc and came to rest against a heap of slate. Sandy made another noose and hitched it to one of Railgrinder's buffers. He returned to the cab and they both climbed back in.

Sandy released Railgrinder's brake, and with a hiss and jolt, it started to pull away. They leaned over the back of the cab and watched as the cable grew taut. Railgrinder hauled against the weight of the pithead, steaming, its fire glowing white. The cable pulled tight against the corner of the first shed and bit into the wood. Railgrinder strained and began to gather momentum. Sparks gushed from beneath its boiler. The cable tore into the side of the shed and started to slice through it.

Wood splintered and the cable sang like piano wire. It carved through the planks, splinters flying, and suddenly the entire structure collapsed. The cable dragged against the side of the next shed and sliced it in half as Railgrinder gathered speed. The third shed shattered in an explosion of decayed timber and now Railgrinder was pulling hard against the leg of the pithead. There was a moment of resistance when Railgrinder's fire seemed like a handful of tiny stars, blinding and tremendous, and Sandy and Alex had to cower against the heat, but then they heard the first screams of tortured wood and felt the sensation of something giving way.

The pithead buckled and the leg attached to the cable tore from the ground. The flywheel at the top of the mast flew off its axle and plunged down into the shaft trailing chains and a jangling constellation of cogs. The drill snapped like a stick of rock and flew into the air, ricocheting against the legs of the pylon, shattering them like driftwood. It soared up, arcing over the yard and harpooned the roof of one of the factories. There was an explosion and screams from the creatures working within. Gas cylinders blew in a succession of flat, punchy detonations and the entire building was engulfed in flames.

Railgrinder used its power to take down the entire structure. As they rode off into the forest, Sandy and Alex watched the pithead topple and crash down into the dry, rutted yard, flung to ruin in the grey earth.

Sandy reached over, lifted the slackened coil of cable from Railgrinder's buffer and dropped it onto the rails. Railgrinder took them away from the yard and the chaos, back into the trees, before their presence was ever noticed; its back end, its fire and steam, its crew of two, all gone rocking down the rails, cloaked by the forest.

Alex increased Railgrinder's speed and they made quite a pace. Sandy leaned against the side of the cab and squinted into the draught. Sparks landed in his beard and glowed like fireflies.

"Where does this line take us?" Alex asked.

"To the sea," Sandy said. "There's a line that runs the length of the Quays. It's been destroyed and the bridges are out East of here, but it should still be running to Quay-Endula. There are precautions in place."

Eventually they left the forest and Railgrinder crossed a dark moor. Immense, serrated tors rose from the earth, and bitter-smelling ferns grew in abundance, smothering the land. Visible in the moonlight, through a gap in the distant mountains, was a level horizon of ocean. The line where it met the sky appeared elevated, owing to their altitude, and it looked to Alex like a fractured dam, its pent waters about to inundate the moor. But the waters held; the sea drew nearer, and soon they were travelling a pass through the mountains and emerged, panting steam and throwing metal light, onto a sweeping line that took them down, and down, in grace-ful curves, to the edge of the sea. They passed a boarded, derelict town, and a castle, red as rust, rearing up from the beach. Crimson lights shone in some of the windows and shadows flexed in the lines between the shutters. Alex shiv-ered and felt a strange tingle in his belly, an excitement he had not experienced before, an anticipation of something inside him wanting to mature, to find expression.

"Is that a bad place?" he asked.

Sandy was also looking up at the castle. His eyes shone with those snug, crimson lines of light.

"It might turn out to be," he said. "See the light, there's a battle raging in there."

"Should we help?"

"No. That needs to take its own course. We've got our own agenda, Alex."

The castle receded, and with it, so did Alex's sudden and powerful sense of longing. The light, though; those warm red gashes of light and the limber shadows that moved within them, they stayed with him for a little longer.

"Stop the train a hundred yards from here," Sandy said. "There's a siding and a shed. I want to show you something, but we have to go there on foot."

As they slowed near the siding, Sandy jumped down and ran ahead, towards a set of points. He pulled a lever and Railgrinder clacked off the main line and onto the siding. Sandy jumped back into the cab. The train shed was long and high with a curving corrugated metal roof. Alex engaged the brake and Railgrinder drew to a halt halfway along the length of the shed. He and Sandy climbed down onto the narrow platform.

"This way," Sandy said, and led them the remaining length of the shed and out onto the siding.

Once outside, and with the Railgrinder's noise no longer dominant, Alex could hear a new sound. Again, it was that of hectic industry; clangs and thuds and squeals. It was coming from farther along the beach.

They slid down a bank and onto a fractured concrete promenade.

"Keep close," Sandy said.

The high half-moon shone bright enough to throw shadows. They reached a row of storm-damaged beach huts where they crept along the promenade keeping to the cover beneath the awnings of the beach huts.

"There," said Sandy, and pointed down onto the beach.

The beach was teeming with activity. In the moonlight they could see hundreds of creatures dragging pieces of wood and metal across the pebbles. There were wrecks piles against the rocks, the remains of dozens of ships driven up onto the beach. The creatures were plundering them, ripping off planks and struts, sheets of steel, throwing huge chunks of machinery over the sides, burrowing into the engine rooms and tearing the mechanisms and instruments out. Alex watched as a group of three creatures tore a great, rusted propeller from the stern of a ship and sent it spinning up the beach like a wheel.

"What is this place?" he asked.

"Contraption Beach. This is where the Toyceivers make their war engines, the Uproar Contraptions. When they're constructed, they'll be driven through the remaining Quays and used to destroy them. "

"What can we do?"

"Nothing here," Sandy said. "We need to reach Quay-Endula. That's our goal."

They continued to creep along the promenade, looking for some steps to take them back up to the rails. The beach huts were dismal looking things, more like garden sheds than cheerful cabins. Their wood was splintering and the roofs sagged. They each had a small, railed veranda, just big enough to sit on and some of them had no door. Inside they looked cramped and damp and unwelcoming. Alex could smell the mildew. As they passed one of the huts, Alex heard a sound from inside. It was a furtive scrape, like twigs being dragged across the plank floor. He turned and looked and as he did so, the door opened and he saw what was making the sound.

It was a dreadful looking thing. It had a small torso, like a child's and a white, skeletal face. It wore an absurd crimson woolly hat, pulled tightly down over its bulging forehead. It had eight spiny, segmented legs which ended in sharp points that scratched and scraped on the concrete. It hissed at Alex, and grinned.

Alex reached out and grabbed hold of one of the wooden railings running around a veranda. He pulled and it came away with a soft, splintery crunch. It was nearly rotten, but he held it up and brandished it as the creature strutted towards him.

Alex stepped forward and jabbed the railing at the creature's head. It darted to the side and rose up on four of its legs. It growled, its horrible pale eyes gleaming deep in their sockets. It fenced with its front legs, using them as four articulated spears. Alex clouted two of them out of the way and kicked it in the chest. It yelped and flipped over onto its back. It flailed its legs, the knee joints rattling against the concrete like hollow seashells. Alex ran towards Sandy.

Sandy looked pleased. "Well done, son," he said. "A good clean fight! If you can take care of Bom-Bertil, you can hold your own against others like him."

Alex looked back at the struggling creature. Its legs sounded like a teaspoon rattling in a china cup. Suddenly it sprang over onto feet and spun around. It was glowering and furious. Its hat had come down over one of its eyes.

"Bom-Bertil?" Alex said. "You know him?"

"Oh, I know them all, Alex," Sandy said. "I've been dreaming about them since I was a child. Let's get back to Railgrinder, and I'll tell you more about it."

They went up the steps, leaving Bom-Bertil strutting in fury, but cowed into inaction, humiliated by the boy, its hat sagging over its eyes. They retraced the line back to the shed and climbed up onto Railgrinder. Sandy took over the controls, disengaged the brake and took them out in a grey tempest of steam and smoke.

"I'll tell you what happened, when I was a boy not much older than you are now," he said.

And while he did, on they went, to Quay-Endula.

*   *   *

I was out playing with my best friend, David. It was getting on for evening and we were down on the railway tracks that ran past our village. It was summer and the day was long and we were getting tired and hungry. All day we had been picking stuff up from amongst the pebbles alongside the line, examining them, pocketing the odd treasure. David was searching for pieces of jettisoned engine parts. We were making models in my dad's shed: robots, machines, gearboxes, spacecraft; all junk but good oily fun.

I was feeling distracted. I had been having nightmares for weeks. Nightmares about awful places that felt like dimensions full of gloom and menace. I was being chased by something that wanted to take me up, absorb me and drag me inside it, deep within these dimensions, forever.

David was a good lad. We had always been close, best mates for years even, and he knew I was troubled. He was sensitive like that, gentle. I had told him all my secrets. I used to be kind of small. Weedy. Vulnerable. David protected me from bullies, but he couldn't protect me from what happened that evening.

We were standing at the tunnel mouth and suddenly I experienced an effect on my mood so profound that I realised complete hopelessness and despair was all I would ever know and that this was my lot in life. My mind emptied of everything other than utter doom and I got one thought, like a black firework going off against a dying sky: It would be best for me to die.

I remember turning to David and seeing the expression on his face. My heart broke because I knew he had seen it too. My future. No child should have such existential insight. Life stretches too far ahead to sustain it, an impossible slog towards nothingness.

But I was wrong; David was looking past me, at what was coming through the tunnel. He stepped back, his hands raised above his head and he nearly fell. I stood, passive in the path of it, feeling the dark wind rush by as it pressed against the air. It stank of death. But it was a death that would always be alive.

David fled. Somehow he managed to clamber up the bank and I was glad to see him go. I understood. I reached out to him but he was gone. I loved him and I was glad to see that he was going to be safe.

I turned and watched as Junction Creature swelled from the tunnel and engulfed me in its black, eye-filled mouth. I hung in the guts of Junction Creature as it roared back through the tunnel. It was vast, and the whole of its mass was filled with eyes. They drifted up to me in thousands and gazed at me, lidless and full of blood, but still seeing – seeing forever. I felt Junction Creature's fury at being thwarted. I could hear its hideous, thundering mind as it raged. And all the time I could feel it, planting nightmares all over the world, pieces of it constantly feeling, probing, budding out and using the dimensions of dreams to be everywhere, at all times. But it needed more. It had been after David, not me. I could sense it, calculating, fuming, to take away David's future and the good things he would do, the hope he would give people, and the son he'd have. I saw them all, through Junction Creature's million stolen eyes, in a future place. I wanted to cry, to fight, but it was hopeless. It needed David, and others like him. Not feeble little boys like me. It wanted Firmament Surgeons, and it wanted the Dark Time they controlled. It wanted to be everywhere forever, not just constrained to doing this endless labour, this reaching. It was missing things. It knew it was limited and it loathed it. And it was those limitations that saved me.

I heard Junction Creature roar. We were no longer in a tunnel. It had emerged onto a plain of ruins, a bombsite pitted and populated with blown buildings and fragments of ancient machines. Junction Creature slid through the wreckage. It was enormous. Junction Creature was supreme here.

And then it fixed its eyes on a building and swarmed towards it. It was a tower block, and as we drew closer, Junction Creature saw the man standing on a splintering parapet. I felt its hate grow immense, and with it a determination to destroy this man. The building was collapsing. Junction Creature pressed against the block and it began to crumble, the man falling.

As he fell, I felt something. In my darkened mind, against the despair like a lamp held up by a distant guide, I felt a splinter of hope lodge there.

Junction Creature screamed and I experienced a wave of pressure as its entire mass flexed against the awful irritation of my hope. It bucked away from the building and as it reeled I felt myself moving through it, pushed to its rim, where I drifted, terrified.

And then the balloon rose alongside me, buffeted by the air stirred by Junction Creature's rippling flanks. It was a hot air balloon, piloted by a little girl. The man was there, and a tiger, a massive, beautiful tiger. I thought I was dreaming again, of course, and I must wake up soon. And with that the hope in me grew, and Junction Creature was enraged by it. It ejected me like vomit.

The man caught me as I fell. He pulled me into the basket and the girl opened up the burner and we floated away. It was so serene. Junction Creature dropped away beneath us, flattening like a cumulus cloud full of all the storms left in the world to be spent.

After our descent they set me down in an apple orchard by a stream. There was a house there. It was a large house, sprawling with an annexe with French windows that opened out onto the orchard. The man took my hand and led me through the orchard and into the annexe. It looked like a doctor's office. He told me to wait five minutes and then go out through the door facing the French windows. He told me his name was Doctor Mocking and that the girl had been his daughter, Lesley. He told me that when I went through the door I would be different. I would have a new ability. He took something down from the wall and gave it to me. It was a long, slender tube. As soon as he gave it to me, I knew what it was. It was a pontil rod – a glassblower's blowing tube. I liked the feel of it immediately.

Doctor Mocking told me that I should hide it somewhere when I left because I wouldn't need it for a long time if I was lucky. He also told me that I wouldn't see David again and that when I left this office time would be very different for me. I understood what he was saying. This man had saved me from an eternity in Hell and I accepted the new life he was freely offering me with gratitude and joy. As Doctor Mocking turned to leave, he said, "You don't have to go through that door." He smiled and walked out into the orchard.

"I opened the door and awoke, in my bed, in my house. Nothing was different. Lying across the foot of the bed was the glass blower's pipe. I sat up and held it, turning it in my hands. I could hear someone coming, so I rolled over and slid it beneath my mattress.

The door opened and my brother came in.

"Your breakfast's ready," he said.

I was delighted to see him, relieved, euphoric. I leaped out of bed and followed him downstairs. Mum and dad were there. Nothing was different. I ate my breakfast and got dressed for school. I looked in my bag; it was the same books, same teachers' names on the covers.

I left the house and walked to the bus stop. The bus came, number 5, nothing had changed. The children were the same. I went upstairs and looked around, my heart beating faster. All the bullies were at the back, a tight-knit group of spiteful little faces.

"There's Sandicap!" one of them shouted the length of the bus. "Still seeing the doctor cos you wet the bed?"

I backed down the stairs and sat on a seat nearest the driver. I hugged my book bag to my chest and turned my face towards the tinted Perspex partition of the driver's cab. I could see my reflection and the tears that ran down my face.

David wasn't on that bus, nor would he be on any other one. Everything was different.

*   *   *

"So I had to toughen up," Sandy said. "I had no option. Look at me now."

"You're a brute, Uncle Sandy."

"Heart of gold. Just don't get in my way."

"Does Aunty Jean know all this?"

"Of course. I hold no secrets from my Jean."

Railgrinder clattered through an abandoned station, past a derelict kiosk and a waiting room hung with faded posters, the signal boxes filled with cobwebbed levers. They travelled in silence for a while and then Sandy said, "There she is."

Alex was unsure for a moment what Sandy was referring to. For a wild half-second he expected to see Aunty Jean standing at the side of the line, silver hair shining in the sizzling magic of Railgrinder's irondust.

But instead, he saw the lights.

"Quay-Endula," said Sandy.

"Wow!" said Alex.

Quay-Endula was everything Alex had imagined it to be. It sprawled around the bay like jewels poured in profligate adoration about the throat of the most indulged woman in the world. Even at night – or perhaps especially – it was magnificent. The esplanades and pavilions were lit with gleaming spotlights; cyclopean viaducts, cable car pylons, funicular railways bestrode the Quay and the parks glittered with delicate, twinkling installations, a million coloured bulbs strung through the night. The pier stretched to a point towards the horizon, white light blazing from the arcades and stalls all along its length, the spinning colours of its electrifying rides, the stately revolution of its immense wheel, the specks of its tiny gondolas visible like a constellation rotating against the night sky.

"Looks good to me," Sandy said.

"Are we stopping here?" Alex said, breathless before the beauty of the Quay, his eyes wide to take it all in.

"Yes," said Sandy. "Well, come in on the East side, through the Old Town near the docks." He patted the side of Railgrinder's cab. "Our ride stops there."

Railgrinder rocked over a set of points and took a right off the main line. They rumbled along dark rails past sheds and junction boxes, beneath soot-blown signal boxes built on scaffolds across the rails, their windows softly flickering with the light from oil lamps within. Railgrinder no longer ground; at some point during its descent towards the Quay, its grinding wheels had disengaged and they approached Quay-Endula without glamour or row.

They entered a large train shed and as they eased alongside a low ironwrought platform, Sandy engaged the brake lever and they came to a stop where Sandy and Alex dismounted. They stood on the flaking ironwork platform and looked around. Hanging above the rails, roughly at the midpoint of the train shed, by a rusting mount made from welded scrolls, was a large station clock with black numbers just visible on the sooty parchment of its face. It read ten past three. Lamps mounted on columns along both sides of the track fluttered and spread delicate clam-shells of yellow light across the walls and onto the arching scallops of the corrugated roof. There was a café to their left, its windows opaque with steam. As Alex and Sandy walked past, with the muted clanking of their boots, they heard the sound of chatter and could make out that it was French, but one of a rare and scholarly dialect nei-ther could interpret. Beneath the platform's iron lattice, the shadows of tiny mice blew about like balls of dust. They came to a large door propped open with a maga-zine rack. It led into a foyer, which was dark and cool and unoccupied.

"Is this the ticket office?" Alex asked, looking about for a kiosk, or posters advertising sights and activities, or a chocolate vending machine perhaps. He was feeling hungry. He hadn't eaten since…When had he last eaten? Breakfast, but when was that?

"No, this is just the way out onto the docks," Sandy said. "There are no tickets here, this station is all about industry."

"I'm hungry, Sandy," Alex said. The word industry seemed to have a physical effect on him. It was a wintry and functional word, but also full of work, of machines and heavy labour. It was laden with endless, thundering energy and it worked its way from his brain and into his stomach.

"Okay, of course! Hang on," Sandy said.

He guided Alex back onto the platform and took him to the door of the café. He held the door open and they went in; everything was steam and silence. The burner under the

great brass urn behind the counter roared, jetting bursts of
steam towards the low yellow ceiling. For a moment it felt
to Alex as though he had walked into the reading room of
some odd, convivial library. The place was full of men and
women reading books, magazines and newspapers. Some
sat at small Formica-topped tables, others sat up on stools
at the glass-topped counter. Upon their arrival, everyone
had all stopped what they were doing and were staring at
Alex and Sandy with curious, open expressions. A man
stood behind the counter wearing a white apron. He was
tall and slim and wore wire-framed spectacles. He smiled.

"Sandeee!" He said, breaking the silence. "Bonsoir!"

"Bonsoir, Johnny," Sandy said. He led Alex up to the
counter. Alex felt the gentle scrutiny of the people sitting
around the café as he walked between the tables. "Voici
Alex," Sandy said.

"Bonsoir, Alex. Bienvenue à mon café!"

Alex knew enough public school French to understand
the welcome.

"Merci," he replied, smiling. He suddenly knew where
he was. This was the Triangle Bar that Sandy had told Alex
about during one of their evenings over games back at the
farmhouse. It was a Lacan-café and Johnny the owner and
his partner Peter could make it appear anywhere in the
Quay where there was a sufficient derelict site or vacant lot
to host it in the meantime. It was somewhere for strangers, foreigners, and dreamers to go to catch up on news
and developments in their life and around the Quays. But

like everything in dreams, Alex recalled Sandy telling him, news was vague and sometimes unreliable, or at least always open to interpretation. Alex looked over at a table where three men sat reading newspapers. They all wore long suit coats and trilby hats. They looked like spies clustered in a wartime cellar bar. One was holding his newspaper open in his lap and Alex could read the heavy black print of the front-page headlines: Quai-Katavothron tombe. Robin Knox craignait perdu.

Anyone who wanted to go to the Triangle bar had to speak French. French, Sandy said, was the best language to use when speaking of secrets in dreams, and for some reason the Autoscopes detested it. All peoples had the ability hardwired into their brains to speak all languages and in all accents, and the French part of the brain could be accessed when visiting this part the Quays.

Alex wondered for a moment why his French was so stumbling, and why, when they had heard the conversations from outside it had been impossible to understand, but then he realised: he wasn't dreaming. This time he was really here. He'd have to get by on his own accord, and not by some dream-magic.

"Y at-il des nouvelles?" Sandy asked Johnny.

Johnny shrugged and nodded towards the newspaper headlines. Sandy frowned and wiped a hand across his face.

"Ce n'est pas bon," he muttered. "Vraiment pas bon."

Whatever had happened at Quay-Katavothron had caused a disturbance in the remaining Quays.

"Pouvons-nous avoir deux croissants?" Sandy said. Johnny smiled and reached into a glass cabinet on the end of the counter. He produced two of the largest, softest, crumbliest croissants Alex had ever seen. He placed them on two glass plates and slid them over to Sandy. Alex thought they looked like juvenile pangolins curled up sleeping nose to tail. They smelt wonderful, sweet and buttery. He picked his croissant up in one hand and took a bite out of the middle. Paper-thin shards of pastry unravelled and floated to the linoleum floor. It tasted like salt and butter and honey and melted in his mouth.

"Merci, Johnny," Sandy said, and turned to go. Alex made a muffled sound and widened his eyes above the remains of the croissant clutched in his fist.

Johnny laughed. "Mon plaisir, Alex," he said.

Alex nodded. "Berthee, 'Onny," he said.

As they left the café, the conversation started up again, a heated discussion of some sort, and the man holding the newspaper balled it up in his fist and threw it to the floor. He was crying and some of the others moved in to comfort him.

Sandy pulled the door shut behind them.

"It's not our business," Sandy said. "That man has lost a friend. He comes here to make sense of it, but it's a long journey home for him."

"How long has he been coming?" Alex could hear softer sounds, soothing words spoken in the sweet and elegant tongue.

"Twenty years," Sandy said, "twenty full years."

"Come on, let's get going."

They left the station by way of the foyer and went down a short flight of wide concrete steps that led onto a barren and grit-blown square. They could not see any of the glory of Quay-Endula from where they stood. Just ahead of them stood a row of low buildings that looked like factories with some heavy machinery standing sentry behind chain-link fence. Sandy led them across the square and into an alleyway fenced on both sides with more of the sagging chain-link, harping and jangling softly in the night breeze. The dark yards on either side were storage for large metal containers, the kind carried onto ships and the backs of articulated lorries. They were piled three high with narrow alleys between them and when the wind rose, dry leaves and litter blew along the alleys, clattering like the trot of small, clawed beasts.

Alex was glad to emerge from the alley onto a path lit by a few weak streetlamps. They passed through a mist of muted orange light until they came to the docks. The docks were quiet at this time of night but not deserted. Groups of men sat along the docks, around oil drum fires and Alex could hear the low murmur of their voices. There were ships in their berths too, container ships loaded with freight whose gangplanks and ropes rattled cleats in the wind. At the far end of the dock, its bridge lit up like a beacon, a small battleship lay moored. As Alex watched, a

wedge of brilliant white light pulsed from the bridge forcing him to shade his eyes and gasp. It was as if a lighthouse
had just rotated its mirrors and shone its beam directly
into his face. Sandy took Alex's arm.

"Come on," he said. "I know what that is!"

They ran the length of the docks. Alex had to mind
his footing – the after-image of the flashing light just now
fading from his eyes. They reached the battleship and stood
at the foot of the gangplank. It wasn't a large ship, but sat
sleek and low in the water. Alex could see racks bolted to its
deck that ran the length of the side of the ship, and a huge
harpoon gun mounted on the bow.

Sandy was looking up at the ship, mesmerized.

"You ok, Sandy?"

Sandy nodded. He pointed to the ship.

"That, my boy, is the Rogue Angela."

Alex glanced back at the ship. He certainly had seen bigger ones. He'd been to Portsmouth once, with his school,
and seen an aircraft carrier there. This one looked beaten
up, scraped and dented. There was crush damage to the
bow beneath the harpoon gun, where the steel plates looked
to have been impacted. Maybe it had hit a rock.

Sandy was looking at Alex, frowning.

"She doesn't look like much, I know," he said. "But,
trust me, she's a legend, this old girl. She and her Captain
both."

Alex pursed his lips. Squinting he saw a giant emerge
from the bridge and descend the steps onto the gangplank.

Sandy whistled, loud and piercing, and waved his arms.

The giant stopped and turned. He was bald, naked from the waist up and streaked with oil and dirt. Beneath the dirt he was covered with the easy, heavy muscle of a warrior, and tanned as dark as the hemp lines that moored the ships to the pitted iron rings on the walls of the dock.

At first he frowned, and then he smiled and raised a hand. He stepped down onto the deck and descended the gangplank. He stood a foot taller than Sandy. Alex gaped up at him. He could see where the legends of the same might have come from.

The two men grinned at each other, and then the giant pulled Sandy into a crushing bear hug, Sandy's feet dangling inches above the concrete dock. Sandy exerted as much pressure as he could around the trunk of the other man but couldn't quite get his hands to reach completely around his back to get a decent grip. He was turning red.

And then, just as suddenly, they stumbled apart and were both laughing. Sandy's shirt was streaked with oil and his beard was flattened on one side. He ran a hand through it and straightened his moustache.

"It's good to see you, Sandy!" the giant man said.

Sandy cleared his throat. "You, too, Grode, you too."

The giant turned his gaze on Alex. His eyes were small, fierce, the dark brown of turned earth. Alex shrunk back a little, terrified of being scooped up in the same manner as Sandy and crushed against that immense chest. But Grode just smiled and lifted Alex a hand.

"You must be Alex," he said. "Sandy has told us all about you. You're very welcome here."

"Thanks," said Alex.

Sandy turned towards the ship. "We've just missed her, haven't we?" he said, looking up at the bridge.

Grode nodded. "She's gone over to meet the others. Took a boy with her, and a dog."

"Shame," said Sandy. "I would have liked Alex to meet her."

"Who is she?" Alex asked.

"The Captain." Grode said smiling, his big teeth a crooked henge.

Alex raised his eyebrows.

"You thought I was the Captain?"

Alex shrugged. "I guess I did," he said.

"Just a humble First Mate," Grode said.

"Do you remember what I told you earlier, Alex," Sandy said. "About the girl and the man, and the tiger in the balloon that rescued me from Junction Creature when I was a boy?"

"Yes."

"That girl, Lesley, she's the Captain of Rogue Angela."

"Wow."

"That light we saw coming from the bridge was a Gantry opening. She's gone back over to our world to meet others like herself – like you – and deal with a great and ancient evil."

"The Autoscopes?"

Sandy looked at Alex.

"Worse," he said.

"Much worse," said Grode.

"Junction Creature?" Alex whispered.

"That's just what I call him," Sandy said. "He's the devil-in-dreams, and he's trying to destroy you all."

Grode led Alex and Sandy along the side of the dock.

"He's terribly hurt," Grode said. "It's a mortal wound. I couldn't tell Lesley."

Together they walked up a gangplank that led onto the deck of a huge cargo ship moored to the dock wall. They walked through high corridors made by the stacked containers until they came to an area towards the stern where some of the containers had broken from their midlocks and slid apart, creating a narrow atrium. The container facing them was open and they walked up to it.

"Oh no," said Sandy.

They stepped up into the container and walked towards the back. Two other men stood at the rear of the container. They both had lamps that illuminated what lay at their feet. Alex gasped, held his breath, and leaned into the pool of light to see better what lay there. It was a tiger – Lesley's tiger.

Bronze John.

"We had a run-in with an Autoscope," Grode said, "Just before you got here. It managed to get Lesley, nearly killed her too, but that lad and his dog found her in time and brought Bronze John to her." He knelt down and put a hand on the tiger's flank. There was a wound there, deep and ragged. The bleeding had stopped – or been stemmed by some intervention from the men attending the tiger – but Alex could see the severity of it.

"He's barely alive," Grode said.

"Let me see," said Alex.

Grode stood up and stepped aside. Alex squatted beside the tiger. He ran his palms over the fur on either side of the wound. It was soft, incredible. He had never been so close to an animal of this size, or one this magnificent. He felt an enormous, primitive respect, but no fear.

"I need you here, Sandy," he said.

Sandy knelt beside Alex, his eyes wide. "Poor old fella," he said. "He's so old, and so brave. Lesley's had him all her life. He's helped her so many times."

Alex slid along until he reached Bronze John's huge head. The tiger's eyes were shut and his teeth were showing along one side of his jaw where his lip curled up, baring them in his pain.

"Bronze John," asked Alex, "What should I do?"

He waited, and the tiger sighed. It opened an eye and looked at Alex. The eye was glazed and very tired.

Then it spoke, in a tiger's whisper. To Alex it sounded like that of clouds gathering to bring thunder, of a moment of twilight trembling on the world's rim and all its coming night sounds building.

"Bring me your Instrument, Alex," it said.

Alex gasped; the hand that was resting gently on the fur at the tiger's throat froze. Had he expected the tiger to speak to him? To know his name? Alex wasn't sure, but a part of him had hoped, a deeper part of him that was growing now, rising to the surface.

Bronze John closed his eye, and relaxed his lips, covering his teeth.

Alex stood and turned to Sandy. "Did you hear that?" he asked.

Sandy was looking at Alex with an expression of calm anticipation.

"No," he said. "But tell me."

"We need to get Railgrinder down here. Now."

Grode took Sandy back up onto the dock. "There's a service line that runs parallel to the dockside," he said. "It runs from the station along the back of these buildings," he said, indicating towards the low wooden structures, which were mostly storage and stevedores' quarters, "and then on out to the far cove where there's a terminus.

"We used to have so many ships trading here once," he said, and his face was greatly troubled with a mix of sadness, regret, and, not least of all, anger. "The ships used to come down into the bay and we'd unload them straight onto the beach."

"I can bring Railgrinder up as far as the ship," Sandy said. "Tell Alex I'll not be long."

Grode nodded and stamped back over the gangplank onto the deck of the container ship while Sandy took off running, heading back towards the station.

Grode returned to the container in which the tiger lay, and where Alex stood waiting.

"Sandy's gone to get the engine," he said. "What's your plan, son?"

"I think we need to get Bronze John out of the Quay. I think he'll die here. If we put him on the train I can take him out."

Grode looked down at the tiger. The other two men who had been tending to Bronze John stood back in the shadows, their lamps guttering. The two were wiry, with strength in their bodies, but together they were not all capable of lifting a tiger.

"I can fix a flatbed truck to the engine and we can tow him out," said Grode. "But we've got to get him on it first."

Alex walked past Grode and stood in the mouth of the container. From where he stood he could see, moon-lit through a tunnel of stacked containers, a wedge of the glittering Quay, the place of marvels and monsters, according to Sandy. "Get the truck ready, please," he said. "I know what to do."

Grode took his two men and they went up to where the rail-way line ran behind the buildings. They took their lamps and walked up the embankment and along the line like night-workers, looking for the points that would switch the lines onto a siding that held the trucks they needed. Grode found the points and took the lever in his huge fists. He strained against it and the lines clacked over. He told the men to wait by the points and he went into the yard and hung his lamp from the buffer of a flat-bedded truck and then returned to the main line. Then they waited.

From his position behind the firebox Sandy saw the lamps up ahead. He slowed Railgrinder to a crawl and felt the engine rumble over the points and then take the rails in a sharp curve off the main line. Grode came alongside and jumped up into the cab. "The truck's straight ahead," he said, pointing to the lamp hanging from the buffer of the truck.

"Okay, easy does it," Sandy said, and slowed Railgrinder some more until he had nosed it up to the buffers and they touched with a slight jolt. He put on the brake.

They climbed down onto the cinder floor of the yard and chained the truck onto the front of Railgrinder's engine, and then Sandy returned to the cab and released the brake. He put Railgrinder in reverse and eased it back out of the yard onto the main line, where he braked again and stood leaning out of the cab, looking towards the ship, waiting for Alex.

Alex spoke to Bronze John and in his head Bronze John spoke back to him too.

"Before," the tiger said. "Before this, it was I who helped. Now I am too weak. I am but Lesley's toy. Her toy tiger. A small toy."

And Alex heard Bronze John laugh.

"If I could I would make myself small again. But I cannot."

"I know what to do," Alex said.

"Yes, that I know," Bronze John said. "But hurry. I don't have very long now. Take me out of here. So I can be a toy again. So I can heal."

"I'll get you help," Alex said.

Alex left the ship and went up onto the embankment where Sandy and Grode waited. He could feel the heat from the engine; smell the coal white-hot in its furnace. He stepped up into the cab and looked for the cord that hung from the roof. He saw it above the brake lever and reached out, took it in his fist and pulled.

Railgrinder's whistle sounded, high and sweet, then modulated to a lower tone as Alex slackened the cord, blowing the note into the night like a lament. Alex pulled the line tight again and the note rose, wavered, and then fell again until he released the cord and stood back. The note echoed across the docks and out, over the whole of the Quay.

"What was that?" Sandy wondered.

"A request," said Alex. He stepped down from the cab and indicated that the men should follow him. They returned to the ship and waited on the dock.

The first of them came with the heaving of the sea. More, by way of the air; but most came walking. With slow steps they came together, down from the hills surrounding the Quay, and from the woods thereabout. They came from the old quarters of the town and from the shadows of the buildings, from yards and alleys and the black attics of homes. There were those that were huge: great sentinels striding with caution, or one rising from the water lifting its tentacles and a mouth filled with teeth the size of legionnaires' shields. There were those that were smaller, truck-sized, on hooves and claws, easing from the shadows to gather at the side of the dock. And the smallest, no bigger than Alex, in tatty shawls, drifting like ghosts above the ground, with bugging eyes, gashes for grins and long, black lolling tongues.

Alex and the men watched the creatures one by one. They flinched beneath the spray flung up by the beast from the sea and blinked seawater out of their eyes to watch the others come by road and down from the hills.

Sandy put a hand on Alex's shoulder. "These," he whispered in awe, "are the Quay-Endulan Paladins."

The creatures were all around now, milling on the side of the dock. Alex could feel the night air trembling with their presence. He could smell them, too, the sweat in their pelts, motes of black dust shed in the air from their dark resting places, the heat of their breath commingling on the wind. These were the epic things, the creatures of renown that lived amongst the men and women of the Quays, and made known their presence to dreamers on the other side as both subtle counsel and restraint, prompting them to think of the marvels still evident in the Universe, their places in it, and the expectations that they bring.

Almost in a daze, staggered by the enormity of this convention, Alex walked alone amongst the creatures. He held out a hand and they nuzzled him, lowered their heads to be caressed. He touched their manes, horns, antlers and spines. He felt the wet, warm pulse of their nostrils against the palm of his hand. He stood and looked up at the giants, his arms limp at his sides. He felt his own breathing, slow and regular. Their silhouettes blotted out the lights from the Quay behind them. It was like looking up at great gaps in the air, and the air shivered around them as though they were pulling themselves together from the black fabric of the night. They inclined their faces down towards Alex and he saw their eyes, glowing like vapour lamps against the starless sky.

"His name is Gregory," Sandy said. He had walked across the dock and now stood by the gangplank leading up to the container ship. He was looking up at the biggest of them all. Alex turned. Around him the wraiths floated in their air, grinning. They reached out with their thin white arms and touched Alex's head, shoulders, face. Alex smiled. "The Rippingales," Sandy said, his voice little more than a whisper.

"They're sad," said Alex. This came to him with a sure and profound force. "They're the sadness of the Quay."

"And they will fight for it," said Grode. "We can hold things here a while longer, but you will need to take them back with you. If you ask, they will go with you."

Alex walked to the gangplank. He went up onto the deck of the ship and waited. The giant called Gregory moved from the company of his fellows and stepped across the gap between the dock and the side of the vessel. The ship moved in the water, pulling taut against its ropes and settled again lower in the water as he came aboard. Alex followed the path to the stern through the stacked containers. Gregory came behind, head and shoulders above the three-high stacks. Alex stopped at the opening to the container in which the tiger lay. He stepped aside and watched the giant creature stoop and then kneel, his great lamp eyes shining in, illuminating the container with a grey metallic light. The giant reached forward, his black-pelted shoulder bracing against the side of the container, and then withdrew his arm and a hand considerable enough to lift a tiger on its palm. Away from the container, Gregory stood, Bronze John curled like a toy asleep in his hand, turned and strode back towards the bow of the ship. Alex followed.

With great gentleness and care, Gregory set Bronze John down onto the flatbed truck. The men had thrown rough sacks and nets across the wooden slats to make the bed more comfortable. The tiger did not stir, his breathing shallow and irregular.

Alex and Sandy climbed up into Railgrinder's cab and opened the throttle. Grode and his companions watched as the engine backed away, towing the truck with the tiger upon it, and then stood aside, their lamps held high, and lit the way for the creatures to make their way up the gradient from the dock to the rails. They followed the engine, a titanic and dutiful circus, and as they strode behind, Railgrinder engaged its grinding wheels and lit them all with a standard of golden sparks that glittered like foxfire in their manes and tails.

Soon the ghastly parade reached a good marching pace and trundled through the dock station. The creatures, the Quay-Endulan Paladins, passed the now empty lot where Peter and Johnny's Lacan-Café had been. The front was boarded with fractured sheets of plywood. They would be set up somewhere new, a warm hearth for haunted dreamers to gather around in some forgotten, unlocked region of the Quay. The giants ducked beneath the clock that hung from its iron scrolls, its parchment face still set at ten past three. And on they went, out of Quay-Endula, climbing the hills that led past abandoned stations and the ransacked mayhem of Quay-Fomalhaut's Contraption Beach, where it was quiet now. The scant remains of the beached vessels lay sprawled across the rocks like the ribcages of tragic iron whales.

They passed the castle that rose from the beach and Alex saw how the red light still raged behind the shutters. He felt something in his belly drop like a weight and he closed his eyes and turned away. Whatever fumed in there like a sick temper was in its terminal throes. Alex hoped that it might be a battle worth waging for whoever was in there. He held fast to the rail that ran around the sides of the cab and fixed his eyes on the dark procession of shadows that followed the engine. In the light thrown back from Railgrinder's sparks Alex thought he saw Bronze John move. It might have been an accident of shadow and pale golden light, but he thought he saw the tiger flex his claws, and move an eye beneath one of its heavy lids.

You know what's going on in there, thought Alex as he watched the tiger. He could feel the stirring in the tiger's core, as if matching his own. You want to go in there and fight it, and I want to watch! But Bronze John settled and Railgrinder rocked past, the creatures in step behind, trudging and trotting as Alex watched the castle recede.

The tracks continued to rise and they started out across the moor. It was beginning to lighten now; dawn was coming in dim, smoky bands beyond the hills, rising and filtering the density out of the dark. The creatures looked less like fantastic shapes formed from the bitter black rafters of smoke blowing downwind from Railgrinder's stack and became more distinct, their outlines sharper. The radiance of their eyes softened with the rising twilight and Alex could see everything in more detail: teeth and horns, plates, scales and folded wings. The Rippingales flitted alongside the giant Gregory and his brothers like threadbare hummingbirds at the faces of immense black flowers.

Sandy had been quiet throughout the journey, content to settle against the wall of the cab and gaze out of the porthole above the engine at the passing Quays. Now he said, "Alex, take the controls," and he stepped aside.

Alex went to the throttle and put his hand on it. As soon as he touched the lever he felt the power of the engine vibrating through it. He felt something else, knew something more about this place and the power it gave him, even as the throttle trembled in his fist and made him clench his teeth. He knew what he must do. He would open a Gantry and take them all back, him and Sandy, and the tiger, and those creatures he was sent to fetch, but the vast wonder of this home trip was that now he could take them back to a time of his choosing. He felt time flow around him, and another kind of time, a Dark Time full of eddies and dimensions, the collective chronologies of all the dreaming people in the world, and all that had ever been or were to come, and it was truly eternal. Alex gasped and his knees buckled. Sandy was there, and held him up.

"Hang on, son," he said. "You've felt it, haven't you? Control it. It's yours to control."

Alex stood straight, looked up at his uncle.

"I love you, Uncle Sandy," he said. "I love you –"

And the Gantry opened and took them across Dark Time.

They passed through a corridor made from stanchions of light. Sandy stood swaying on the footplate, staggered by the scale of the Gantry. He glimpsed a great distance curving away either side of the luminous pillars, something like a limitless factory structured for immortals, populated with uncountable numbers of machines, pumps and turbines. A labyrinth of brass looms shuttling and weaving across an impossible distance. And through all these strung golden threads, like dewed cobwebs catching the first rays of an early morning sun, were the Gantries, the networks of nerves in the minds of all the world's dreamers.

Sandy stopped looking, afraid the distances would overwhelm him. He closed his eyes and held onto the cab's cold, reassuringly sold rail. He felt a jolt and opened his eyes. The jolt was not purely physical; it was temporal. They were out, and he was a child again.

Railgrinder came to a full stop on a curving stretch of rail at the bottom of a steep cutting. Alex released the brake and looked down at his uncle. He smiled, then stepped forward and hugged him, laughing. Sandy was now a good three inches shorter than Alex, but the wiry curls of his red hair gave them a sort of parity in stature. He looked down at himself and sighed. He held out his scrawny arms. "Look at the state of me," he exclaimed. "What a weed." But he was smiling as he said it, his thin face pale in the low light of a twilit day that had once been long ago.

"Nice footwear," said Alex.

Sandy lifted a foot and beheld his hand-me-down galoshes.

"They were my Granddad's," he said. "Is it any wonder I used to get a right kicking?" Then he looked up at Alex. "That was after Dave."

"I know."

"Speaking of which," Sandy said. "I'd better go. It's nearly time." He might have looked a little paler, but the sun was setting and shadows were sifting down the cutting like smoke.

"Do you want me to come?"

Sandy shook his head. "No, I have to do it."

"I don't want you to be alone."

Sandy smiled, his eyes watery and almost colourless in the remaining light. He looked over his shoulder, back to where the monsters stood in a dark throng behind the flat-bed truck.

"I won't be," he said.

Sandy put out his hand, and Alex shook it, feeling an uneasy understanding take hold of him. Sandy turned and climbed down onto the gravel at the side of the rails. He walked on ahead, towards the curve and what lay beyond, to when lay beyond, and the monsters followed.

"Alright, Dave?"

The other boy turned, still holding the piece of rusty metal he'd found at the mouth of the tunnel.

"Oh, there you are, San. Where'd you get to?"

Sandy stood looking at the boy, at his kindly face, and said, "Just been around the bend." And he laughed at that, and so did David, and Sandy felt an immense happiness flood his whole spirit, a happiness that was as fine as gauze and just as delicate, just as capable of tearing. He felt tears prickle his eyes and he sniffed and wiped his face with thin fingers that felt absurdly fragile and small.

"You okay?" David said. "You look like you've had a shock."

"I'm fine," Sandy said and waved his hands, his funny little hands, and walked up to his friend.

David held out the metal object. "What do you think, San? I reckon it's a piece of gearbox. Or part of the breaking system of an old steam train. What do you think?"

Sandy looked at the piece of metal. It looked like the flush off an old bog.

"I reckon you're right, Dave," he said. "Reckon it's an instrument of some kind."

David grinned, and put the piece of metal in his already bulging pocket. Sandy went past him and stood at the mouth of the tunnel. Behind him the monsters gathered, unseen by the other boy, dark things with eyes brightening as the light failed, fists like boulders clenched and claws and stings unsheathed; tusks lifted, gleaming like sickles, spines rattled as they rose quivering; antlers lowered and hooves pawed at the gravel between the sleepers.

"David."

David looked up, a sooty pebble dropping from his hands.

"You need to run, David," Sandy said.

"What, San?" David said, but he was already taking steps backwards. His brow creased and he wrinkled his nose. "What's that stink?"

Sandy spun around. He held out his arms. "Run!"

David saw the blackness racing through the tunnel towards them, pushing its storm-ruptured grave stench ahead of it, felt the utter malignancy at its heart and its sole intent to corrupt. He screamed. David turned and ran.

Sandy stared into the cauldron of eyes that swarmed at the tunnel mouth. His eyes watered at the smell, his mouth was dry with fear. The membrane of Junction Creature's rim pulsed and all his stolen eyes flocked there. The sick air moved around Sandy in thick ripples as if all its molecules had bonded with atoms of hate. Hate became fury. Fury became despair. Despair became hate. Hate. Fury. Despair.

Hatefurydespair.

Hatefurydespair   who are you?

Hatefurydespair   get out of my way

Hatefurydespair   I don't want you

Hatefurydespair   I want the other

Hatefurydespair   I want the other

Hatefurydespair   I WANT THE OTHER

"You're not having him," Sandy said, and felt

Peacejoylove

And Junction Creature screamed.

David ran for the side of the cutting. He tripped on a sleeper and went to his knees. He scuffed his palms in the dirt. His mouth was open, his eyes wide with terror. He could hear the thing at his back, could feel the pressure of its mass as it bulged towards him. Sandy was gone. He knew his friend was gone. His mind raged with a blinding panic. He struggled to the bank and tried to grasp a handful of grass but his fingers were suddenly slick with sweat and the clumps he grabbed slid through his fists and he slipped back to the gravel at the side of the tracks. He could smell it. It had the smell of old meaty bones left to rot in a sweltering, months-unemptied bin, the rich, inglorious stench of decay. David choked and rose trembling to his knees. He looked back, knowing it was coming for him. And as the world swam and he felt he would go mad long before that thing swallowed him up, he glimpsed something standing at his side. His eyes moved in their sockets, everything else was frozen. Something was there, a shadow, a shading of the air, and lamps for eyes high up, in a smudge like a face, a wide blur against the twilight sky.

Sandy walked forward and reached out a hand. Junction Creature welled at the tunnel mouth, a fuming, and ten-drilled darkness rippling out across the floor of the cutting. The tendrils were tipped with raw eyes. They rose and quivered in the air, seeking to slip past Sandy and latch upon the other, the boy on his knees. Sandy turned his head and saw Gregory and the monsters looking towards his friend. There was a moment when he knew they would have to choose. Sandy would have to choose for them. He closed his eyes and stepped forward, through the membrane, and into the heart of the devil-in-dreams.

David felt the ground fall away. He went slack, losing consciousness for a moment as he felt himself lifted. And then he was back, awake and blinking, his body lying fifteen feet away from the cutting, at the edge of the field that led back to the village. He lay back against the grass, his eyes clenched shut and full of tears. He rolled onto his belly and stumbled to his feet. He ran. He did not look back.

*   *   *

Alex heard the scream and jumped down from Railgrinder's cab. He ran along the cutting and around the curve. He shouted Sandy's name, stumbling as his feet kicked up gravel and stones, and came out of the curve where the tracks ran straight for a hundred yards and disappeared into the tunnel. He skidded to a stop, his knees locking, and stood swaying. Gregory stood at the edge of the cutting. The monsters surrounded him, their size and number blocking Alex's view of the tunnel mouth. Gregory bent and lifted something from the side of the track. It was a boy.

Alex watched as Gregory stepped up onto the steep slope of the cutting and reached out, lifting the boy high over the bank, and placed him a good distance away, out of sight. Alex walked forward, but the creatures barred his way. He tried to push through them but Gregory knelt and put his huge head down and looked at Alex with his smoky fog lamp eyes. Alex looked up into the giant's face and understood. Gregory put out his hand and Alex climbed onto the giant's palm. Gregory lifted him, just a few feet, so that he could see over the backs of the smaller monsters. Alex dug his fingers into the hairs on Gregory's palm and watched as the boy that was his uncle Sandy disappeared into the living darkness that filled the tunnel mouth.

Alex walked up to the entrance to the tunnel and stood beneath the crumbling arch. He peered into the darkness – a true darkness now, just cold, lightless air – but he could see nothing. Junction Creature was gone. Sandy was gone.

"This time's different," Alex said. "This time he knows where he's going. He knows what to do." He wanted the words to be reassuring, but they sounded as cold and lightless as the air in the tunnel, and their soft echo did little to reduce his uncertainty; they sounded like the secretive whispers of doubters hiding in the belly of the rock.

The monsters were still standing in the cutting but Alex sensed their agitation. He went over to where they milled. He reached out and touched some of them, stroked fur and hair, ran his fingers along hides and scales, felt the hot breath on his hands and arms.

"Go," he said. "With all my love."

The monsters began to climb the cutting. Gregory and his brothers and some of the larger creatures made it in one step, others corralled and pushed and clambered until they had all made it to the top. The Rippingales drifted up like ragged kites. Alex watched them disappear from sight as they headed out across the field. They would disperse, he knew, and find dreamers to counsel, now that they were here. And there were people to warn, and children to protect. And one especially: David. And the son he would have, who would be just like Alex, and would together one day have to face that thing, that Junction Creature, and bring it to account.

Alex walked back to Railgrinder, and thought about his uncle Sandy.

Alex went to the flatbed truck and peered over its side. The sacks and nets were still piled there but Bronze John was gone. He clambered onto the bed of the truck and pulled some of the nets aside, unfolding the sacks where they had rucked beneath the tiger. He lifted a flap and there he was. Alex smiled and picked him up. Bronze John rested on Alex's palm as he had on Gregory's, but the scale was much different here because now Bronze John was a toy again. Alex looked at the plastic tiger, poised in a leap, the tail crooked, the mouth open to reveal painted teeth, the eyes shining black. Along its flank was a twisted scar about an inch long, where the plastic had sealed itself into a neat keloid ridge.

Alex climbed down from the truck and got back into Railgrinder's cab. He put Bronze John on the floor next to the firebox and then he released the brake and opened the throttle. Steaming, Railgrinder reversed around the curve and took them into the tunnel.

They emerged from the Gantry onto the moor. It was still dark and the soft wind moved the ferns like a tide. Bronze John stretched, and sat, and lifted his head to look over the rail at the back of Railgrinder's cab. Alex was astonished by his size. He filled the cab and was unable to stand in the space, merely cramp himself into an uncomfortable-looking crouch, his great head resting on the back of the cab, his tail curled around the pressure-gauge pipe next to the firebox, twitching in the heat.

"How are you?" Alex asked.

Bronze John turned his head and looked at Alex with one almond eye.

"Healed," he said. "Thank you."

Alex noticed the scar beneath his ribcage. It dragged a furrow through his stripes, but seemed otherwise closed and uninfected. In fact, it looked old.

They rode on across the moor and then dropped down through the pass towards Contraption Beach. Ahead, Alex could see the castle, pitched up on the edge of the beach, and its windows still blushed with that uncomfortable red light. Alex slowed Railgrinder as they approached, squinting to see what might be throwing those flexing shadows against the shutters.

"Do not stop," Bronze John said, "but let me off."

Alex managed to drag his gaze away from the castle.

"Why?" But he remembered before, when they had brought the tiger past the castle on the back of the truck; how the tiger had moved, had unsheathed his claws despite his pain. He had known then that the tiger had felt it, too.

"Do you want me to come?" Perhaps the tiger could hear something in Alex's voice, a misplaced excitement that shouldn't have been there. He looked at Alex and said,

"This is my fight, not yours. Go on to Quay-Endula."

Sandy had said something similar, Alex remembered, but still, that light... it was entrancing.

Bronze John roared, and Alex cried out and fell against the side of the cab. The sound was so primal, immense and incapacitating, Alex felt all the strength drain from him in an instant. He felt like he was made of paper – edible paper.

The tiger was watching him expectantly. Alex was trembling. The shock of the roar had taken his mind off the castle and its warm and worrying lightshow. He reached out for the throttle and slowed the train to a walking pace. Bronze John turned in his crouch and leaped from the cab. He landed on the bank and took off towards the castle in great loping bounds. Alex watched him go, but did not look up at the castle again. Still trembling a little, he opened the throttle and took Railgrinder back into Quay-Endula.

Railgrinder went through the dock station, beneath the iron clock (ten-past three forever, there) and past the boarded up café. It ran alongside the dock until it came to the truck yard at the back of the stevedore's cabins where Alex had last seen Grode. He slowed the train and came to a stop. He looked out, down the slope to the dock, to where the ships were moored in darkness and silence. There was no sign of anyone. Even the cabins were dark. No fires burned in braziers along the dockside. They had been quenched. Alex frowned, and then looked beyond the edge of the dock, and the ships, out to sea, towards the horizon. There were lights out there and they were heading inland – hundreds of them. Looking at the lights gave Alex a headache. It was sick light, nightmare light.

He heard something, footsteps treading carefully through gravel. He looked to his right and saw another light, but this time it was coming from a lantern being carried by someone walking the track towards the train. Before Alex could say anything, the lantern swung and threw light across the face of the man carrying it. Alex laughed, and leaped down from the cab. He ran to the man and jumped into his arms.

"Good lad," said Sandy. "Good lad!"

They stood together in Railgrinder's cab and watched the lights approach from the horizon.

"Toyceivers, in their Uproar Contraptions," Sandy said. "Don't look if you can help it. That light's mean. It'll make you ill." He shovelled a load more coal into the firebox and kicked the iron door shut. "They're coming to attack the Quay."

Alex looked away and watched his uncle work by the lamplight.

"There's a cove at the far end of the Quay," Sandy said. "That's where we're going next."

He let out the brake and opened the throttle. Railgrinder's firebox blazed and a cloud of grey ash blew from its stack.

"We'll meet others there," Sandy said. "Others like you. And we'll wage war. On those." He jabbed a fat, callused thumb in the direction of the horizon. "Just one more thing," he said. He reached down and pulled something form a narrow channel that ran alongside the firebox. It was a slender tube about four feet in length. He held it up so that it shone in the lamplight. It was his glassblower's rod, his Instrument.

"I kept hold of it this time around," Sandy said. "We're going to need it."

Sandy looked down at Alex, his eyes creased at their corners with soot and concern.

"You up for this, son?"

Alex took his uncle's hand – his big, strong hand – and pointed ahead, towards where the track curved around the headland and would bring them out onto a hidden cove.

"Yes, Sandy," he said, which was all he needed to say.

And Railgrinder moved off.

AN OCEAN BY HANDFULS

Well, God knows where I was; some dream or other I suppose, with me at the centre of it all, in control, with friends around me all coming out of the factory and set up for the rest of the day to do something. And there were these pretty girls from the bombsites with dirty legs and sticky fingers. I had these really strange clothes on, sort of 1950s. Jacket, white shirt and trousers. And I never favour trousers, only ever bluejeans. I don't know what I had on my feet, because of the nature of the dream. I had fags, too. Rollups. I can taste the sweetness and dust of them and feel the bits on my tongue. This makes me gag and when I do my breath frosts out in clouds so it must be late on. By the look it's October or maybe into November, the old dark grinder, shoring up the brittle end of the year like a stanchion. Oh, and everything's in black and white. This is strange because I always dream in colour. But it suits the whole mood. Somehow I know everything is coloured underneath, but this seems oddly more real, timeless. I love the chrome and steel magnitude of it. Less blurred; focused.

We're at the Triangle bar, so we're all talking French. All the papers on the glass-topped counter are French and the wireless is tuned to French stations. Peter and Johnny only ever talk French and if we want to get served we have to speak it, too. It's such a great place, we are all learning to speak French.

Later, we go to the ambulance station down the road. There's a big courtyard sort of like a petrol station and then a main building and garages.

Outside, Reg is sitting in his cab, as usual, smoking and reading the paper.

He sees us and nods.

We're always coming here because there's a big barrel of sump oil in the corner of the yard and we try to see how much we can steal in little cups and waxed paper boxes, because Johnny pays us in extra French vocabulary for every pint we can get.

They use it for the burners, which boil the water, and last week we got *assiette*, *feuilleton* and the conditional tense conjugation of *boir* for just the one visit.

We stretch up on our toes to peer into the sump oil. Overhead the clouds are dark like a lid over us and it starts to snow.

This is perfect. Quiet, just for Reg's paraffin heater clunking. When we look into the sump we see our faces shining back like negatives. It's like the stillness of space in there, not a disturbance or sense of depth. Then the snow starts to land around our faces like stars appearing, making tiny ripples and sucking up the dark and sinking into the depths.

When we get back to the corner it's snowing so hard we have to shake it out of our hair. We nip under the awning and stand there shivering.

"Il fait neige," says Johnny.

I nod and give him a cupful of sump. "Merci, Johnny."

It's then that Stan comes hurtling around the corner. He scatters the old timers reading their papers and sets pastries flying.

"Adam's dead!" He cries.

Snow blows up and down the road around our feel like talc. The chrome and Art Deco interior of the bar glints and reflects the snow like static on its surface. Johnny stops what he's doing and turns around. The gas burners roar under the urn. Everywhere there's steam and silence.

From the look of things it's like nobody around here ever dies.

There's a look of horror on everybody's face. Everyone starts talking at once. I'm not sure I know how to feel. I obviously belong here, although I have no discernible past, at least none that I can recall, but this does not disturb me. And this is real and it's unfolding now, although not in any sense I can fully understand. Stan grabs my arm and pulls me out into the harried snow so we can escape the limiting discipline of French.

Reg drives past, exhaust blowing. He waves.

There's a feeling like time has no place here, which is why I feel so located, like this place is all I've ever known, yet I'm conscious of no history to properly situate me. I know everybody and they know me, yet I've never been here before in my life and I've never, ever left. And at last somebody's dead.

Peter and Johnny are brewing something for everyone. Someone balls up a newspaper and hurls it at the ground. The wind picks it up and bundles it out across the road.

Stan points down the arcade which runs off the main road, the corner of which is sheared off by the Triangle bar. He takes off again with everyone at the bar watching him, crying, their eyes wide and bewildered as if the impossible has happened.

I look up at the industrial sky and widen my eyes to let the snow blur them, then I follow him.

We get to the end of the arcade and run out across the bombsites.

I get to the top of a heap of rubble and stop. I turn around, strafed by snowfall, and look back. Pitched under the pewter sky I can see the backs of the tenements and shops, denatured as rainbombed sandcastles. Stan calls me, so I go on.

We reach a wrecked corner. The only buildings left standing are a few tenements and a pub, which gives the road stretching ahead of us some sort of line and angle of definition.

I look through one of the tall windows, my eyes wide between ground glass advertisements for ales and spirits. All I can see are people sitting there, crying.

I turn to Stan and his white face. His lower lip is trembling and a tear has tracked down his cheek. A snowflake lands on his teardrop, drifts momentarily on its taut surface and is consumed.

Stan shakes his head.

"I can't go down there," he says. He appears stricken. I look past him, down the road, which I now notice is bombsites one side and wrought iron railings the other. Over us the sky is as black as the sump Johnny cooks with. I feel cold. Stan's hands, when I take them, are blue. He is trembling and unable to grip my hands in response.

I tell him to go inside the pub and start a fire in the empty grate.

"Promise me you won't go past the railings," he says. "Walk by the bombsite. Promise me!"

I have no idea why he is so afraid, but I promise nonetheless.

I watch Stan as he goes into the pub. As the big doors swing inwards I can hear sobbing.

What has happened here to cause such despair? As the snowfall shifts and compacts, strangely synthetic beneath my feet, an ill feeling of loneliness tears through me like an infarction.

I have lost something here.

Or rather something has been torn away and the pain is at once cold and utter, yet compels in a way that leaves me gasping.

I trudge over the rubble. Everything to my left has been flattened by the concussion of explosions. I have no knowledge of conflict, but waves of despondency again wash over me. I have to stop and close my eyes until the sensation ebbs.

As the snow blurs the demolition away into the distance, I turn to my right and look over at the railings. Regardless of my promise to Stan, I cross the street. I make footprints over an inch deep.

I peer through the bars. Rust flakes off on my cheeks.

It's virtually lightless in there but I can make out it is some kind of park, stifled by trees. They bunch and crowd, with nothing but the smallest of paths winding between them, right up to the railings.

Something moves deep within the trees.

I jump, surprised, then realise I cannot release the bars I hold at either side of my face.

Alarmed, I retreat back across the path until I reach arms length from the railings. I am gripping the bars with all my strength and cannot surrender them.

My attention is drawn back to the trees, which are now beginning to thrash as things force their way through them.

Sweating, despite the snow whipping against me, I tug and pull to no avail. I can make out forms now, although indistinct, like chunks of softened, sooted glass, limbed, mouthed, rangy. I am suddenly terrified.

I look back to where I have come from. The corner of the street, indeed all but a few yards to either side of me, is obscured by the silent blizzard.

My thoughts are hectic. They are so close now I can feel their urgency. I rock back on my heels and pull, the muscles in my shoulders screaming, but I can only look on, caged.

As they approach, I hear music. It is the beguiling tinkle of the ice cream seller's chimes, enticing and relentless and, here, horribly misplaced.

And finally, as some stodgy thing with a face torn into it begins to press inexorably through the bars to be taken in my fixed embrace, I sense the true force behind all this.

Sense it before seeing it, easing its way through the trees beyond, bark and trunks fracturing in its stead, branches thick as arms splintering against its jaws. Sense its dispensation for grief, the remorseless, prowling motive that drives it, and the trauma and confusion conditioned by it as clearly as I hear the sweet and entrancing music issuing from some unseemly place within it.

I have heard that if one scoops a handful of the sea then replaces it, allowing the water to churn and blend for a century, then lifts a second handful from an arbitrary place, one will find atoms from the first handful resonant within the second. Thus, it is said, that there are more atoms in a handful of seawater than there are handfuls of water in the sea.

So, I came awake, disentranced on that blasting street.

Stunned, I looked into the park. Nothing stirred except for the sound of weighted branches shrugging off their stoles of heavy snow cover.

I could barely remember why I had started off down this road.

But I could remember the death of my friend.

There is nothing to distort the mind like grief.

At first there had been a wave of energy, a blaze of clarity in my thinking, but energised with inefficient, hungry fuel at a monstrous cost. I was borne on an ever-lifting wave as I displaced my new, terrible and unpredict-able feelings into this highly conductive yet fearsomely empty realm ahead of me.

A realm I had to fill, to load, like a new thing birthed, bloody, raw, clenched out into a staggering and aghast light. I came complete with memories, a story already concluded which, wherever I strained, could not focus on what I yearned to find. I was a revolving panic in a geo-metric square and if I turned this way quickly enough I might, just fleetingly, glimpse a fifth angle. I had breathless sight, the wrong eyes and could not distort my percep-tion enough to seize on the one thing I most desperately needed.

But I have at last come to an edge of land and look out across an ocean.

The terrain I have covered, the bombsites, the mon-strous shapes, the bewilderment, is at my back. The snow is thinner here and blows like dust into the waves, leavening the salty, tearful sea.

It is not the ocean I dipped my hand into all those years ago, but his memory.

Now I do so again and what I find are moments distilled. Clearer for their toss and tumble through my heart and mind. Sharper for the processes they have undergone, but also sweet. Sweetness, like peace, I would not have been able to surmise, but sweet it is indeed.

If I turn back now, which I must, I will see a changed landscape. I will walk back through it a thousand times, ten thousand, and sometimes encounter the bombsites again, or, more likely, some threatening, brittle thing, but I have the better of them now.

My ocean dilutes them ever finer, ever more translucent as it sways and lifts throughout itself.

I make my way back to where people are wiping their red-rimmed eyes. I see Stan's small face bob up behind a window as I turn the corner of the street. His eyes are alight and as he sees me, he leaps down from whatever it is he is standing on and disappears. Moments later the doors heave inwards and he is running for me, arms wide, feet kicking up snow like smoke in a cartoon to connote speed. The image is perfect.

As he throws himself into my arms, I see firelight gleaming off the brass and dark shining wood of the bar. I hear a man laugh deeply, just once, from within.

I hold onto Stan and he is warm.

ACKNOWLEDGMENT

Thanks to David, for the introductions; one written generously for this book, and the other he made to Charlie at Montag books on my behalf. Also, thanks to Charlie, for allowing me to take this strange contraption out for a run again.

AUTHOR BIO

Paul Meloy was born in 1966. He is the author of the short story collection Islington Crocodiles, and the novels The Night Clock and its sequel, Adornments of the Storm. His stories have been published in various magazines and anthologies including The Third Alternative, Black Static, Interzone, Adam's Ladder, House of Fear, The End of the Road, Prisms, and Cinema Futura. He works as a Community Mental Health Nurse and lives in Devon with his family.

www.ingramcontent.com/pod-product-compliance
Lightning Source LLC
Chambersburg PA
CBHW031102030726
47496CB00002BA/341

9 781940 233840